UPSIDE DOWN IDIOTS CLUB

A NOVEL

LEO MAXWELL

UPSIDE DOWN IDIOTS CLUB

LIFE IS COMPLICATED, LOVE IS SIMPLE

LEO MAXWELL

PALMARIUM PARTNERS

Upside Down Idiots Club

Copyright © 2023 by Leo Maxwell

All rights reserved. No part of this book may be reproduced in any form or by any electronic or mechanical means, including information storage and retrieval systems, without written permission from the author, except for the use of brief quotations in a book review.

This book is a work of fiction. The characters, incidents, and dialogue are drawn from the authors imagination an are not to be construed as real. Any resemblance to actual events or persons, living or dead, is entirely coincidental.

ISBN. 979-8-9893065-3-4. (Ebook)

ISBN. 979-8-9893065-1-0. (Paperback)

ISBN. 979-8-9893065-2-7. (Hardcover)

*This story is dedicated to
those around me who encouraged
my artwork and writing.*

*And to those who read through the pages,
enjoy this crazy love story and
the many influences that affect our daily lives.*

INTRODUCTION

JACK MOHR is a good looking, talented entrepreneur from a hard-working family in the Pacific Northwest. While growing up, he studies science and medicine and immerses himself into ways to make his love for science make a difference in the world. Along the way, he is influenced by a group of young autistic kids, a beautiful woman who is an undiscovered artist, and a high-wealth venture capitalist. After his first taste of new money, he enjoys the spoils of five-star night clubs and evenings with lovely women. Then along comes Ava and brings him into her world of art, erotic massage, and romance. Together, they share heightened moments of physical and emotional love. She introduces Jack to her artwork, sculptures, and the naked vulnerability of each other. However, she hides something from him, not knowing he may be her best path to a cure.

Over the course of time, Jack discovers many things about himself and those close to him. His love and devotion to science is rewarded by a special group of kids who forever changed his life. One life is saved through the kindness of another path to a cure.

PROLOGUE

HOW IMPORTANT IS *it to turn things upside down? There is an upside-down bikini trend where women turn the coverup triangle and point it down, thereby covering up much less of the breast. Diana Ross made the lyrics famous, suggesting, "you're turning me upside down." And Jack Johnson made it very clear in his song that "I want to turn the whole world upside down." How is it that turning something upside down has such a significant impact? The bikini is suddenly sexier. The song lyrics suggest you're turning my body upside down, inside out, and round-n-round. It is crazy fun.*

This team had no leader, kingpin, or ruling order. No bylaws, no regular meetings, and certainly, no structure or hierarchy in the group. They were the most unique and (soon to be) most influential people in his world and would be affectionately known as the "Upside Down Idiots Club."

"Oh my god," Jack thought, "this journey (with the Saints) is going to be fantastic."

This story begins in a rather unexpected way, with Jack in the company of a remarkable group of individuals, immersed in a diverse range of literature, from romantic Shakespeare to obscure Einsteinian theories. It's fascinating how this seemingly innocuous hospital reading group would eventually lead to one of the most groundbreaking advancements in medical science.

PART ONE

CHAPTER
ONE

BEGIN WITH TWO

IN FIRST GRADE, there are numerous aptitude tests for math and verbal skills, marking the beginning of gifted and talented student assessments, typically undertaken between ages 5 and 8. This period initiates the evaluation of intelligence quotient (IQ) rankings. The average IQ for children under 8 ranges from 80 to 120, with gifted scores falling between 120 and 145. Scores above 145 are considered extremely gifted. Jack and Robbie both scored between 160 and 165.

During a classroom discussion, Jack confidently stated, 'I'm going to save the world!' Some kids chuckled, while a few nodded. When it was Robbie's turn, he said, "I'm going to help my brother."

Born just a few hours apart, these two young prodigies would eventually become influential agents of change, effectively 'saving the world' in their own ways. For now, they cherished their time together, whether at school, home, or their favorite pastime—being on the water in a boat.

Their family owned various boats, ranging from canoes and dinghies to prams and a nearly seaworthy twenty-five-footer for fishing. The

family's prized possession, handed down through generations, was the 'Mohr is Better,' a semi-luxury cruiser. This boat could circumnavigate the world, reaching up to 30 knots, accommodating six adults, and carrying the esteemed Mohr legacy."

CHAPTER
TWO
EARLY YEARS

JULIA WENT into labor with her twins in the morning and rushed to Tacoma General Hospital. Her first son, Jack James was born just after dinner. He was 5 lbs. 7 ounces and came through the birth canal as easily as planned. Headfirst and smiling. The nurses wrapped him up and placed him in a nearby incubator.

As she rested between births, there was an uneasy sense of calmness. Her body was relaxing when it should have been gearing up for the next challenge.

Then there were complications. The second twin, Robert Joseph, was tiny, stubborn, and unwilling to leave. There were two separate umbilical cords (one for each twin) and although the afterbirth was intact, there was blood coming from her vagina. Julia had effectively been in labor for over eighteen hours at this point by now.

It was after midnight. Robbie's heart rate was 150 bpm, and Julia's had dropped below 60. The nurses monitored her medications carefully as there must have been a change in her condition. She was given a shot of Demerol before Jack's birth and managed the pain for Robbie with a light drip of Fentanyl. These narcotics were common and had little or no effects on the mother or newborn if used properly.

Tom recalled when the girls were born years earlier in what seemed like a walk in the park. Julia had Amara and Gianna two years apart with natural childbirths. Amara was born in July and weighed 5 lbs. and 6 ounces and Gianna was a September baby weighing just over 6 lbs. In both cases, the girls and their momma were at home in their beds after just an overnight in the hospital. Easy peasy.

By 1am, Julia was exhausted. She was on an IV for fluids (mostly sugar water) and her face looked tired and her shoulders limp. The nurse called the doctor announcing that her heart rate was below 50 bpm, and the baby was in danger.

Her doctor, Dr. Holmes, specialized in multiple births. Her visits to the doctor's office were exciting in the months leading up to their birth. Julia looked forward to the ultrasound view of the twins and the positioning of each baby in her womb. She began reviewing names as soon as the pictures revealed they were both boys. James and Joseph were family names and she wanted to use these. But the J&J in the naming seemed a bit too cute for the twins and moved these to middle names. Jack and Robbie soon became favorites. Their bedroom had pillows and blankets with their names stretched across them. They each had twin beds, and although they shared a room, Julia and Tom ensured the boys had their own belongings.

Dr. Holmes probed her tummy with a handheld ultrasound. He pushed the probe over Robbie and viewed his curled-up body. He looked fine, but his HR was now 165 and his head was facing up. Then he looked over at the monitors and Julia read 40 bpm and she had spiked a fever. He adjusted the bed to see if he could help her push the baby, but there was no change.

"Get me an operating room," Holmes called to the nurse. "We need to move her now."

The nurses quickly made a path for the stretcher. The tubes and monitors were easy to gather, and she was rolling out the door in seconds.

Robbie was happy to stay right where he was. The doctor made one last attempt to induce labor and see if Julia might start contractions. But there was no response. Tom was watching through the viewing room. Somehow, she was losing blood and it showed in her face and body. Now, seven people crowded around her stretcher, three on each side of Dr. Holmes.

"Her heart rate is 35, blood pressure 90 over 55," said the nurse.

"The baby's heart rate is back to 150."

"We need to get him out," said Holmes.

"Prep her for a C-Section."

The team moved quickly, rolled in new tools, and readied the patient for surgery. A second nurse stepped out to tell Tom what was happening. They would perform surgery to remove the baby and keep him informed at key intervals. It was now nearly 2am.

Dr. Holmes performed the surgery. It was a routine incision and Robbie was removed with ease and placed into his clear plastic crib. He rested peacefully.

During the following 2 hours, three doctors and four nurses used every resource to keep Julie alive. She was a very strong woman, a native American, and a fighter. There were several moments that day when her heart could have stopped, her blood pressure would not rise or her heartbeat might have slowed too far, but her will to live was even stronger. After one of the most grueling childbirths over 24 hours, Julia would rest, and her vital signs would return to normal. This family had angels watching over them.

Tom looked in from the maternity ward window at the boys. Months ago, he and Julia knew it would be exciting and yet challenging to bear twins. When Jack was born, Julia glanced up at Tom with a reassuring look that she was alright and could handle birthing Robbie.

Jack opened his newborn eyes and glanced over at his brother. Robbie was awake and peeking back towards him. Before birth, they had each other in darkness and now they loved each other even more in the daylight. With their mothers blood still circulating in theirs, the boys looked over to their father. What lay ahead for the Mohr family was a lifetime of amazement and wonder.

~

The twins were born in February of 1992, in Pisces, the year of the Monkey, Miley Cyrus and Kyrie Irving. They were born in Tacoma, Washington and grew up in a small town near Seattle called Reston on Puget Sound. The population was less than 1000 and most folks made easy introductions simply by saying they were from nearby Tacoma. Their family owned a few acres of land on the waterfront and a home-made boat dock stretching over forty yards on a finger of the Sound. From the kitchen window, you could see for miles on a clear coastal day. The view faced true north, across the islands with Seattle in the distance. It was close to the city yet far enough to be perfectly isolated. Jack's father, Tom, was from Long Island, New York, and the son of a German immigrant. Their family history traced back to the early 1800's when they arrived from Europe and settled in New York. Most of the men in his family worked in construction, brick laying, or some form of building. Jack's great grandfather was the first to move west and raised his family near Chicago. As a child, Tom enjoyed the big city and exploring nearby Lake Michigan. One of his fondest memories was a long car ride from Chicago to Milwaukee along the lake. He remembers stopping at every major harbor to watch the boats. Jack was fascinated by navigation and the fact that a ship could travel over 2000 miles from Lake Michigan to the Atlantic Ocean. He would stop at gift shops, buy postcards with pictures of all kinds of traveling ships, and pay extra attention to any card with the backs of the boats. It was all about the "names" of the boats that told the story. Jack shared this love for boats and the significance of their names. He had his list of favorites.

Jack's father owned a very successful lumber yard in Tacoma. Most of his customers were interested in high-end home building and bought custom laminated wood beams that were typically longer than the bed of an 18-wheeler. He also specialized in hard-to-find exotic wood used in bespoke projects, including cabinets, desks, and unique items for yacht interiors. He catered to builders who wanted authentic, thin, clean wood and were particular to avoid veneer. His selections included mahogany, burl wood, teak and some exotic Asian wood with elaborate patterns of light & dark wood grains. Tom had a passion for finding hard wood from all over the world and his customers knew he had some of the finest inventory.

He also maintained a showroom that displayed the woodwork from several of his clients. Jack's favorite was a scale-model of a wooden yacht that rested near the front entrance of the lumber yard. It was nearly three feet long, and carefully hidden drawers were pulled out from the various parts of the yacht. There were three masts and multiple sails. Whomever crafted this yacht was a meticulous craftsman and a magician to hide all the secret compartments. Jack once counted over 30 known drawers with a likelihood of several more that were hidden or required a form of unlocking. The yacht was a treasure and symbol of their joy for vessels that sailed the open waters. And the back was signed Wet-Ev-Oar.

Jack's mother, Julia, was a model-like beauty from head to toe. She was born a Native American Indian in the Utah mountains. Her parents were from the Navajo and Ute tribe. Julia's birth name was Aiyana and meant "Endless Beauty." Her thin lines were elegant as she could dress up or down to match any occasion. Her choice to sell real estate was second to modeling. She managed a small real estate group of independent brokers in the Pacific Northwest. Their specialty was finding undervalued homes and matching first time homeowners who needed to stretch their incomes.

His mother was tall at 5'10," with an hourglass figure, and striking brown eyes. Tom and Julia managed two separate and fulfilling careers that allowed them plenty of time to raise children. Jack had 2 older sisters, Amara, and Gianna. Growing up, they were both taller than him until middle school when he finally passed Gianna just before high school.

Robbie was special. He had the best features of Julia and Tom, and depending on who was judging, a bit more handsome than Jack, especially head-n-shoulders good looking. Although his body could not keep pace with his brother, Robbie had more sense of presence and commanded attention without trying. He was autistic, but that seldom mattered in the Mohr house.

~

Jack's friends always commented on the beautiful women in his family growing up. It was natural gifts that gave them gorgeous heads and shoulders atop their slim figures. They looked like they were meant for a fashion magazine or runway. Once, during a family vacation, they stopped by a 5-star hotel and the owner called them out in the lobby. He was intrigued by the children and asked them over to the main desk where he described the hotel's origin, pointed out some of the upscale amenities, and waved his hands past the view of the grounds as he continued to gloat. He wanted them to stay and have a closer look and invited them to a drink and appetizers at the bar. Tom was taken back by the man's forwardness but felt like they were given a gift. They looked at the kids and said,

"How about a fancy drink and snack with the owner. Anyone want to join me?" said Tom.

"Absolutely," Amara exclaimed, "that sounds awesome."

They zig-zagged to the garden patio and positioned themselves around a flowing fountain. The owner greeted them and swung his arm in a welcoming manner to have them join at the bar.

"Please help yourself to whatever you like," he said.

The twins and the girls were still underage and ordered soda. Tom had a cocktail and they toasted to a special evening with an unusual encounter. The owner made his way over to Tom and leaned in to ask a favor.

"I wonder if I could ask a special favor? He asked.

"We are having a photographer come in this evening for some shots of the hotel and I wanted to include your family as my guest. Would that be ok…?"

"Of course," replied Julia, "We'd love to."

After several camera flashes and group poses, the owner returned with an envelope and handed it to Tom. It was a gift certificate to stay at the hotel, including a suite, dinner, and a note from him at the bottom. It read, "You have a lovely family, and it is my pleasure to invite you to stay with us." He added, "My daughter is a professional photographer doing a shot for the Langham Hotel chain. Normally, they would want to shoot on their properties, but I couldn't pass up the opportunity to have her include your lovely family." Later that year, Jack's family was put on the cover of a brochure for the grand opening of the Langham Hotel in San Francisco.

Growing up in a small town in Washington was simply wonderful. Jack's father built their house and made sure that there was plenty of room for everyone. The Mohr's had an extreme love for being part of a family and enjoying being together, especially in their home. They used very special math to calculate the space required in their home. It went something like this: Multiply the number of family members by 2, which is the approximate total number of rooms required. The typical house for 4 kids would be a 4-bedroom, three-bath (aka a 4/3) house, yet Jack would enjoy an enormous 11 room home with enough bedrooms, baths and living areas, basement, and a gorgeous kitchen with much room to spare. Robbie once asked his mother why they didn't have 12 rooms and Julia replied, "we knew you and Jack would share a room for life, and eleven is a perfect number for our family. It is a number of enormous mental and physical power, and people who embody it often display heightened intuition, natural intelligence, and spiritual insight."

"Ok," said Robbie. "Eleven rooms are perfect."

The twin's room was extra-large with plenty of windows and room for all their hobbies and creative projects. They shared common interests in fish aquariums, train sets, and musical instruments. Their bedroom furniture was insignificant and positioned in opposite corners. Along the long wall facing the backyard, were two long rectangular windows that stretched nearly 10 feet each. It was more than just a room with a view. It was their window into passion and exploration. It was their looking glass into their lives. They would spend endless nights together looking out to the night sky and wondering about the future.

~

After age five, Robbie began nonverbal language skills. Hand gestures and face and eye contact covered most of his needs. Jack asked him again if he wanted to learn sign language and Robbie said, "No, I can speak just fine."

At age nine, just before entering the third grade, Robbie bet Jack they could pass all the requirements in Boy Scouts to be an Eagle Scout. The Scout requirements said you needed to be age 10 to join and it took most boys till age 13 or 14 to become an Eagle. It was unofficial, but the boys met all the requirements in less than a year and became "honorary Eagle Scouts" before the age of nine. They were now in good company with Ashton Kutcher, William Gates Sr, (Bill's dad), of course, Bill Gates is a Life Scout.

On their tenth birthday, Tom gave the boys a gift for them to share. It was a true astronomy telescope and could see the star maps the boys knew by heart. It was a refractor telescope with a 2-inch eyepiece, a 10" aperture, and fitted with equatorial mounts - enough magnification to see what was happening as far away as Mars. Together, they used their Night Sky app on their iPad and their new telescope to see several favorite constellations and imagine a few of their own. Life looking through their telescope brought new joys into their minds. The sky expanded their imagination into a 3D world that extended to the end of the universe. Through stargazing, Robbie began to separate his mental journeys from Jack, and these stars brought them back together years later after an exotic night club in San Francisco.

Julia served the family breakfast by 7am, even during the summer months and kept the dishes and meals moving for the six of them. The girls were looking into colleges, Tom was always busy at work, and the boys had bounds of time to soak up their summer. Their routine was simple. Breakfast fed the brain, followed by reading in the mornings which was mandatory for at least 2 hours. Subjects varied from classics such as "Lord of the Flies," "Huckleberry Finn," and "Call of the Wild" to non-fiction subjects of interest and, finally, to trashy fiction novels about action, mystery, and even romance. The boys were voracious readers and could read and swap a novel daily. Call it speed reading or overly fast readers; they shared at least one skill with almost exact precision.

Lunch was served promptly at 11:30am and then a long walk to the community center.

"Why do we always walk to the center when Mom can easily drive us?" questioned Robbie.

"I'd rather walk than be stuck in a car; besides, it's less than 2 miles and mostly flat," replied Jack.

"I still think walking is boring."

"Ok, let's make it less boring," said Jack. "I'll bet you I can stump you in three questions or less."

"I can beat you in two." Jack knew he would take the bait.

"Ok, then let's agree to the following. We each get to ask each other 2 questions and to keep some boundaries, the context must be from our readings in the past week."

"Game on," said Robbie.

The first time through, they each came up with incredibly obscure questions and each found their opponent worthy and capable. It also made the walk seem quicker and their destiny to the center an easy trek. The center was only fun during the summer months when the boys mingled with kids from other schools and worked on their social skills. They played sports such as kickball and wiffle ball, creative endeavors like painting, making candles and weaving, and then a few sports strategy games such as miniature pool and Robbie's favorite, the carrom board game. Carrom was a game that elegantly mixed strategy and luck such that you could gloat if you were winning and just look away when you were losing. The perfect game. And for some reason, no one ever owned a board at home. Again, a perfect set of circumstances and challenges.

Maybe the one advantage Robbie had (on any opponent) was his extreme love for this game and the magic of circle pieces that fit nicely

into his complex brain. When he played carroms, he was in his element. Like the game of pool, there were only 2 degrees of freedom for the game pieces. Interestingly, carrom comes from pool meaning to strike two balls in succession using a single cue ball is "to carrom" off one another. As a perfectionist of the game, Robbie knew to bring graphite shavings to keep the pieces sliding effortlessly across the board. He would challenge anyone in the Center. The take was usually for 25 cents up to a dollar. Most kids had some spare change and were willing to play a smallish kid like Robbie. Looking back, it was likely one of the few traps the boys set amongst their willing opponents. Not every day was a carrom challenge, but certainly once a week and winnings could exceed $5 on a good day. Reading and Community Center visits were focused primarily on Mondays, Tuesdays, and Thursdays.

Wednesdays were dedicated to music and included studying, practicing, and performing. The boys were expected to know piano, guitar, violin and at least one wind instrument. And to know an instrument in the Mohr family, was to be a master. The girls played piano and flute from elementary through high school and performed annually in concert. Amara had a slight advantage in piano, and Gianna was the first chair violinist at Reston High. Both boys could sight-read and would often have a rehearsal listening to recorded music and then practice on one of many instruments. Pachelbel's Canon in D major was a popular duet that Jack and Robbie played and would evenly switch from piano to violin. Julia was a concert pianist, and the children were expected to have some playing time in their repertoire to include Bach, Beethoven, Chopin, Handel, Liszt, Mozart, Rachmaninoff, Tchaikovsky and Vivaldi. The music room was the house's second largest room, with plenty of room for a baby grand piano and a miniature stage.

And of course, the Mohr Performing Arts would occasionally have a Christmas or Easter concert with local neighborhood folks in attendance. Tom was the gracious host, Julia the conductor and the twins and girls would play piano, violin, cello, clarinet, flute, French horn, piccolo, and the guitar or drums when required. The boys performed jams every Wednesday after lunch when not in concert. It was a mix of favorites from Elton, Billy Joel, George Michael, Phil Collins, Sinead O'Conner, and Gaga. As a backup career, they agreed they would start a band and pull in the sisters to help with the female solos. Interestingly, before they completed middle school, the boys had written enough of their music to make an album.

The week ended each Friday with inventions. Tom would stay home an extra hour after coffee and lead the conversations which typically had a core subject and then a light discussion on technology, value, and where there was a gap or need for improvement. While other kids learned about mousetrap cars, Jack and Robbie challenged themselves with energy conservation (alternative fuels, energy storage), health or medicine, and sustainable foods. Tom selected these group topics for discussion knowing full well they were more important towards the end of one's life and he wanted the boys to understand and own their future constraints.

Their summer explorations included breezing through the infamous potato battery experiment, a host of homeopathic medicines and antibiotics using herbs from the garden, a makeshift windmill that used the wind power to drive a mechanical pump (for well water), and some homemade rockets with very inventive fuel supplies. Before his coffee had cooled, Tom would leave the boys with some minimal directions and hoped that when he returned for dinner, that chaos or mischief had not taken out any house structure or any electrical, plumbing, or significant repairs. The trebuchet experiment went terribly wrong after a few test flights of a golf ball that flew through the window in a smashing fashion. The boys knew this invention originated in China before Christ and made its way through parts of the middle east and Africa before having a greater impact in Europe in the Middle Ages. The invention of gunpowder followed this weapon, and it is now mostly used as a physics experiment.

"It's a bad experiment, if you ask me," said Jack.

"It feels like the most difficult way to make a simple catapult," replied Robbie.

"Oh great, so why did Dad make us build this contraption? It's more of a nightmare than any kind of threatening weapon of choice," said Jack.

"I believe Dad wanted us to learn and understand they each played a part in the world. The reason for using the more complex trebuchet was to hurl a heavier object farther than any catapult would deliver, allowing soldiers to destroy enemy walls from a longer distance." said Robbie. "He wants us to remember that there are many times while inventing where there may be a specific solution to a unique problem."

"I know you're right, and we still have a window to repair," Jack smiled.

Most people assumed they were brothers separated by a few years. And, outside of the classroom, this was about the right measure. Standing side-by-side, the gap was over a foot, with Jack nearly 62 inches and Robbie closer to 50 inches (just above 4 feet). Their weight differed by over 30 lbs., ranging from 115 to 85 lbs. However, their good looks were remarkable, and people didn't seem to care that they were odd to be twins.

Over the next few years, there were two areas where the boys began to grow apart. The first was in sports where Jack excelled in almost any sport involving athleticism. He was fast and used his quickness to dominate in basketball, baseball, and flag football. The family was big on swimming and tennis, and Jack managed to play nearly every sport in middle school. However, Robbie could not keep up with Jack or many sports where speed or agility was an issue. He was a fast swimmer and held his ground in tennis but was never selected for elite teams or contests. However, he continued supporting his brother and attending most competitions. By high school, Robbie was limited to walking, bicycle riding and casual tennis. In contrast, Jack was winning in both team and individual sports as he entered his next school phase.

The second area of divergence was with girls and soon-to-be girl-friends. From head-n-shoulders view, the boys looked like identical twins with dark brown, straight hair, blue-green eyes, and gorgeous smiles. They each were worthy of winning the best-looking girls in school, and they did, but not quite in equal fashion. Jack's groupies were infatuated with his sports and physic and Robbie's followers were more into his charm. Interestingly, the Mohr boys and their attracted girls were divided in their interests, which made for easy double dates, aka the playground hookups. Robbie's was the politest of anyone and got his training from his older sisters. Certainly, Jack was a young gentleman too. However, he was also the primary instigator for areas such as touching and kissing games, early interest in smoking, target shooting (with any sort of homemade weapon), and electrification of bikes and other moving objects. None of these areas were mischievous, rather their young age allowed them a pretty long leash. The boys never got hurt and always treated others with respect and safety.

During the summer of their 11th year, there were many firsts including their first cigarette, first time in an R-rated movie, first kiss and first sleepover with the opposite sex. Even better was that the sleepover was with Samantha Miller, who they knew from the church camp. On her birthday, she invited her best friend and the twins to play water games in the backyard and spend the night in a family-size tent. Robbie innocently taught them how easy it was to zip two sleeping bags together and the night ended with each boy getting to sleep with their first young woman. Jack would remember his first kiss with Sam and the chance to spoon in their joined sleeping bags.

Surprisingly, with all the curious and brilliant ideas Jack and Robbie produced, they never crossed the line into theft, property damage, or any sort of wrong behavior. They knew of other mischievous kids, mostly from the Community Center, who had knives, bb guns, pornography, and recreational drugs, but the Mohr's were clear about virtues and keeping on a straight and narrow path.

At 12, Jack the entrepreneur, had converted a paper route delivery job into a joint mail/newspaper/package delivery service. He called it "Jack's Daily Delivery Service or the Triple D's. He made money from sales and service from the nearby homes within a 3-mile radius. He rode a modified mountain bike with a sidecar with enough room for his delivery materials and his co-pilot, Robbie. He quickly learned that people wanted special services and if it meant getting their mail to the post office after hours or bringing a hot loaf of French bread home for dinner, there was always a need and associated fee. This was years before Door Dash! Jack & Robbie made over $1000 in their first year and managed the business to over $2500 before they turned 13.

After being easily identified as gifted children in elementary school, the boys attended the same middle school, which began their slow separation. They took very different classes and had few friends in common. They were both incredibly smart, but as opposite as any two twins could be, at least at school. Both attended a small, public school in Reston where everyone knew about Robbie's condition. He had autism spectrum disorder or ASD and was supported through the school's IEP team. The crazy truth was that Robbie was far more intelligent than his peers and going to school was more for the social aspects.

During the summer of his freshman year in high school, to obtain volunteer credit hours, Jack spent time at a hospital clinic where he focused on kids who were not sick but came to the clinic for company. He worked with gifted children and found that interactions with these kids were incredibly easy.

At one of his shifts, he brought Robbie along to assist him. He brought his backpack to the room and left it on the table. One of the kids took out his textbook and gestured for Jack to read to him. "Are you sure you want me to read this textbook?" said Jack.

Three of the four kids nodded and with simple instructions, Jack opened his biology book and began reading about cell division. The reading was "textbook-boring" and as he continued to read, more kids joined the small group until nearly a dozen kids were all listening. It was an advanced textbook, yet they watched Jack read as if the material was an exciting story about intrigue or mystery. He continued to read and after nearly an hour of page turning, he put the book down to give the kids a rest.

Then Luke, one of the more animated ones of the bunch, gestured to Jack a hand motion to keep reading. So, he read for another chapter and wondered how this group of young kids were so enamored with him. Some of the material was complex, but Jack kept feeding their listening appetite.

Robbie was seated next to Jack and watched the group intensely. Throughout the readings, Jack would look over to his brother and be comforted as Robbie gently nodded his head, acknowledging it was working. Throughout the summer, Jack brought several books to read to his young class; each time, they were fascinated by the new topics. Jack was only 15 years old and reading advanced college textbooks. This was supposed to be hard work and very difficult subject material. Instead, the group seemed to know the material before Jack read aloud. Their faces looked on with eager anticipation. It was like feeding baby ducklings.

When Robbie joined the group, it was like an adult entered the mix. However, he was Jack's twin and since they shared a womb, he had clout. Robbie would sit in different places around the group to keep some form of rotation around Jack. It was his way of shaking things up a bit. The team knew the drill and they put up with him. In private, they would always chat, and Jack would often be their center of attention. From the beginning, Jack felt like there was something of great significance in this group of children, but it took years before he realized was in the presence of incredibly brilliant minds.

Jack was especially intrigued by several of the kids who demonstrated an extraordinary ability to solve complex problems He recalls the boy named Michael, who wanted to explore the earth's gravitational pull, but could not figure out how to solve his problem at the clinic. He asked Jack to help him with permission to go on a field trip to the local planetarium in Seattle where he could study the planets and better understand the relationship with the solar system. Without any textbooks or training, Michael drew a problem set of the night sky and scribbled his findings over several sheets of paper. It was a waterfall of calculus math equations that used more Greek symbols and squiggly lines than individual numbers. It was amazing. Jack wondered how one of his students could have the body of a teenager and the brains of an astrophysicist. Michael addressed the group and said, "I wanted to thank you all for taking me to the planetarium to see the beauty of the night sky, especially during the daytime.

There is more to learn from the stars and our universe, and I truly understand why Einstein spent so much time looking upwards to the heavens." The boys knew Einstein was on the spectrum and like many people, likely spent the better part of his life being misunderstood.

"These are the celestial bodies," said Robbie. "And your mind travels beyond this Earth and carries your dreams to the orbiting planets and stars.

"And if billionaires like Bezos and Musk have it their way, we will colonize the Moon and Mars in less than a decade," smiled Jack.

"Maybe we will all go to the Moon together?" asked Luke. His curiosity was always filled with hints of kindness.

Eventually, the immaculate reading group of boys whittled down to five, including Robbie and their distinguished ad hoc teacher who constantly wondered who was learning amongst this special group. Jack knew firsthand that Robbie was unusually smart, but now he wondered if he may have underestimated the depth of his intelligence. Over the past couple years, Jack was spending more time on his own life and neglecting time with his brother.

Attendance in the group was always perfect, so when Paul, the youngest member at 13 years old, was conspicuously absent, it raised concern. Paul had always been present, using his infectious smile as affirmation. Jack looked to him for approval when it came time to decide to continue or conclude their sessions. On this particular day, Paul was missing. Jack asked the group about his whereabouts, only to be met with blank stares. He continued reading until there was an opportune moment to wrap up the session, then went to find him. He went to the nurse's station, seeking information about Paul's condition. The nurse checked her records and informed Jack that a Paul Simpson had been reported sick and was in room 218. Jack hastened to the elevator and arrived at Paul's room. Inside, a doctor and nurse tended to him, asking gentle questions to gauge his condition. When Paul spotted Jack, he smiled. Jack reciprocated, saying,

"Hey, we missed you today. I read the next chapter on human and plant cells and wanted to keep you up to date with the others. Maybe I can catch you up on the material when you feel better."

Paul grinned again, with an awkward wink with his right eye.

"Are you ok…?" Jack asked.

He nodded in return and smiled. Jack followed as the staff left the room and spoke softly to the doctor to get his attention.

"Excuse me, Doctor Thomas, I work with Paul in the ASD classroom and just wanted to know if he is ok."

"He will be fine," the doctor replied. "If you need the full report, you might check with the desk as I can only share with family members."

Jack returned to Paul's room and shared some details of his hectic day as work and studying for upcoming exams. Paul watched Jack's face and took in the movement of his lips and eyes. Jack could feel his intense focus and knew that his complex daily life story fascinated Paul.

"You know, I think we have a lot in common," Jack commented.

Paul turned his head and gave a sideways smile. At first it did not seem so obvious. Jack was a gifted, tall, handsome student with about every option available in life. Paul, at just over 4' tall, was barely noticeable in his hospital bed, and required several pillows to prop up his body to look normal.

"Sure, we do," said Paul.

"We both have endless fascination with the world, we like facts without the sugar coating and our blue-green eyes are the envy of all the nurses."

Paul returned a huge grin and moved his head in a gentle half-circle.

"Let me try to get an update on the status and how long you'll be hooked up to these tubes. I'm guessing you got a little dehydrated and will be back with the group tomorrow."

The team witnessed Paul's weakness earlier in the morning, and his face looked far too white. When Jack returned, the group was very anxious for a status report, and he had them circle their wagons for these words. "I'm still getting more information on what happened this morning. From what I can surmise, this was the first episode for Paul. The doctors are checking to see if it was just a matter of dehydration or what caused the blackout. I did get to see him, and he looks just fine. He should be back in the group by tomorrow. I will be sure we can all see him soon.

CHAPTER
THREE

UPSIDE DOWN IDIOTS

THIS INCREDIBLE STORY begins in a rather unexpected way, with Jack in the company of a remarkable group of individuals, immersed in a diverse range of literature, from romantic Shakespeare to obscure Einsteinian theories. It's fascinating how this seemingly innocuous hospital reading group would eventually lead to one of the most groundbreaking advancements in medical science.

In the realm of intelligence, a plethora of antonyms exist for 'genius'—words like imbecile, inability, dunce, and nincompoop spring to mind. These terms often label someone as an outsider, excluded from the team, or worse, made to feel unintelligent by those who consider themselves more astute. Yet, when it comes to personal experience, being called an 'idiot' can carry vastly different weight depending on who utters it. For instance, in a random road rage incident, when an enraged driver hurls the epithet, it stings far more than if it were a casual comment from a passing acquaintance.

How would you feel If you were called an idiot? Does it really depend on who called you an idiot? Let's say there was a random road rage incident on the way home from work, and an enraged driver swerved and cut you off, calling out, "Hey, you idiot, I was here first." So, when is it ever justified to label someone a 'jackass,' 'fool,' 'dummy,' or 'idiot'? Perhaps never. And what about when one directs such derogatory words at oneself? In moments of self-frustration, many of us have, at one point or another, called ourselves a 'stupid idiot' or a 'dumb jackass.' But why? Is it some peculiar form of self-soothing? The historical tendency to brand those with cognitive differences as 'stupid,' 'foolish,' or 'idiots' only perpetuates harmful stigmas.

What if we tried to acknowledge outstanding achievements, commend amazing talents, and celebrate genius instead? Would anyone take offense at being told, "Your idea is fantastic. You are really smart"? Interestingly, most intelligent individuals already know their capabilities, so external comments can either bolster their ego or leave them indifferent.

This brings us to the crux of the matter. It's more about the person making the statement (the barker) than the one receiving it (the recipient). When a genius receives praise from peers, it is met with gratitude and a sense of deserving. Yet, if the same compliment comes from a grocery clerk at Walmart, it might be met with a touch of smugness. Until that genius exits the store only to find a rogue shopping cart has careened into the front of their car.

"What kind of idiot lets the cart run free?"

"Almost any idiot," said a passerby.

How profound is the question; Are idiotic things more likely to occur near Walmart than Whole Foods or Nordstrom? If someone makes a mistake, large or small, who is to say whether the impact is large or small? If a clerk at Walmart shortchanges you $1.95 and the manager of the men's suit department at Nordstrom overcharges your card too much or $195 (100x from Walmart), who has made the greater mistake?

To the Walmart receipt, "Oh crap, who cares?" and then toss into the trash.

To the Nordstrom credit card mistake, "Oh crap, what a stupid mistake. You're an idiot for not watching the total as they rang up the suit."

It was all so trivial and yet part of everyday life. There are invite-only clubs dedicated to people considered intellectually smart. On a spectrum, they include Cerebrals, Colloquy, Intertel, Mensa, Poetic Genius Society, and the Prometheus Society. Most are measured using the IQ score with Mensa at 130, Prometheus at 160 (including Einstein and Hawking), and the Mega Society with IQ scores above 170 or about one in a million individuals. One of the smartest US politicians was John Sununu, Governor of New Hampshire, who served under President Bush and has an IQ of 175 (member of Mensa and Mega). Genius IQ is >140. Charles Darwin was about 165, Bill Gates was around 170, Galileo was at 185, and Isaac Newton was closer to 190. Chris Langan has an IQ of >195, dropped out of Montana State University - and is currently a farmer in Missouri. Chris Hirata, circa 1982, worked for NASA at age 16 with an IQ of 225. Terence Tao teaches math courses as a professor at UCLA with an IQ of 235. Jacob Barnett, circa 1988, was diagnosed with Asperger's and has an IQ of 189. And finally, autistic children regularly score above 160 IQ.

How important is it to turn things upside down? There is an upside-down bikini trend where women turn the coverup triangle and point it down, thereby covering up much less of the breast. Diana Ross made the lyrics famous, suggesting, "you're turning me upside down." And Jack Johnson made it very clear in his song that "I want to turn the whole world upside down." How is it that turning something upside down has such a significant impact? The bikini is suddenly sexier. The song lyrics suggest you're turning my body upside down, inside out, and round-n-round. It is crazy fun.

"Oh my god," Jack thought, "this journey (with the Saints) is going to be fantastic."

The words are simple, but the meaning is exquisite. The group of rare, unique, one-of-a-kind individuals had to be given an identity to represent their unending wisdom and wonder. A name that ties them together and separates them from other "typical" groups. Nothing as corny as Fabulous Five, Genius Gentlemen, Wheelhouse Wizards, or his worst favorite, Guys without Gals, would serve these amazing characters. This team had no leader, kingpin, or ruling order. No bylaws, regular meetings, and certainly, no structure or hierarchy in the group. They were the most unique and (soon to be) most influential people in his world and would be affectionately known as the "Upside Down Idiots" Club. There were 5 in the club, and amongst themselves, they were known as the Saints.

Jack was their lifeline to the everyday world and forever an upside-down club emeritus. Robbie told Jack,

"I hope our brains will always be connected through common pathways we understand, and our hearts will remain together no matter how far our brains get disconnected." So, here our story begins.

CHAPTER
FOUR

ROBBIE & JACK

THE CHANCES OF FRATERNAL TWINS, where one has autism and the other is neurotypical, are less than 10%. Autism is considered to have a genetic component, often inherited from a parent. However, there are instances during pregnancy that might trigger autism, particularly if there's an existing genetic vulnerability. Despite being twins, it was their differences that made them extraordinary. Julia and Tom deliberately nurtured their individuality, even down to their clothing, avoiding the common reference to them as "the twins." Julia viewed it as allowing them to shine individually, rather than being lumped together. Their distinct preferences, tastes, and thoughts were celebrated. In family photos, they flanked their parents, alternating between boy-girl-boy-girl. Even the arrangement of Christmas stockings reflected their birth order, and their yearbook photos were side by side.

One of the most obvious and fabulous overlaps with the boys was their amazing brains. Julia would disagree and point to their good looks. However, the passion and wit from these two was incredible.

The boys shared an immense vocabulary and to keep their edge, they also created new phrases to push each other's boundaries. Like a game, they sometimes translated common or complex wordings to their own. Some examples included Artificial Intelligence = Neurological fake out, Headache = Pain in the brain, Headstrong = One way street, the list went on and on.

Genetic engineering was a daunting subject for most, but not for Jack and Robbie. Their solid foundation in various scientific disciplines, including anatomy, biology, physiology, and a host of other "-ologies," served as a springboard to becoming experts in the field. Robbie harbored aspirations of becoming a doctor, perhaps even a neurologist. He had already delved deep into the intricacies of brain anatomy and function, and was now exploring disorders, injuries, and medical interventions.

CHAPTER
FIVE

FIVE SAINTS

NONE of the Saints were particularly athletic. While they enjoyed watching sports and delved into game stats with a certain fanaticism, when it came to physical coordination, they'd be hard-pressed to execute a play, catch a ball, or make any significant throws. Due to their autism, they tended to have lower motor skills, which made individual-player sports like swimming, tennis, horseback riding, and martial arts more accessible. The extent of their basketball prowess was usually limited to playing NBA 2K on the PlayStation, hardly enough to get their heart rates above 90 bps. Walking and hiking were their preferred forms of exercise.

As a group challenge, Robbie once brought a surprise activity to the park.

Robbie told the group, "I wanted to try our skills with a balance and speed drill. It's called the Ickey Shuffle and is used for improving both forward backward and lateral movements. And while none of us plan to play football or tennis soon, we can try our luck with speed and agility."

Robbie spread the 12-foot ladder on the playground in a perfect straight line. There were 11 "steps" to jump over and various running patterns or "shuffling" to perform.

Robbie added, "Let's begin with the simple straight pattern by quickly stepping across the ladder. I'll time each of you and record your best time out or 3 runs. Luke you'll go first."

Luke, followed by Michael, Joseph and Paul ran through the ladder with impressive speed and accuracy. In every case, their times improved as they learned their skill. Robbie taught them 4 other drills involving side-stepping, speed hopping and arm swinging.

"Oh my God," yelled Joseph as he watched Paul zip over the ladder course. "You look like a crazy chicken flapping your wings."

"Wait till you try it. I'll be laughing at your every move," replied Paul.

This craziness went on for over an hour with the Saints in full stride with competitive spirit for each new Ickey dance. They were in their element working and playing together with improvements in form and speed. On the last run, Robbie challenged them.

"Ok, it's time to tighten this up and get real. Each of you are making strides (with a big grin from Robbie), in your approach to the ladder runs. However, it's time to increase your performance to elite levels."

"Oh, sure we can improve," said Joseph. "Maybe you can show us how."

Robbie decided to spend a few moments on the mental and physical aspects of these drills. He reviewed the elements of speed including reaction times, distractions, and an odd factor of starting while breathing out vs breathing in. He went on to show how repeated training and exercise, like breaking Olympic records, happens over time and practice. Literally, these athletes put in over ten thousand hours of dedicated workouts. Robbie reminded the team that none of them had reached their full potential and that a 10% improvement could be achieved through focus and eliminating distractions. He asked each Saint to close their eyes for a minute and see themselves completing the ladder exercise more efficiently and quickly than ever. It was now time to prove his theory.

Luke was first to the line. Robbie asked him to breathe in and out slowly three times and on the fourth breath to be ready to run. As each ran their race, they seemed more confident and excited with a true sense of confidence to lower their time. Watching the intensity on their faces was amazing. Their bodies glided over the ladder with new speed and grace. Robbie put their times down on the board, showing their previous best and last race.

"Wow," said Luke, "It really works. My last race was the fastest."

Joseph high-fived Luke and said, "Excellent run my friend."

Luke slapped his hand with a smile and cocked his head slightly backwards and closed his eyes to thank him.

What happened on the playground was wonderful. These boys experienced a new sense of achievement and pride in competition. No one questioned Robbie's role as the timekeeper as he seldom moved his little frame beyond a fast walk. He was also a teacher at heart and being a team lead was perfect. If there was ever a chance to volunteer to be in charge, he would jump to the front of the line, which was his competitive advantage. He was the leader of athletes, or at least the leader of his peers in competitions with various landscapes. As a group, they were always encouraging to the point of supporting each other to win. They were each their brothers' keepers and there was never any end for praise.

It was time to reconsider the idea that the Saints weren't athletes. Each of them possessed physical strengths, tailored to their sport. Being born with autism wasn't their best attribute, but it guided each of them towards their passions.

It may be time to mention the amazing talents in language and music, starting with the Saints path for foreign countries through history, reading, and language. Every one of the saints, including Jack, had grown up learning about history naturally, albeit with a voracious appetite to learn about every period and visualize landscapes, villages, and live through the characters of their research. Joseph and Michael were always proud when a ruler carried their names into battle as kings of certain monarchies, dictators, and emperors. One of their favorites, Emperor Joseph II, sibling to Marie Antoinette, ruled in the 1700's in Austria and spoke German, Belgium, Austrian, French, Spanish and slight influence from Russia. He was a revolutionary in war, religion, and equality.

Our Saint Joseph would gather history books and recount his emperor's travels, battles, two marriages, and assume that in every case there would be the need to speak in the appropriate language. Once in their group session, Joseph announced,

"Lass mich ein freier Mann sein, frei zu reisen, frei zu bleiben, frei zu arbeiten, frei zu handeln, wo ich will, frei, meine eigenen Lehrer zu wählen, frei, der Religion meiner Väter zu folgen, frei zu reden, zu denken und zu handeln Ich selbst – und ich werde jedes Gesetz befolgen oder mich der Strafe unterwerfen," or in English,

"Let me be a free man, free to travel, free to stop, free to work, free to trade where I choose, free to choose my own teachers, free to follow the religion of my fathers, free to talk, think and act for myself — and I will obey every law or submit to the penalty."

"Your German is excellent," said Michael. "You've mastered the accent and are ready for another language."

"Austrian is very similar, and I think I might need another character before I learn French, but I can't do Marie Antoinette's voice," Joseph smiled. Holy Emperor Joseph II's sister would eventually be the Queen of France through marriage to Dauphin Louis (King Louis XVI) and Joseph would find a historical path to more French phrases.

Jack and Robbie were trained at home in French, Spanish and German. Each Mohr family member spoke at least 3 languages and the boys managed to take on Chinese. For any Eurasian business dealings, knowing Mandarin as a minimum and perhaps short forms for Korean, Japanese and Taiwanese would be required. In some cases, they mixed in reading graphic novels, learning characters, and swiftly turning pages in a backwards fashion.

Playing and listening to music were everyday occurrences for the

Mohr family and it was inevitable that the group of Saints would one day jam together. Michael played a few chords to "Piano Man" and Paul followed with a raspy harmonica duet. They were an awkward but elegant twosome who required no practice to play beautiful music by ear. The hospital had an old piano, probably donated by someone rich since it was a baby grand and stayed relatively in tune. Eighty-eight black and white keys, 88 hammers, and 230 strings made up the most universal percussion instrument. The piano was invented in 1688 by Bartolemeo Cristofori. He was an Italian and at the age of 33 was recruited by Prince Ferdinando de Medici as a lover of music and possibly for casual occasions like the Carnival in Venice. Piano means "softly, with a little force of loudness."

After a few bars, Michael switched to Blues Traveler, "Run-Around," to see if Paul could improvise in quick steps with his mouth-piece. They were very sharp runs and each player kept pace. In a few seconds, Michael went into a medley solo with Elton John's "Tiny Dancer", to the Beatles "Let it Be," and then back to Piano Man. This time, Paul took over and reminded everyone that the harmonica was the key instrument in the song. It was time to take over this gig and he moved quickly to "Love Me Do," and started the awkward Paul dance. Robbie kept the beat with the tambourine and over the next hour, the Saints held their jam session adding guitar, trumpet, flute, and violin.

In the annals of musical history, countless examples of composers demonstrated their genius in ways that left their competitors astounded. Beethoven once won a sight-reading piano competition by playing the sheet music upside down, then improvising on one of its themes for half an hour. His opponent, Daniel Steibelt, never returned to challenge him again. On another occasion, after hearing a piece just twice, Mozart played a 12-minute choral composition from memory.

Neurologists teach us that certain musical pieces affect the patterns in different brain regions and influence different memories and subjects. It means we should better understand which music is more helpful when doing math, foreign language, or English composition. Yes, music matters. Although he lived before ASD was part of his diagnosis, Wolfgang Amadeus Mozart was certainly in the autistic spectrum and is now part of the controversy involving his music and a variety of mental processes known as the "Mozart Effect." Interestingly, the Saints seldom looked at themselves through the ASD lens or had anything other than their pure love for music. They each played multiple instruments and performed organized recitals for school or after-school audiences. They were but a drummer away from starting a band.

CHAPTER
SIX

SMART BEGINNINGS

JACK WAS an academic overachiever as a student, but in his heart, he wanted to pursue great dreams and considered his drive normal. Ha. He took advanced classes in biology, chemistry, math, physics, and early junior college courses (while in high school) in anatomy and physiology. Jack was fascinated with the human body's biology and each part's kinesiology. To some, the challenge was complicated and stressful as the terminology of anatomy was like learning a foreign language. For Jack, it was exactly like learning a foreign language; he was anxious to be as fluent as possible. The process was no longer about learning, rather it was focused on how to understand and apply the information to a path forward. Jack became fascinated with blood and created a self-experiment to evaluate the efficiency of blood flow throughout several activities. He knew from extreme marathon runners that one could condition themselves to deliver oxygenated blood to working muscles (e.g., the arms and legs) well past exhaustion. Conditioned athletes could endure lactic acid build-up to the point where the condition of the blood in the system, aka; the blood oxygen saturation point would be limiting speed or endurance function. Normally, this results in a body collapsing on the running path.

However, with elite runners, they push past the pain utilizing mental techniques to conquer physical pain.

On to Jack's high school senior experiment. His goal was to evaluate his entire body as a platform where he could exercise extreme conditions to create responses from each area of his body. Some of the challenges were stresses on bones, organs, or blood circulation. Part of his data collection included distance runners who proved they could push through the pain and run until extreme exhaustion. However, Jack wanted to isolate his experiment on the path of a droplet of blood and as it traveled through the circulation system. The starting line was the heart's left ventricle at the peak of the systolic pulse wave. For the droplet of blood, it was like a downhill ski racer looking down a snow-covered hill. Whoosh! The dynamic push from behind as the valve compresses and pushes volumes of blood forward through the major veins.

Jack's mind was filled with questions. Which way did the droplet go? How many possible paths are there, and does it really matter? How can I control the flow? Does the blood move fast or slow change the property of the droplet. Since red blood cells are toroidal, will the droplet change shape due to stress or damage. If blood is a mixture, what other elements or nutrients surround the droplet? How could the droplet journey be documented? Jack imagined an intense awareness where he could feel the droplet of blood passing through his body. Beyond inhaling and exhaling and monitoring his heart rate, he imagined that he could feel the micro-droplets' path in his body as they traveled.

At age 18, and 6 foot 3 inches tall, Jack Mohr was considered tall amongst his peers. Weighing in at just under 160 pounds with a lean and athletic look. Jack graduated his senior year in high school with varsity letters in both basketball and tennis. He won the "Mr. Basketball" award for the best shooting guard in Washington State with an FG percentage of 67% and tied the school record for free throws with an average of 11 per game. As good as he was in basketball, his love was to play tennis. Jack was self-taught and found that his determination and work ethic on the courts were sufficient to put him in the top of his class. He was state tennis champion 4 years straight and was ranked in the top 20 on the west coast.

At the end of his junior year, he had full-ride tennis scholarships to Stanford, USC and UofW. During his senior year, Jack was undefeated. He won the Washington State High School tournament and competed at the USTA junior invitational in Southern California, placing first amongst the top players under 18. After the tournament, Jack recalls spending time on the beach and falling in love with the sights along Pacific Coast Highway. He drove from Los Angeles through Orange County to Laguna Hills and sat with his coffee and egg breakfast waiting for the NBA crowd to show up. By 9:30am, a few hundred folks lined the outdoor basketball court and suddenly Anthony Davis and LeBron James appeared. It was shoot-around time and after a few minutes, the court was filled with Lakers and the show began. They would have a casual pick-up game and Jack had one of the best seats in the house.

CHAPTER
SEVEN

FOUNDER PRIDE

THE UNIVERSITY OF WASHINGTON (UoW) Department of Biomedical Engineering was one of the top programs in the Pacific Northwest. It was expanding their facilities with the help of local philanthropists (aka Gates and Allen). When Jack applied for college, the only three campuses of interest were Stanford, Northwestern and UoW. He sent applications to all three in hopes of being able to make a difficult choice of where to go and the math made it very easy for him. UoW was his only acceptance, so the Bay Area and Chicago would have to wait.

While most kids in college ground through the material, he seemed to soak up every morsel of new knowledge. His passion has always revolved around biomedical engineering, including human, plant, and animal interventions. During his first few years, he managed the up-and-down grind of roommates, classes, labs, intramurals (basketball, tennis), ran an occasional 5k & 10k race and a random party with fraternity brothers. Strangely, he didn't enjoy alcohol and thought it must have been an acquired taste for all his heavy-drinking peers.

On his 21st birthday, he was guided through the Miracle Mile drinking gauntlet and after his final shot of Wild Turkey, he realized he had not missed anything. With head-spinning moments and careful control of his stomach, Jack was glad to have close friends to carefully shove his drunk ass into their cars and even kinder to carry him up the apartment stairs to a soft floor where he slept off his special day. As crazy as it sounds, in the coming years, he would be introduced to incredibly exotic alcoholic drinks. Combined with increasingly important social engagements, he would elevate his drinking with famous cities including Manhattan, Brooklyn and even Moscow (Mule).

The distance from their home near the waterfront to his freshman-year dorm was about 40 miles. Jack drove his very used, quad cab Sierra pickup with Robbie in the front seat and most of his belongings shoved on the back seat. He parked his pick-up as close to Willow Hall as possible. His dorm room was in a hallway-type layout with group bathrooms at the midpoint. Somewhat like walking down the halls of a Holiday Inn with industrial-strength carpet, painted brick walls and light-colored wooden doors at each entrance.

The move was, in part, rather easy as he only brought the essentials of clothing from half his closet, basketball, tennis racquets, a messenger-style city bike, an old-fashioned clock radio, and decorative wall hangings with dreams of superyachts, a resto-mod Camaro, and a majestic log cabin on a lake in Canada. Jack loved the 1967 Camaro he bought at age 15-½. It was a "poor man's Corvette," but gave him an amazing sense of pride and ownership. He had outfitted the car with many extras including a custom paint job, Crager mag wheels, and some diamond-tuck stitched seats. To make the experience more exciting, an 8-speaker stereo with a 12" LCD screen was years ahead of Tesla's instrument cluster. Interestingly, Jack had written a program interface with his cell phone like early CarPlay with applications appearing on the screen as if it were his phone. For now, the Camaro was in the garage back home, a poster-size picture on his wall and his F-150 quad cab was his college ride. He also brought a fancy bicycle with him in the rear bed. It was modified for racing on the streets of Washington State where Jack competed in local races from 25, 50 and

100 miles in distance. It's unclear if there would be time to ride in college, but he would keep up with running, swimming, and biking to help burn off excess calories. And of course, he brought several computers including Mac, PC, and an older game console.

He was assigned a new roommate named Kevin from Montana. When he and Robbie opened his dorm room door for the first time, they walked in to see two suitcases, a backpack, and some sealed cardboard boxes. The top shipping label read Kevin McAffee and the city was Bozeman. Kevin had arrived and claimed the "left side" of the room. Everything looked symmetrical to give each roommate their fair share of space. Jack loaded his closet with clothes, shoes and sports equipment and raised his bed to about waist height to leave room for storage underneath the bed. He pulled off the wheels of his bike and tucked them towards the back and then filled in the rest of the area with a small dresser and cabinet.

Robbie watched in silent amazement as Jack played organizer extraordinaire. Everything fit into place a bit like puzzle pieces. It was well organized with manly touches, including his favorite pics of cars and sports heroes and a special portrait of Louis Pasteur. Jack admired him for his major achievements and especially, the minor ones. Pasteur loved fishing and sketching and would have been right at home in the Pacific Northwest. Imagine the dreary weather in Arbois, France - a small town near the Switzerland border where Louis grew up. After settling down and marrying Marie Laurent, they had 5 children, Jeanne, Jean-Baptiste, Cecile, Marie-Louise, and Camille. Only Jean-Baptiste and Marie-Louise survived typhoid. Oddly, the invention of pasteurization for food processing would later be invaluable to Jack and his inventions.

For now, the bedroom was nearly complete with a few minor things like figuring out if he should rent a small refrigerator, knowing where to wash his clothes, and knowing the password to set up the WIFI connection. All this could certainly wait as it was after 5pm and time for food. Jack gestured to Robbie to follow him and then went on a food-finding expedition on campus. Classes had not officially started, yet there was a frenzy of students and what looked like a group of small restaurants. They were both hungry and settled for some sort of chicken-fried steak and fries for dinner.

"Are you ready to start school?" Robbie asked.

"Of course," said Jack. "I plan to learn new things and be surrounded by folks as smart as you. I hope you know you are welcome here anytime you wish and welcome to join in the fun."

"Now, I get my own room and plan to dive into my studies," commented Robbie.

"You'll be the smartest student Berkeley has ever seen on Zoom!" smiled Jack. "I'm guessing their professors will ask you for answers in no time. And do me a favor. Please be smooth in how you treat all these common folks. You are a unicorn's unicorn!"

"Maybe you should worry less about me and more about how you're gonna get to classes tomorrow," smiled Robbie.

"As usual, you're right. I should take you home and get some rest before tomorrow." Jack replied.

The drive back home was easy and quiet. Jack played some tunes to drown out the pick-up noise and cruise back to Reston. He got Robbie back to the house before 9pm and a quickly hugged Julia, Tom, and Robbie before the return drive. Dorm parking was easier than expected, and he returned to his room in no time. The light was on under the door and when he opened, he met his roommate in Montana cowboy clothes and the friendship began with ease.

First day as freshmen is a bit like the running of the bulls in Spain. Students looking down at their phones for their class schedules and then up to the oncoming human traffic. There was an abundance of awkward bobbing and weaving, ducking and covering. Jack had two classes on Monday; the first was an introductory biochemistry class. He went to a huge class of 200 students and sat about midway down the stairs. Coming in from a side door was the professor who intro-duced himself as Dr. Koppelman (aka: Dr K.), with a tenure of 22 years and the head of the Biological Sciences Department. He was a very tall professor at 6 foot, 5 inches and had that Abe Lincoln look with silver goatee and always dressed to impress. He turned to the board and outlined the complete semester of work. Then back around to begin his lecture and with a case study-like approach to including origin, key contributors and the three key disciplines for biochemistry including structural biology, enzymology, and metabolism.

"The key thing to remember is that biochemistry is the chemistry of the living world. Plants, animals, and single-celled organisms all use the same basic chemical compound to live their lives. Biochemistry is not about the cells or the organisms. It's about the smallest parts of those organisms, the molecules," said Dr K.

The next hour was filled with foundational material where the professor added color to areas with influencers in medicine and nutrition. Jack was captivated to hear someone with an approach to both science and real-world applications. It was day one, class one, and the best experience of his young college student life. After class, Jack made his way to the dining hall and scooped up more than he should have, but it was fun to have an all-you-can-eat buffet. His next class was at 3pm, which gave him a little time to walk the campus.

The University of Washington is ranked #7 in the world for public colleges. There are over 50,000 students per year and strength in the most challenging scholastic categories. Both Paul Allen and Bill Gates were key financial contributors and had their names on buildings in Computer Science and Engineering.

The following lecture, Dr K. begins by reading the following list of Ingredients: Enriched flour, Niacin, Reduced Iron, Thiamine Mononitrate, Riboflavin, Folic Acid, Palm Oil, Salt, Dried Carrot Flake, Autolyzed Yeast Extract, Citric Acid, Concentrated Green Cabbage Juice, Dextrose, Disodium Guanylate, Disodium Inosinate, Disodium Succinate, Dried Corn, Dried Parsley, Egg White, Garlic Powder, Hydrolyzed Corn Protein, Hydrolyzed Soy Protein, Lactose Maltodextrin, Natural and Artificial Flavor, Onion Powder, Potassium Carbonate, Potassium Chloride, Powdered Chicken, Rendered Chicken Fat, Silicon Dioxide, Sodium Alginate, Sodium Carbonate, Sodium Tripolyphosphate, Soybean, Spice and Color, Sugar, TBHQ, Wheat. Contains: Wheat, Soybean, Egg and Milk. Contains Bioengineered Food Ingredients. Manufactured in a facility that also processes peanut, tree nuts, sesame, crustacean shellfish, and fish products.

"How many of you know what I might be talking about? For most of you, life is very busy, and nutrition likely takes a back seat. Any ideas of what this college late-night staple might include these yummy ingredients?" Between the fact that he read this exhaustive list too fast and that he was still a bit of an intimidating professor, there were no raised hands.

"Here are a few hints, to help you." he read again. "Rendered Chicken Fat, Dried Carrot Flake, Dried Corn, and the most common ingredient is enriched flour. Finally, just add hot water."

Then there were many hands raised. Dr K. asked, "How many of you stock this product in your dorm rooms?" Jack scanned the room as most of the hands stayed raised. It was rather obvious now. Dr K. returned to the front of the hall and reached under the platform to reveal a plastic-wrapped item. He held up high and announced, "Yes, this delicious, nutritious food substitute also known as Cup (of) Noodles. An amazing treat that includes a host of man-made chemicals, and the all-important bioengineered food ingredients." Dr K. then provided unique insights about periods where we were heavily influenced by artificial substitutes to achieve corporate results over human interest. His references were unbiased and blended historical events into biochemistry. In passing, he brought up his thesis as a quick reference to the influence of natural and derived plants as a food source. Jack picked up on this and decided to look up his thesis work for a deeper dive at another time.

His freshman year was filled with advanced learning experiences from math, science, general arts, English and humanities. Jack took a full workload with five classes per semester and maintained good grades each quarter. It was time to think about what would lie ahead for the summer. His options included staying on campus for some sort of academic reason, heading home to be with dad and Robbie, or finding a new endeavor. He already had his sophomore year mapped out with classes towards his major and another class with his favorite professor Dr K. This time, his class would be smaller and more focused on cell biology. It was a required course for his major, and the material was intense.

~

Mid-terms were in play and Jack had his fill of preparation and execution. Spring classes were less of a challenge, or he was getting good with the system. He had five finals, three were basic challenge questions and the final two had more essay and thought processes. The exams ran through mid-March, and it was time for a week off. Jack wished his roommate (Kevin) a safe trip back to Montana and wished him well locking the room for a week away. Jack hit the road by late Friday afternoon. He stopped for wine on the way home and arrived at the smell of steaks grilling.

"Hey, who's running this place?" Jack yelled, grinning. "I'd like to order the finest steak on the menu!"

"Oh sorry, we only have leftovers," Tom grinned, but it was obvious that the joy of Jack's arrival was messing with his speech.

"Oh, I see," Jack replied. "Maybe another night would be better."

"Maybe you'd like a filet?" called Robbie.

"I would like a steak, a baked potato and red wine."

"We have a rare special this evening and I think we can accommodate one more to join." Robbie smiled.

"Hey brother," Jack grinned, "it's been too long." Jack laid down the wine and went straight to Robbie for a bro hug. "It's really good to see you, my friend."

"It's my pleasure," Robbie goofed around. "I hope you can stay a few days and we can talk."

"I am here for the week, and we will walk, talk and live to the fullest. I have no homework and only a few tiny to-dos, so we can hang out as much as you can afford. How is your schedule?" Jack said.

"I'm done with midterms too," replied Robbie. "Let me send out a request for a group meet-up. Maybe we can grab a few Saints to join us."

Saturday morning came with bird voices through the windows. The Mohr family house brought song and joy into the kitchen as the men brewed coffee. Tom prepared a full carafe for the ever-slow-moving college kids who dragged themselves to the brew. Tom poured three cups and distributed them to Jack and Robbie.

"Mmmmmm, this is perfect," said Jack. "A Saturday to enjoy with all its glory."

"You know it's just another Saturday," said Robbie.

"Yes, but it's all ours and I want to head to the lake" replied Jack.

"Wow, slow down tour Meister. Some of us are still waking up," Tom tried to reel him in a bit.

"Hey dad, where is the small boat?" Jack said.

"You mean the dinghy?" replied Tom.

"I want to take Robbie out on the bay and need whatever boat we can find," said Jack.

"Ok, give me a few minutes to figure this out. We have a few options, and I need to walk around back to see what is okay to put in the water," said Tom.

"Sorry, Dad, I just know it would be great to be on the water today," said Jack.

Tom found the small pram meant for short trips and ideal for two. It was on a trailer with bicycle wheels and easy push to the pier. He grabbed two life jackets, walked the trailer around front, and softly yelled, "Here's the fastest boat on the bay," Tom said smiling.

Jack and Robbie stumbled out onto the front porch and down to the grass. They surveyed the boat situation and then nodded. They went off without plans, lunch, snacks or even water. It was impulsive and just like two young kids on an adventure. The walk was not too far, and they both climbed into the craft with skills of plenty. It was the family pram and was only 7 feet long. Two small oars, two life jackets and then Tom yelled from the pier. "Here, catch!" He threw a brown paper sack and Jack grabbed it with luck. It was their lunch and fixings. Jack rowed about 70 feet and then slowed.

"This should work," he said.

"Wow, that was some Olympic rowing," said Robbie.

"You're now an expert," replied Jack. "We are surrounded by water and the rest is easy. Besides, I must talk to you about something and can't row all day."

"Is everything ok," Robbie replied.

"Oh ya, I just want to let you know about some developments at school," said Jack.

"Of course, let me know what's on your mind," said Robbie.

"You know about my studies and the path to a biomedical engineering major. It's complex, and nothing too much for the Mohr clan. It's my freshman year and feels like a good major. The grades are easy, most of the student body is filled with narrow social norms, and my roommate is cool."

"Ok, you seem set for the next few years," said Robbie.

"So, here comes the rush," Jack replied. "I have a new idea that might be a big deal. About a month ago, I contacted a professor about my theory, and he provided enough insights to nearly validate the hypothesis. I need your help on a few things and more importantly want your opinion."

"This sounds serious," said Robbie.

"I'm wondering if it might be important. It falls under the category of a nutritional substitute and mixes a few common elements with technology advancements and could produce amazing results. Remember the impact of artificial sugar and corn syrup," replied Jack.

"I thought you wanted to save lives through biomedical engineering?" Robbie said.

"I still do," said Jack. "I want to understand all there is to know about science and apply it to making lives better. This happens to be a steppingstone towards my goal."

"I'd love to hear more details," replied Robbie.

~

Then the dialogue dam broke, and the next hour was filled with Jack describing his invention. In between bites of his sandwich, he would call out areas where he needed more advanced thought - or more directly, Robbie's help. His idea included many steps of investigation or experimentation where each outcome determined the next path forward. For a nineteen-year-old kid, he seemed very confident in what would normally seem like a long shot to success. In their back and forth, Robbie responded to every question with a "physics-like" foundational approach that would take all possible variable outcomes and allow Jack to direct his action. Growing up, the two brothers would share stories before bed and blend their ideas into one. They would add another chapter or two during breakfast in the morning if it was a good enough story. This boat ride chat felt similar with triple the intensity.

"Do you trust Professor Dr K.?" asked Robbie.

"I do," said Jack. "I've studied his work, attended his lectures, and would like to invite him into the process. UoW has several programs for entrepreneurs and one of interest. The Paul Allen Foundation sponsors it and provides funds and lab time to support research and development. I've already downloaded the application and it's an easy submission. We need a novel idea, an enrolled student, and a "sponsor" professor. Bang, bang, bang, we got it!"

"You know the idea makes a lot of sense and makes me wonder how you came up with such a novel idea, Robbie grinned. I think it might be time to invest more of your time into the plan."

"I'm on it," replied Jack. "Now, let's talk about you and the boys."

The title of the application was simply; "Reconstructing Rice." The abstract outlined a plan to support further investigation into ways of processing brown rice, using rice as a carrier, experimenting with alternatives to mechanical processing (grinding, milling), methods of heat or liquid (drying, impregnating) and outputs including rice, and gelatinization. A thorough review of the genetic novelties of the IR8 rice program and side effects of chalky and hardened grain. Initial results include math models. The study will drive conclusions towards better intestinal health. Team members included Jack Mohr (sophomore),

Professor Koppelman (Science), and co-inventor, Robbie Mohr (UC Berkeley, sophomore). It was the end of midterm break and Jack uploaded the application. He was invited to present his idea to the application committee two weeks later. He laid out his plan with excellent details for a first-time entrepreneur. It was clear he was ready for an audience. Dr. Dr K. stopped him in the hallway on the day of this presentation, wished him luck, and reminded him he was ready, and the committee would like his approach. Jack walked to the appointment room and entered a panel of 5 senior professors. They read their opening script with support to new ideas and gave him early confidence to begin. After 15 minutes of slides, one of the professors asked, "Jack, you are a very young entrepreneur with a challenging idea ahead of you. The world has many views about rice, and you want to challenge the scientific community for a new outcome?"

"Yes," said Jack. "It's about time for new ideas. Rice makes a lot of sense as the foundation where the novelty is in what we do to enhance its value. Wheat and corn have taken their massive platforms to market, but rice makes more sense." Jack was exuding confidence while the committee huddled together. After a few minutes, they provided immediate results.

"Your idea has enormous potential and an equal number of challenges. We have decided to approve your submission with further details on the award later this week. Congratulations, and we look forward to hearing more."

Jack immediately sent a Snap to Robbie; "The rice is approved. We got it."

Robbie replied, "Another step forward, congratulations."

On Thursday, Jack received an email from Dr. K. asking him to stop by Friday morning. The subject line read "Good News." After breakfast, Jack walked briskly to Dr K.'s office. Jack knocked on his door, was told to come in, and swung open the door. Dr K. was behind his desk working on some messy lecture notes and reached over to pass him a sealed envelope. It was from the Allen Committee and Jack broke the seal. He scanned it quickly and smiled. Looking at Dr K. he spoke, "This is wonderful news. We got $500,000, 250-300 hours of lab time, unlimited computer time and three milestone deliverables. Now, I need to re-evaluate my summer plans!"

"Congratulations Jack," said Dr K. "You should be proud. I will assign another couple of students to help with modeling and experimentation. Let's meet next week to review your plan and develop a high-level schedule."

"Agreed," exclaimed Jack. His early entrepreneurial dream had begun. He returned to his dorm room although he felt different this time. He was starting a new adventure that would change his life forever.

So, back to the minor issue of what to do with his summer months. Over the next few weeks, he kept his focus on schoolwork with a crazy distraction about his immediate future. He stayed close with Robbie and his "remote studies" in physics at Berkeley and checked in with his dad on circle of life issues. His last call with Tom was rather dull talking about investments, retirement, and healthcare - the most important topics in later years. Ugh.

With Robbie, they had their different ways of communicating including SnapChat (for fun), text (for serious) and an archaic voice-mail app christened by the saints as worthy. Of the few things to do each day, one is remembering to check in on the app. The "boys" use it almost daily for obvious and missed communications - meaning most communications with Jack. It was an easy path to Mr. Busy and although there was seldom a response, they knew he would eventually listen. The beauty of this conversation was the removal of time and the need to speak to someone knowing they will respond with clarity and essentials in their own time.

Jack's message to Robbie was with a slight hint to the team. He collected his thoughts and spoke into the app, "Hi Robbie, I wanted to let you know I'm doing well with school and studies. It's coming to the end of my first year and I have the summer months to consider. I'm really enjoying some of the challenges in science and have a few ideas that are still early in thought and want time to speak with you in person. I trust you are well and that we can connect soon. Love, your favorite brother."

Over the coming sophomore year, Jack would live two simultaneous lives, including being an incredible academic student and an impossibly skillful entrepreneur. The bias was never more obvious than at the lab where advanced thinking was harnessed. After completing the first two milestones, the final prototyping stage would begin soon. The pressure was on to deliver and the best way to deal with the stress was a multitude of jokes involving the word "rice." In the morning, it was "so rice to see you," and for lunch, "would you like a rice of pizza" and while shopping, it was "how much is the "purr-rice?"

Robbie sent Jack a Snap; "hoping there is not too much sacrif-rice, in your day."

Over the coming year, the "rice project team," published results, academic papers, and a few journal articles that gained some attention. The most significant interest came from a fellow student in the graduate program who was from mainland China. He wrote to Jack and asked if they could meet to discuss some of his findings. His American name was Alex Sun, and he met with Jack for coffee to explain the following. Alex was the first of his family to leave the mainland and study abroad. He was one of 2 children (he had a sister), and his parents were in the food and agriculture business. They had been successful in raising beef, chicken, pig, and other unmentionable animals for food or food substitutes in the China market. Their clients included both restaurant and fast-food chains, making millions of yuan as one of the market's finest providers of protein-rich foods. Alex had mentioned a path to potentially augment farm-raised animals with a plant substitute and they were very excited to learn more. They asked their son, Alex, to inquire about a business proposition or convenient way to discuss potential business for his research.

Jack quickly convened with Dr K., raising the concern about what to do. Their project was for research and development. However, a commercial deal might be attractive. In the coming 3 months, they worked a deal with Alex's parents to license their project into their China market (exclusive) with royalties back to Jack, Dr K., and the university. At age 20, Jack had signed a licensing deal that would eventually grow to over 7 figures.

Jack was among the smartest kids in his graduating class at the University of Washington in Seattle. Upon graduation, several folks wondered if he would become an accomplished doctor or a world-famous scientist who might invent a new medical procedure or find a new cure for a complex disease. He never acted like a brainiac, but he certainly had the brains to do so. He was able to memorize and recall detailed information to the point of amazement. He once bet his classmates that he could recite word for word any 10 pages in print. His bet was a dollar per word and the challenge was often accepted, yet the winners were few, if any.

The rules were quite simple. Jack was given 24 hours to prepare for each contest, and then he would recite the selected 10-page section to his betting audience.

"Get your credit cards ready," Jack joked.

He breezed through Paul's passage from an advanced clinical textbook in neurophysiology in 17 minutes and then the word count was determined. He completed over 5000 words without a single mistake. Then it was time for Jessica's "Iliad" and again he whizzed through the text without a hiccup. When he was done, Jessica announced his score of 100% and announced the word count at 5127. His collective win was valued over $10,000. Jack knew he couldn't take this friend's money, so he suggested a compromise.

"Enough gambling for a while," Jack announced.

"Memorizing is very easy, and I'd like to teach you guys some tricks."

The team was pleasantly surprised and curious to learn. He proceeded to share a few techniques in speed reading and word association. Jack described a way to create a long string of characters (such as a 10-page document) and then attempted to have everyone grasp the memorization hurdle of such a long string of information.

"The brain is highly underutilized and if you use it correctly, you will amaze yourself with additional knowledge." Jack commented. "Once you gain more confidence, the results will increase, and you'll be reciting pages of text without mistakes."

The team was in awe of his ability. What Jack left out was the amazing ability of the Five Saints. It was his secret for now and his "other team," would be available when the timing was right. For now, it was about the newbies learning to find unique investments and managing the chaos of information overflow.

Then came his real genius. Jack was describing his brain-strengthening methods that were well known, (7 Easy Steps to Memorize the NY Phonebook, etc.) however, he wanted to add a slight improvement using a 3-dimensional view of the brain. He took a moment to share with his students how the mind works and compared it to a computer.

Jack said, "We use computers for many purposes, but the most basic use is documenting our work. Why can't we ask our brains to do the same...?"

In the coming 20 minutes, there was a mixture of extreme focus, hypnosis, and cerebral electricity. Jack explained how the brain was filled with excited neurons and our job was to harness these electrons for our benefit.

"Over half of what we hear and see is just noise," he said. "What if we removed this distraction and just concentrated on what mattered? When you push yourself to this upper level of consciousness, you will find some tasks which other folks consider difficult or impossible, are now routine."

The group had many questions for Jack. The evening went from a teaching lesson to a group-sharing event as Jack realized that some of his techniques were more challenging than he led on. At 21, Jack was advancing the science of human artificial intelligence without realizing his full capabilities. He was able to model the brain as if he had a PhD in computer science or an MD in neuroscience. His gift was being "wicked smart" combined with the "attitude of gratitude" to realize that it was a gift, and he would spend his life sharing, teaching and giving to others.

Jack understood the layers of intelligence in normal day life. The noisiest top level consisted of everyday chatter including small talk, social media, and television. These represented inputs with slight significance; however, nothing that could not be overlooked. The next level was the sincere level where someone important spoke and needed to be heard. It could be another student, a good friend, a family member, or a loved one. These conversations were held close to the heart and had a meaningful impression on the soft tissue. Then came the challenging third layer, which forced the brain to study or change to advance. It was commonly used for scholastic works, job stress, competitions, and strategic planning. This area was a small slice in the brain and yet carried significant power. Those in power often had control over all these elements of work, stress, competition, and strategy as if to enjoy the experience. The fourth and final layer of intelligence was likened to lucid dreaming and hyper-inclusive thoughts, and it leveraged the connections of the super-intelligent.

This was, of course, the experiences with the Five Saints. Jack knew that 98% of the time spent on work and life's daily challenges did not compare with the 2% of Saint time. He would imagine if he could somehow expand these times to be a bigger part of this life and how he would relish these experiences. An enormous part of his life was in a magic bubble with Robbie, and it then grew to include the rest of the magnificent gang. This was a spoiled richness in time with the Saints where conversations amongst the group were held as normal.

However, the subject matter was often far different than normal. Jack recalled a conversation about Reginald Dwight (aka Elton John), where the boys discussed Lady Gaga's influence as the godmother of his 2 boys, the mystery of their surrogate mother, and who was the biological father. What sounds like a tabloid headline, was treated with sincerity, curiosity, and concern. There was a common interest and collaboration about growing up without parents, his idols Elton Dean and Long John Baldry, and the lyrics to the song Jack. As the five of them spoke with Jack, the words were more than a tapestry of trivia and more like a complex map of how someone like Elton John can be part of our lives. The finale was about the piano and how it was his instrument and perhaps Elton's most significant influence since age 4.

What was it about the brain that allowed us to memorize things from recalling a lengthy recitation from a textbook to recalling the lyrics to an Elton John song? Biologically, the cerebrum contains the information that makes up your intelligence, memory, personality, emotion, speech, and ability to feel and move. And then a deeper layer suggests the hippocampus supports memory functions including sensory, short- and long-term memories. What is known and unknown about how the brain's memory functions are well documented and yet always a mystery.

In the Hollywood movie "Rain Man," Dustin Hoffman is an autistic savant with an incredible memory to recall nearly everything from his past. The movie is about two brothers who often battle their way through uncommon ways of communication encircled by a cross-country ride in the family's restored 1949 Buick Roadmaster. The main character Raymond's brain was wired differently, and each crazy scene depicted his brilliance in memory recall for the number of Roadmasters produced, match sticks in a box and counting cards with multiple decks. It is based on the real-life of Kim Peek, who could speed read books using his left eye to read the left page while simultaneously reading the right page with his right eye.

~

For over 20 years, Jack and Robbie played memory games without knowing it. They conversed on subjects that required memory recall to the extreme depths that would commonly have them diagnosed with hyperthymesia. As a twin, Jack often assumed that he and Robbie had some sort of biological path to common ground in conversations. They never argued. Their relationship was built on the sincerest brotherly love and affection that two brothers could ever hope to achieve. Physically, they were true opposites, yet mentally, they were a complete mirror image of each other.

Jack DM'd Robbie: "How far back can you recall memories from our childhood…?" After a moment, Robbie replied, "You mean inside or outside the womb?" It was unclear if he was joking, so Jack returned the following: "Can you remember any particular details of when we were young…?

"I can remember our times in the crib," said Robbie.

"Enough," replied Jack. "No one can recall memories before the age of 2 or 3. What's in your memory?"

"I remember wearing a blue onesie and you were in green. We each had our own crib, and they were close enough that I could reach over and touch you between the rails. I'm guessing we were around 1 years old."

"You know this is impossible," said Jack.

"Ok," replied Robbie. "I won't tell you the lullaby's Dad used to sing to us or your favorite stuffed animal stuffy."

"What's to say that you remember Dad singing to us, but we were actually 4 or 5 years old?" replied Jack.

"Just ask Dad why he sang "Carolina in my Mind[1]," by James Taylor, and how you moved when he sang.

~

In my mind I'm going to Carolina

   Can't you just see the sunshine

Can you just feel the moonshine
Aint it like a friend of mine to hit me from behind?
Yes, I'm going to Carolina in my mind.
Karen she's the silver sun
You best walk her way and watch it shinin
Watch her watch the morning come,
A silver tear appearing now I'm crying aint I?
I'm going to Carolina in my mind.
There ain't no doubt in no one's mind that loves the finest thing
around
Whisper something soft and kind
And hey babe the sky's on fire
I'm dying aint I? I'm going to Carolina in my mind.

"When Dad sang James Taylor, you would look over to him as if he was singing just for you. He would start with a song with a lesser-known whistle and then jump into the words of a homesick song. And you would reach out to try to touch his lovely words. I'm sure Dad sang to us about our entire upbringing, and trying to convince you how far back I can recall is tough since there is no way to know for sure. But hear me now, I can remember what we wore to bed, who sang to us, and the crankiness when we both started teething."

And without any disagreement, Jack moved on to another subject. He wondered about the relationship between memory and intelligence. Both he and Robbie had astonishing memory recall and were both highly intelligent. He remembered a school paper about Hermann Ebbinghaus and The Forgetting Curve. Unfortunately, these studies referred to the more common individual and he and his brother were far from common. However, the science behind these two gifts would have to wait for another day. As an amazing factoid, autistic savant Jack Tammet recited 22,000 decimal places of the pi sequence. It took more than 5 hours.

PART TWO

CHAPTER
EIGHT

WORK & PLAY

WORKING in venture capital could be isolating. Days were consumed by reading and analyzing data related to early-stage developments in medicine, biology, medical devices, and pharmaceutical innovations. The constant stream of research was overwhelming. Jack's goal was to decipher trends and big ideas before they attracted the attention of other investors. He recognized that the data source was as crucial as the data itself. He scoured technical papers, combed the internet, and devoured newspapers and magazines to soak up any information he could. In-person meetings were essential to validate his findings.

During one of his team's review sessions, he arranged a stack of newspapers and magazines in the center of the group. The pages were well-worn, as if they had all been thoroughly digested at least once. The newspapers included NY Times, Wall Street Journal, Silicon Valley Journal, SF Chronicle, SJ Mercury and the Seattle Times. The pages were ruffled as if each had been read at least once.

He gestured toward a journal and said, "Make sure to read the article on the operating room of the future. It outlines some fascinating devices involving robotics and AI that will revolutionize the OR."

"Where did you get the Seattle Times…?" said one of the associates.

"I started reading this paper as an undergrad and became a loyal reader ever since Paul Allen retired and started dedicating his time and money to medical research."

Jack provided insights about the Pacific Northwest and how the early movers and shakers such as Microsoft have been long since replaced by Amazon, Facebook and SpaceX. He reiterated that Paul Allen's real estate fortune was worth over $10B and he shifted his investment company's focus (Vulcan Capital) towards medical research after he was diagnosed with Hodgkin's disease.

"His key investments included cancer research, brain science, and 3 mega-yachts," Jack commented as if describing his hero.

Paul Allen passed away in 2018, remembered as a Microsoft founder, an astute investor (DreamWorks, Seattle Seahawks, Vulcan Capital), and a philanthropist dedicated to bioscience and cancer research.

A second large stack of magazines was then carefully placed at the group's center. There must have been about a dozen magazines with titles such as Nature, Science, New England Journal of Medicine, British Journal of Medicine, Lancet, Journal of American Medical Association, New Scientist, Stanford Medicine, Harvard Medicine, and several more. Jack reached for his favorite and turned to the cover story. He was reading from "American Academy of Neurology Journals," about a research program involving a placebo-controlled experiment to evaluate the effects of autoimmune disorders.

"Some of you may have heard of an unusual immune disorder known as Hashimoto's Disease," Jack mentioned.

"This research highlights key factors that may influence the disorder, drawing on our experiences, perceptions, or even the power of the placebo."

The team was curious about just how much time Jack had to read these journals and whether the large stack of magazines was presented for effect. They each grabbed a small stack of journals and started skimming through the text.

The internet served as their final key source of information. With a few keystrokes, they could access a wealth of data on any topic, person, place, or thing. The internet made gathering information almost too easy. With the talent in the room, this group could review, analyze, and provide critical assessments of almost any investment project. With a computer, a browser, a list of opportunities, and a deadline, Jack's tiger team at Eagle Investments could assess over 50 business plans in a single day. Their proven system was effective.

"I know you've all been through thousands of case studies, but I'd like to walk through this one with you again. It's the case of how the battle for search was won on the internet. By show of hands, who thinks it was Google or Yahoo?"

The team was divided. The "locals" knew the battle between Jerry Yang and the Stanford kids (Sergey Brin and Larry Page) was fierce with Yahoo in the market first (IPO in 1996, early investor Sequoia Capital) and then Google in 2004 (early investors include Sequoia and Kleiner Perkins). Then in 2000, Yahoo agreed to use the Google engine to power searches by Yahoo. Yahoo stood for "Yet Another Hierarchically Organized Oracle." If you mix a browser from Microsoft (Internet Explorer with a license from NCSA, Windows 1995), an early entry from Netscape (IPO in 1995 valued at $3B, early investors Kleiner Perkins), then you must add folks like Marc Andreessen from his early days at the National Center for Supercomputing Applications (NCSA). Jack was running through historical feats in double time and their academic minds were getting rev'd up.

Jack began his short speech:

"Today, we would say Google has won the search battle. There's not much doubt here, as they discovered the core algorithms that displaced Yahoo's rule-based approach and forever changed the future of search. However, I would not overlook the significance of

Netscape's early work. What they developed was much more than a browser. I wanted to have you folks learn from the best and know that finding or approaching the best is not always easy. However, in this case, we got lucky."

To everyone's astonishment, Marc Andreessen walked in. Jack introduced him to the team, sharing insights into Marc's business and personal life, including his recent philanthropic endeavors. Jack suggested that what Marc achieved for the internet through browsing and search was what he wanted his team to do for genomic research, disease cures, and the transformative miracles of medicine. Marc graciously accepted the praise and walked the team through a case study – a small piece of Netscape's history when numerous unanswered questions loomed over the management team, lacking order and clear direction.

Marc opened the floor for questions, and each team member had several. They wanted to delve into the rapid advancements in artificial intelligence, machine learning, gene modifications, CRISPR, and the future of bioresearch. While no one expected Marc to keep pace, his responses were highly informed and offered the team fresh perspectives and newfound enthusiasm.

After an hour, Jack inserted himself with praise to his visitor.

"I wanted to give special thanks to Marc for coming in today. His early achievements in developing the Mosaic architecture paved the way for worldwide web browsing. He proved that a software engineer from Iowa can really make a difference! We are delighted to have you visit our team and share your thoughts."

"It is my pleasure," Marc replied. "We all must start somewhere and the work you are doing here to fund the next big biomedical discovery can easily change the world. I'd be happy to check in on your progress any time."

The team erupted into unanimous applause and swiftly approached Marc as he headed out. They returned to the conference room buzzing with excitement.

"Wow, that was awesome to have Marc come to our office," said Jessica.

"How about Jack as our fearless leader? How did he pull off this visit? Is he well connected in Silicon Valley?" replied Jack.

"No doubt. There is a thing about inventors who changed the world. His first company invented a rice-based substitute and now he is a club member." replied Jessica.

NINE

BLACK & WHITE BAR

HE HAD HEARD about the "Black & White" from the partners at the firm. It was located downtown in a posh high-rise building in the financial district near the corner of Lincoln and Mission Boulevard. Jack had lived in San Francisco for over six months but was new to late-night partying and cruising this part of town. He probably should have just Uber'd downtown, but he was still getting used to the interior of his new ride and first extravagant purchase under new money. As with most investment partners, it was tradition to drive a high-end 2-seater, typically foreign, and exclusive in one way or another. Never could there ever be a time when 2 similar cars arrived on any occasion - this included changing paint color, leather or easier fixes like a body kit or rims. In a nonconforming way, he selected a Lexus, and a gorgeous 2-seater, black coupe. There was a carbon fiber body kit and the body emblems (for what was a prototype, electric LC500e F-type) were removed. It was one of only five prototypes in limited release and Jack was selected for an engineering study to evaluate a new Lexus platform.

He needed to find a decent and safe place to park for all the associated reasons. He found a lot nearby with an attendant that looked like he would keep an eye on his property. Jack walked a few blocks to the front of the glass building. The doors were locked. He leaned in to view the lobby lit up and large enough to fit a basketball court. It looked like a typical high-rise financial building with black marble floors and lighting that accented the entire lobby, but there was no restaurant or bar. Jack checked his phone again to be sure he had the right address. The map address was 525 Mission Blvd, and he was standing at the front door. It was Tuesday evening, just after 10 pm and maybe they rolled up the streets during the weekdays. Something was wrong, and Jack felt weird about standing out in front of an empty office building.

He texted Alex and asked for directions so as not to sound like he was lost. As he waited for a response, a black SUV drove by and turned into the underground driveway near the end of the building. It was the first sign of anyone in several minutes. It seemed too late for someone heading into work, and Jack was curious. He walked towards the driveway and tried to see down the dark entrance. The ramp led downward and curved out of sight. For such a classy building in the financial district, the driveway entrance seemed like it was missing any sort of signage. Jack was expecting a key card or security gate and there was no real clue how to proceed. Suddenly his phone lit up as he almost forgot about the text to Alex.

His phone read, "You must be close. Did you drive to the basement level?"

"I am standing near the front door, and it is locked," Jack replied."

Alex sent a sad emoji face. "This place is invited only, and I forgot to tell you to just follow the driveway. Find the dark driveway entrance and head down to the end." Now, Jack understood the problem.

"Thx" he texted.

Alex's text read, "NP, BTW, I hope you brought your car?"

"Yes, but I have to fetch from a nearby lot," Jack replied.

"You should be fine, enjoy," with two martini glass emojis.

Jack walked a few blocks back to his car. As he handed the ticket to the attendant, he wondered about the night's weirdness. Was this a "newbie challenge," or trick to fool newcomers? It could be an ideal prank by Alex. Jack started his car and drove to the mysterious drive-way. The dark entrance curved downward to the right in a long spiral that felt like several stories underground. Then a straight path down a tunnel for about a block. The tunnel walls were painted black, and the only lighting was from Jack's car. The tunnel was only about one-car width. The LED headlights were extremely bright, and Jack drove as slow as a beginner. He reached the end of the drive where he managed a sharp turn to a small valet area with a circular centerpiece for his car. He still felt very strange about the long drive, but it was even more difficult to think about reversing his path to drive out. Jack checked his phone and the display showed "no service."

Straight ahead were black elevator doors with an embossed logo of "B&W." This must be the place, he thought. Jack switched off his car and suddenly a slender figure appeared to his left. He rolled down his window and a lovely female voice said,

"Welcome to the Black & White Mr. Mohr. Please follow me."

The request was hard to resist from a tall, lovely woman dressed in a sexy black tuxedo. It was not obvious how she knew his name, but Jack was intrigued. He emerged from his car and followed his guide to the lobby. She was approaching six feet tall in heels and walked with model-like grace. He was enjoying the short walk and view from a few feet behind. He glanced at his car as it rotated on the circular floor and lowered to some sort of hidden parking lot.

The second lobby doors opened to a large room with a medium crowd for a weeknight. His guide wished him a lovely evening as Jack started a slow zig-zag towards the bar. This was a very classy place and Jack soon forgot about the strange and challenging entrance he had just endured. The floor was shiny black marble with gold silhouettes of Greek gods embedded in the floor. Jack passed over the first pattern and was then captivated by a glass floor tile with what appeared to be a window into an underground city. He saw images of cars and people moving along the night-lit streets as he glanced down. Jack wondered how these surreal images were possible, then just kept walking and admiring the visuals and the surroundings. The walls had cut-glass fixtures with soft white lighting. The tall ceiling was over 20 feet tall, and cables stretched from corner to corner with down lights. For a first impression, the Black & White was starting to feel unique and captivating.

Jack reached the bar and found a seat halfway around the circular counter. Glancing at the bar he saw dozens of rows of liquor with large, oversized bottles on the bottom and gradually smaller-sized bottles at the top. It was an alcoholic pyramid! Above the liquor were custom B&W mirrors that reflected the light beams around the bar. The mirrored structure had small, white lasers that shot intermittently to the ceiling. It was like reverse raindrops shooting up to the sky. Glancing back to the bar, he thought there must have been over a thousand liquor brands. There were over 50 different Vodkas alone. Jack was busy reading all the labels when the bartender approached him. He was dressed in black and white with a suit vest, shiny black buttons, and the B&W logo. Jack imagined his age was easily over 70.

He laid down a logo'd black napkin and asked, "what can I get for you?"

Jack said, "this is an amazing place, Harry," as he read his name tag. "I had a hell of a time finding my way here, but it looks like the fun begins right here."

"Yes, well, we have a bit of a select offering and tend to cater to those with special taste. How about you?" replied Harry.

"I'd love a Manhattan."

"Any preference for the bourbon?" Harry asked with a casual tone.

"Makers is my go-to or whichever you prefer," replied Jack.

Before he could decide, he noticed a waitress enter the room and walked towards him. She was unusually tall with incredibly long legs. She wore lace stockings with a pattern down to her heels. The stilettos were more than sexy and pushed her over six feet tall. As she passed him, Jack could smell her fresh scent and liked it. This was his second experience in ten minutes with a tall and lovely woman. She walked past him with a tray of drinks and over to a nearby booth. Jack swung his head casually to catch her view from behind. Her ass looked lovely through the lace skirt. Wow, she's another good reason to come to this bar, he said to himself. His eyes returned to the bar, and he waited for Harry. This time, he heard a familiar song playing. It was louder or faster and caught his attention. He realized it was George Michael. The song was Father Figure and Jack remembered most of the words and especially the chorus.

He whispered aloud, "I will be your father figure. Put your tiny hand in mine." The song relaxed him and brought back memories.

He turned back to Harry as his drink arrived and Jack slowly drew the glass from low to high as the alcohol poured down his throat for quick relief. The mix of flavors was perfect and now it was time to explore. "It's time to move up to the top-shelf," Jack glanced back at the row of bourbons.

Harry turned and prepared two drinks including an oversized shot glass and a full glass with an ice ball.

"This one is sweet like your Manhattan. Try this one first," he said.

Jack lifted the shot glass, sniffed it, and threw back the shot. It was smooth. Harry watched his eyes as Jack's head bobbed up and down once. He was not a bourbon snob, but he was starting to enjoy this experience.

"You're a hell of a bartender," said Jack.

Jack knew this drink was for sipping and just swirled the ice ball in the glass. The bourbon aroma was similar, but he had no idea what other flavors he was about to enjoy.

Before he raised his glass to his lips, the waitress leaned into the bar next to him. She gestured to Harry with her index finger curling backwards.

"Is this one ready for a booth…?"

It was only Jack's second drink, but it felt like he had been at the bar for some time. Harry replied,

"Yup, it's about time to find him a more comfortable seat. You should take this," gesturing to the drink, "before he gets started."

Jack was enjoying the small talk and wanted to jump in. Then, Ava put her hand under his glass as Jack lowered it to her palm.

"Follow me," she whispered.

As they walked away from the bar and down the aisle, Jack wondered about sitting at a booth by himself and then realized it didn't matter. His eyes were on the back of a very lovely woman. She walked towards the edge of the room and placed him in a corner booth. Ava slid the drink on the table and put a napkin beside it. Jack approached the curved leather couch and looked up at her with the bar in the background. She leaned across him and again he could smell her lovely scent. Whatever was happening, was turning him on. She reached to the wall and pressed a hidden lever. Suddenly, the dark glass table became a viewing window. Jack looked closely and stars and constellations were glimmering as if somehow the view looking down was the night sky from above.

Ava whispered, "The owner is an explorer and believes that we should always know how to navigate this world. He believes the sky is our map no matter how we travel."

Jack was impressed by both the words from Ava's lips and the emotions he was feeling. His childhood was filled with boating stories and the love of being near the ocean. He recalled the field trip to the planetarium with the Saints. He closed his eyes and felt the slight buzz from the alcohol. His mind tried to piece together the images from the long black tunnel, the George Michael song, and the night sky. Somehow these were all connected, but it was still unclear how.

What would be the first words he should tell his lovely waitress? How should he let on that he was trying to know more about the events of this crazy, wonderful evening.

"Let me know when Harry has another drink ready. Tell him I'd like to try the best in the house." Ava looked back at him as she was leaving and said,

"I'll tell him, but you should know the upper limit at the B&W is quite high."

Jack knew from his venture buddies that the Black & White had bottles of "liquid gold," including rare whiskeys valued at over $50,000 per bottle. He thought briefly about the expense and then decided it was time to relax and enjoy. This was not about money. It was time to have a new experience.

He gave a gentle nod to Ava and then realized he should have tried to push some words out of his mouth, but he was still anxious. She returned with a small dish with decorative beef filet cubes resting on a lettuce leaf. She then placed "her" drink by the dish and said,

"You should eat this and then try the drink afterwards. Oh, and by the way, the view in your table window is from cameras on top of this building. Tonight, you might see the constellation of Virgo. It's my favorite" Ava brought him a second ice ball bourbon as he was not quite ready for her to pour the gold.

Jack picked up the lettuce leaf, scooped a few bites of beef, and dipped it into the peanut sauce. His first chew was delicious as the beef was soft and tender. It was filet mignon, juicy, and tender. He lifted the drink, smelled the aroma, and swelled the ball of ice. Suddenly, the light from his phone came on with a text that read,

"How do you like the B&W?" It was from Alex, his every present associate from work.

Jack wanted to say he was impressed with Ava and the drinks, but decided to just text,

"This place is amazing. Music is perfect and a lovely woman is showing me the night stars."

Alex wrote back, "uh oh, you must be in a booth, ha."

"Yes," wrote Jack, "It's Tuesday night and I have the place to myself. Maybe I came here on the wrong night. Think I'm about done here."

He waved to Ava for the check, and she came over on her next pass. She said, "How did you like the appetizer…?"

Jack replied, "it was lovely, and the filet bites are my favorite, but I think I'm gonna head out."

"Already time to go," she replied. "Maybe you didn't enjoy my service…?"

"Oh, no," said Jack, "you're amazing and I enjoyed everything about this evening. I just have a crazy day tomorrow and need to get going," He was feeling awkward and lonely in the booth. He took a mental note to ask Alex if the B&W was really "invitation only," and what that really meant. Months later, Jack would learn that ownership had its privileges and that someone at Eagle Investments wanted him to enjoy a good bourbon and perhaps meet Ava.

"I see," said Ava as she laid his tab on the table. "I hope to see you next time, and we can visit longer."

Jack slipped two hundred dollars under the tab for Ava and jotted a note on his business card. As he made his way to the exit, he glanced down at the picture windows on the floor and realized this was like no other place he had ever experienced. He only met 2 people including Harry and Ava. Had a few drinks and yet he could not stop thinking about how strongly his emotions were pulling him. Did the experience feel more meaningful because he was tipsy?

As he arrived at the waiting area, a side door opened, and he entered the mid-lobby. The doors opened to find one car in the entry-way. He saw the parking lights of his Lexus. Jack felt the slight buzz from the bourbon, slid behind the wheel, and slowly drove down the underground tunnel towards the exit. He wondered, "what if someone comes along the narrow drive…?" Tonight, it wouldn't matter. He made it to the street and headed towards home. As he pulled into his driveway, a text lit up his phone and read,

"Hope the rest of your evening gets better."

"Just wanted to be sure you are ok as I loved your note and generosity." It was Ava.

"I'm fine & thx for your kindness," he replied.

"Hope 2cu again soon," he pushed send.

"Me too," replied Ava with a lipstick emoji.

When Jack got home, it was too late to speak with Robbie. He would email him, apologize, and hope they could speak tomorrow.

CHAPTER
TEN

SNOBB REPORT

JOINING Eagle Investments as new Entrepreneur-in-Residence (EIR) in the firm was impressive at age 25. Jack's background was uniquely strong in both business and biology, and he would quickly find his way to profitable deal flow.

On the coffee table was the latest copy of the Robb Report with an article on the "Best of the Best." It was often referred to at the office as the Snobb Report since the toys in each article were often the most expensive in their category and ownership was a privilege. There were boats, cars, motorcycles, jewelry, fashion, luggage, food, alcohol, and any other topic where prestige was limited. In this magazine, prices were given more as a path to purchase rather than an indication of cost. Jack remembers flipping the pages and slowing down for the pages with yachts, mega yachts and more. They were called "superyachts," and were typically 200' long and valued in the 100's of millions of dollars. The upkeep and staff alone would set one back over $10 million per year.

Growing up in the Pacific Northwest allowed Jack to get down to the docks for an up close and personal review of the yachts. His home was about 10 miles from the Tacoma Waterfront which included several docking areas for the large boats. On weekends, Jack remembered walking along the elegant boat docks that made it feel like walking down mansion row at the Hamptons or retail shopping on Rodeo Drive. The "common area" had boat slips that stored vessels up to 30 meters (~100 feet). However, the larger boats (or yachts) had much longer docking access and enough room to maneuver the large craft in and out of the harbor. On any given weekend, there were often a dozen superyachts. Lined up end-to-end, they took up about a mile of dock space.

Jack had a superyacht sight-seeing routine which included the following rituals: a) determine the craziest, most obnoxious, or difficult-to-understand boat name, b) guess the length of the craft and then pace front to back, and finally, c) imagine what his yacht would look like if time and money were not important. Of the three tasks, he enjoyed the last one the most and often imagined designing his own boat including an exotic exterior and romantic interior. Unlike most yacht layouts, his would be designed for only a small group. In fact, the ideal for his dreamboat would be for a party of just two. A pool table to relieve any sporting tensions and an endless bar to enjoy favorite spirits. His focus would be on a deluxe kitchen for fine dining and an elegant master suite to make one never want to leave.

During his second day at Eagle Investments, Jack was introduced to the analysts, associates and principals responsible for all the heavy lifting research products. This included data mining, analytics, competitive analysis, business plan screening, deal flow, pitch decks, and about every other tedious task associated with the back offices within venture capital. These were the smartest kids who graduated from the top of their class in B-school. Eagle recruited locally from Stanford and Berkeley and pulled a few outsiders from Harvard, Northwestern and UPenn. Over 30 folks on the entire team averaged about 5 team members per partner. Jack was the newest EIR and hadn't received any information on who might work with him, so he contacted the entire group with openness and interest in their abilities. He was well known for his accomplishments in biomedical investments, and several of the team approached him with their various interests. He was about the same age as the rest of the "data team," although he was nearly a general partner. He had skipped over the grinding part of venture capital and straight to the decision circle. The amazing part was that Jack never really put others in a "box" and treated the team members equally. He knew the value of good and timely information and knew that if he could leverage this squad, he would benefit with increased multiples.

By the end of the first week, Jack had exercised several of his new team including 1 analyst, 5 associates and 2 principals. He was very methodical in his research and leveraged the most from each individual. His new investment research involved a combination of technologies and markets that would hopefully be aligned for major market acceptance. Collecting the data was not trivial; more importantly, piecing together the key elements concerning contribution, cohesiveness and timing would be key. Since he was new to the firm, he wanted to impress the other general partners. However, he knew that venture investing was about playing the odds, taking risks and trusting your gut instincts. After all, he was hired after delivering 25x return to his previous shareholders and now the bar was set even higher for him.

He called a lunch meeting with his virtual team and brought food to the data room where they could eat and brainstorm. After everyone had loaded their plates with Thai food, it was time to start the group session. Jack turned on the extra-large monitor and started his presentation. The title was, "Leveraging DIANA to Mine Your Own Business." Everyone was quite curious about and anxious to hear more. Jack smiled as he began his opening remarks, then a half dozen techie slides, and a summary with concluding remarks. DIANA was the code word for his newest investment strategy and was the basis for his next adventure. As an EIR, he was to assess the landscape of investment opportunities, take a leadership position in one or more, and drive results.

As always, his presentation was just a handful of slides and at the end, he asked if there were any questions about the plan moving forward. There were many. After about an hour of discussion and back-n-forth with the team, it was clear that the team supported his investment idea and would help prepare for the partner review.

Jack was invited to present his research and portfolio assessment to the general partners at the end of his first month. His presentation on "DIANA" received an enthusiastic reception. Managing director Steve Anderson praised Jack's approach, suggesting he look for seed or early-stage investments for the firm's new fund.

CHAPTER
ELEVEN
SUSHI BOATS

THE FOLLOWING day Jack went about his business as usual until lunchtime, when he typically left the office for a change of scenery. Today was different as the memories of the nightclub were fresh and he wondered what all the fuss about the B&W was about. It was a nice club, but nothing to brag about. Curiosity gnawed at him, prompting a text to Alex for more information. He was in the mood for his favorite sushi place; spicy tuna, salmon, and the zing of wasabi were calling. Luckily, it was just a short walk away, and he could snag a seat at the sushi bar, ensuring he'd be in and out in under 30 minutes. His office was downtown and the crowd at lunchtime was always a hassle. Today was special as he reached Kenji's Sushi bar in just a few minutes and found a seat. It was "sushi-boat style", and he loved watching the fresh fish float by in their decorative boats. He grabbed the first spicy tuna boat and swallowed two or three pieces in one mouthful. Jack gave the owner a nod as he sent a cool Sapporo to his station. He raised his bottles in appreciation and then put eyes back on the path of sushi boats. He saw the pink salmon coming with a decorative roll. He grabbed two more bite-sized items and was in heaven. Jack thought this is how life should be – food delivered directly to you as you slurp a cool beer.

He sent a quick text to Alex. It read, "Not sure I got the B&W attraction." He waited for a reply then realized it was the middle of the day and Alex was an exercise freak, especially during lunchtime. Jack waved to Kenji and headed out. He wasn't quite ready to return to work and made his way a few blocks to a men's store. It was an Italian knock-off brand that had excellent tailored shirts.

~

Jack was tall at 6'3" and wore a fitted dress shirt well. He liked a cut waist and often had his shirts tailored to show off his flat stomach. He passed several shirts that were too psychedelic in color – the rack was filled with mostly purples and greens. Nothing in sight seemed to work for him. Halfway around the store, a salesperson briefly asked if there was anything he was looking for.

"Perhaps I can bring out some new things from the back?"

"No, I am just looking and wanted something a little different," Jack replied.

"Have you tried linen and silk shirts? We have some new styles that might work. Let me bring out a few shirts for you."

"Ok," Jack said, "maybe something a bit less vibrant."."

The salesperson returned with three more appealing shirts than anything on the rack. Jack slipped on the first one and stood before the mirror, a newfound sense of satisfaction washing over him. He turned sideways to assess his profile, momentarily contemplating how he might look from behind. The salesperson assured him the shirt fit impeccably and suggested he try all three to get a feel for the styles. Jack complied, and after donning them all, he felt more confident in his appearance than he had in years. The colors were deep, commanding, and straightforward, imbuing him with a sense of empowerment. One even sported a subtle gold stripe from shoulder to shoulder, evoking a sense of military discipline or a white-collar renegade. It was a triumphant shopping expedition, and now it was time to return to work.

After leaving the store and walking for a bit, Jack's phone buzzed for an incoming text. He read the response from Alex. "Hey, what happened at the club…?" Jack was not in the mood for small talk and decided to just let Alex know his frustration. "I thought you said B&W was special, but it was just ok for me. The place was empty and looked like it was going out of business," Jack replied. Alex received the text and realized that Jack's first experience may need careful attention. Alex's job was to ensure the new partners had great experiences in town. The situation was beyond text messaging, and he would fix it.

Alex replied, "No worries, the crowd can vary, and I suggest we try again on another night. Perhaps I'll join you and bring a few friends." Jack received the text and just put his phone away. It was time to dive into work.

Jack pressured himself to stay ahead of the competition and to stay very sharp on significant events in biotech research. He read several blogs on the latest updates including genetic testing, biomedical compatibility, sequencing, and early investment discussions. Wall Street had several public companies including Thermo Fisher, Illumina and Spark Therapeutics who each created significant wealth developing sequencing and gene therapy equipment. Other companies leveraged targeted gene-based medicines such as CRISPR Therapeutics, Correvio, and TransEnterix. And finally, there were a host of startups and venture companies betting on the future of sequencing to be commonplace for public consumption and the benefits of gene therapy to potentially be the central cure to thousands of diseases.

Some recent evidence suggested a possible side-effect of the CRISPR (clustered regularly interspaced short palindromic repeats) technique for gene splicing could give rise to cancer. Long referred to as "the guardian of the genome," the p53 protein was failing to work in the CRISPR tool as a cure and instead, played a key role in creating cancer tumors. However, the potential success of gene editing was by far considered worth Jack's time and investigation, and he knew this was his time to persevere (like Marc Andreessen).

CHAPTER
TWELVE
OYSTER PEARL

FOR AN ENTREPRENEUR OR INVESTOR, it is well understood that the investment that follows a big win is perhaps the hardest of all. Like a casino bet, the odds are against the player and the decision to go big or go home resounds in the back of the brain. For Jack, he had successfully found a winner that catapulted him to early fame and a small fortune before he understood how a business is run.

It was his college dream to succeed in academics and someday be a contributor in the field of biomedical engineering. However, he never imagined that his first entry into a commercial deal would hit the bullseye, with all three darts, aka: the Alan Evans shot. Their ideas to mess with plant proteins involving certain grass strains and a mixture of other key elements to create synthetic meat was ahead of its time.

At the next Friday session with his team, Jack shared his news and asked that a smaller group meet more regularly. This included Naomi Yang (1st year associate) and Adam Bangsford (Sr Associate). They were selected to help with the task of finding new deal flow. Naomi scrubbed the incoming business plans and Alex reviewed the landscape for outside investments that had not approached the firm. The goal was to initiate the first DIANA sequence of investments by exploring the usefulness of DNA to support healthier living. The team knew scouring business plans and data mining may not be as valuable as trusting their fearless leader with inspiration. However, the strategy needed to be played out and for several months, the team did their diligence on the market and collected mounds of data.

In his report to the general partners, Jack wrote the following summary:

"The speed of innovation in medicine is now outpacing the previous 25 years of medical research due to significant applications including artificial intelligence and machine learning. Contributions from Google's Deep Mind (see Moorfields Eye Hospital) and IBM's Watson (see Memorial Sloan Kettering in NY) are showing promise to patient records, pattern recognition and diagnostic treatments. Autonomous driving cars are using state-of-the-art computers and sensors with AI/ML to achieve their goals. I suggest that Eagle Investments leverage technologies in a way that has not been considered. Earlier in my career, we discovered how to leverage our protein supplement, and although we didn't have the end result in mind, it was always in the field of view. We should critically evaluate three fundamental technology building blocks, including sequencing, therapy and editing of human genes. We should invest in one or all to deliver on a next-generation medical advancement."

The summary was simple and provocative. The partners knew Jack was highly intelligent and was anxious to make his mark in the investment community. Although there were still technology risks, Jack would likely drive the ideal path for high returns, and he was worth the risk.

After crafting his email masterpiece, he remembered the lovely woman from the B&W club. Of all the craziness in finding the place, parking the Lexus, meeting Harry at the bar, the most memorable part of the evening was certainly the beautiful woman who waited on him. She had made a stronger impression on him than he realized as he reflected on the evening. This woman knew when to appear and to show the highlights that drew him in. She knew how to wear sexy clothes with distinction and each time she came over to him, she got just close enough to smell her. Jack remembered he was not himself that night and should find a way back if only to see her again. How would he know if she was working or how to reach her? Then, he remembered she had texted him late that night and he just had to recall her number. Jack scrolled through all his text messages until he found it. Now he just needed a reason to call or text her. It had been less than a week and he was hoping she might remember him from his tip or that the place was virtually empty. So, what words of wisdom and charm would be in his text?

It was a Tuesday around dinner time, and a perfect time to send her a note. Jack typed the following text.

"Luv another Manhattan," with drink emoji. "Ru working tonight?"

Then he waited for her reply. But there was only silence on his phone. He tried to get his head back into work and see if there were any work emails or other distractions. He worked in an up-to-the-sky building in the financial district and could always take a few moments out to see the city skyline and view of San Francisco Bay. This was crazy. As the short time passed, Jack remembered every little detail of his evening at the B&W - it was as if he was having a lucid dream. Did someone carefully script his evening so he would see a beautiful woman as he parked his car, hear familiar music playing and then find himself in a romantic bar with no one else to blame? She gave him his full attention, but only later did Jack realize that his night out at the B&W could have had a much different ending. She had made a stronger impression on him than he realized as he reflected on the evening. He left work that night and realized he had her phone number but not her name. His phone was quiet the rest of the night.

Jack was following all the hints and clues from the team at Eagle and yet, the process seemed scripted. After months of fishing with all kinds of bait, Jack stopped and listened to his gut, saying something was missing. Where were inputs from Robbie or the Saints? He was pushing too hard on the process and not using his best resource right in front of him. He convened an emergency Discord call and walked the group through his challenge. He spoke eloquently to the group, "I think you guys have followed my path into venture capital and now have the chance to make a significant investment in what I believe is the future. My passion has always been to improve our world and hopefully make a difference through science and medicine. This all sounds a bit cliche and I need to create a better approach to deal flow and reading a plethora of business plans."

"That may be your problem," said Robbie.

"I agree," commented Luke. "You should look no further than the tip of your nose for answers." The group also commented in the chat window and piled onto the response.

"But you guys need to appreciate that I'm in the center of the universe for brilliant startup ideas and minds that operate differently than the norm."

"That's BS," said Robbie uncharacteristically. "You just happen to be at the center of a large number of smart people, but the real influencer is you."

The conversations went on for over an hour with a common thread. Jack didn't need to shop for a new idea amongst the startup community. He just needed the courage to come forward and lead his own company with his amazing ideas. Time to bounce a few ideas off Dr K. and push his internal team about their inputs.

THIRTEEN

ALEX THE ASSOCIATE

A FEW DAYS had passed since Alex and Jack had spoken at work and after the weekly grind session at noon on Thursday, Alex sent a text to make some plans. It read, "Need some alcohol with some of the team, any interest in socializing, maybe hitting some clubs…?"

"I need to get through this report for Steve (Anderson) and should be done by close-of-business.," Jack replied.

"Great, I'll ping you around 6pm before we head out."

Jack placed immense pressure on himself to stay ahead in genomics research. He avidly followed blogs on the latest updates in testing, ancestry, sequencing, and early investment discussions. Wall Street boasted giants like Thermo Fisher, Illumina, and Spark Therapeutics, which were responsible for generating substantial wealth in sequencing and gene therapy equipment. Companies like CRISPR Therapeutics, Correvio, and TransEnterix leveraged targeted gene-based medicines.

Other companies leveraged targeted gene-based medicines such as CRISPR Therapeutics, Correvio, and TransEnterix. And finally, there were a host of startups and venture companies betting on the future of DNA sequencing to be commonplace for public consumption and the benefits of gene therapy to potentially be the central cure to thousands of diseases.

Some recent evidence suggested that a possible side-effect of the CRISPR technique for gene splicing could give rise to cancer. Long referred to as "the guardian of the genome," the p53 protein was failing to work in the CRISPR tool as a cure and instead, played a key role in creating cancer tumors. It was still early in both research and development and side effects were always part of any significant drug challenge.

In his report to the general partners, Jack wrote the following summary.

"The speed of innovation in medicine is now outpacing the previous 25 years of medical research due to significant applications by artificial intelligence (AI) and machine learning (ML) and computing power. Contributions from Google's Deep Mind (see Moorfields Eye Hospital) and IBM's Watson (see Memorial Sloan Kettering in NY) are showing promise to evaluate and even act on patient records, pattern recognition and diagnostic treatments. Autonomous driving cars (especially Level 5, aka: no human intervention) are using state-of-the-art computers and sensors with AI/ML to achieve their goals by 2025. Just as complex as the plan of record for autonomous driving in dense cities such as San Francisco, has direct correlations to medical advancements beyond the challenges of cancer or other chronic and incurable diseases. Collecting enormous amounts of sensor data is only valuable to those who know how to act on the results whether deciding on a challenging lane change or deciding between invasive surgery, or passive radiation, as both examples risk losing lives if decisions are not made with precision. In 2016, the TV show 60 Minutes hosted details about the IBM Watson Supercomputer to show how a computer might accelerate decisions in precision oncology situations. It was described as a bioinformatics challenge, especially in tackling cancer-causing genetic mutations which can be easily calculated by a brilliant computer platform that surpasses human data collection. The machine produced 99% similar results to the Molecular Tumor Board 30-person team and could learn, scale, and eventually be used for clinically actionable results. The ultimate solution will be one in which patient engagement, professional care, technology, data, and informatics come together to optimize treatment.

We know gene editing research has promising results on single gene mutations and approaching more complex diseases from malaria to cancer. In 2020, Jennifer Doudna and Emmanuelle Charpentier received a Nobel Prize for their breakthrough research in CRISPR gene-editing technology. Let's not mention the IP battles with Feng Zhang from the Broad Institute, and eukaryotic cell editing.

In the near term, scientists are studying the use of CRISPR on cholesterol, HIV, and Huntington's disease. It is theorized that we will see more cancer therapy derivatives from CRISPR methods than any other. Our job as investors of emerging technologies is to determine when the critical time window opens and to place our bets wisely. There is now overwhelming evidence that the technologies surrounding gene editing are contributing to life-saving therapies and a pure play or hybrid investment is highly recommended. Within our investment team, we are evaluating several technology investments that leverage huge data sets to determine useful outcomes. These include a blend from medical research, cybersecurity, bitcoin mining, and artificial intelligence applied to autonomous driving and an effective use of sensor fusion. Data scientists (and significant compute power) can leverage the most complicated algorithms and predict outcomes to fend off a cyberattack, steer a car through dense traffic, provide a cancer therapy recommendation, insert or modify a gene to prevent the onset of a genetic disease.

Jack summarized his paper into a PowerPoint deck and covered the key elements for a new business plan. He was an excellent presenter and used limited words and images per page as he told this story. New business plan topics were presented on the Monday staff call including thoroughly reviewed, external plans and if there were any internal ideas. Surprise.

Jack addressed the investment team, "I suggest that Eagle Investments look for key investments to leverage technologies in such a way that has not been tried before. However, may have new purpose in today's marketplace. When Prof Koppelman and I discovered how to leverage our protein supplement, we didn't have the result in mind. However, it was in the "field of view." Three fundamental technology building blocks should be critically evaluated, and we should invest in a blend across these blocks to deliver on a next-generation medical advancement."

He flipped through a modest set of slides and ended with a key.

Jack spoke up, "Having been with the firm for 15 months, I've seen deal flow on various complex topics that span the risk-reward spectrum. I am mindful that Eagle has an approach that leverages early-stage entry with limited downside risk. As one of the most recent LP's, I also know that our current fund has under $50 million to invest across the team (Jack's eyes scanned the room). We have two preferred investment areas to avoid any portfolio concentration. Saint Newco bridges two investment areas of software and medical which may influence the exit timing. However, there is more emphasis on the software portion in the platform and may trigger sooner. I am confident that this investment will move us into a competitive position as a crossover investment with a potential upside over 25x in under 3 years."

The summary was provocative, mysterious, and aggressive. When they recruited Jack, the general partners knew they had a special genius entrepreneur. His mind was sharp and keenly focused on both value and success. He avoided the techie pitfalls where scientific principles often outweighed the true value in the market. He also had the perfect blend of cockiness and confidence to support Eagle's investment thesis.

Steve Anderson was the first to respond, "This looks very interesting. It sounds like you are counting on a breakthrough combining key elements from nearby technologies with potential levers from your intellectual property. I understand that there are other valuable building blocks in your plan. Trust me, we have looked at several of these businesses. However, a part of this must limit what feels like risk multiplication."

"I'm going to take this as a statement rather than a question," replied Jack. "What I'm suggesting is not to be a better problem solver for the complex puzzles in front of us. I believe a better solution exists to a problem we have yet to define, new to understand, and unlimited potential to solve."

"Now you're sounding a bit philosophical. Can you be more specific," said Steve.

Jack smiled and said, "Of course. We all know the story of how Coca Cola was invented as a counter to morphine addiction and that penicillin was accidentally discovered in a lab as a bacterium-eating fungus. These amazing inventions were discovered by a pharmacist and a scientist trying to solve other unique problems and instead found groundbreaking, world-impacting solutions. We are at an age where massive "unique problem-solving" engines are being produced to solve specific problems of interest. These challenges are so massive that the contributors must stay laser-focused and maintain their course for success."

Andy Weinman interrupted and said, "are you suggesting we invest in a Chaos Theory approach?"

"Not at all," said Jack. "That is more like herding cats as you chase random data. The plan for Saint Newco is to replicate key principles of powerful problem-solving ideas and retarget them to a new solution set."

"Say that five times fast," Steve grinned.

Jack continued, "Paul Allen once said, " It is always interesting to bring scientists together, because they typically have very polarized views." There is a reason for this as the "the scientist" is being used as a problem solver and not a solutions provider. Don't ask them how to solve a problem. That's easy. Rather, ask them what else you can do with your solution? However, to better protect our investment," Jack smiled, "we will start from scratch and use our own scientists to remove bias."

Outside at the table serving coffee, Jack overheard one of the partners suggesting this sounds like the movie Armageddon where Bruce Willis hires a team of professional oil drillers to break up an asteroid. Agreed, I think he's hoping that Mr. Peanut Butter bumps into Mrs. Chocolate for a new candy idea.

~

Per their protocol, the entrepreneur was asked to leave the room so they could discuss the investment opportunity. The partners knew Jack was worth the risk and that he could bring a new and exciting angle to Eagle that was missing. In a unanimous vote, the investment committee passed Jack's Newco and allocated three tranches of budgeted money (or buckets). Jack returned to the room and Steve stood up and spoke, "We are excited about Newco, and you have the green light to proceed. Come see me about the first capital call to the LP's."

Jack smiled and responded, "This is excellent. Thank you for your support."

He returned to his desk and quickly gathered his team for an online chat. Jack shared the news and spoke highly of each member as key contributors to the plan. He said the committee approved their plan with full support. The team had worked over the weekend to prepare the final data package and although it was only midday on Monday, it felt like they had worked half a week. Saint Newco was born.

In the following month, the team set the criteria for a new development platform, the skills required for the team, and the all-important name of the company. Jack proposed the name Seres with the following explanation. I'm sure you have all heard of palindromes and how words are spelled the same forwards and backward. There are also several overlaps concerning DNA sequencing and the GCAT string formations. I always thought an "S" should be represented in genomics since it looks like a double helix and Seres felt like a great choice. Overnight, Newco became Seres, and the company was born.

At 5:30p, Alex reached out again. His text to Jack read, "Hey, I'm counting on your text coming soon before the evening is upon us."

"Ok, I'm on track for close of business and I'll reach out soon," read the reply.

Alex's second job was to be the "initiator" of fun and tonight was all about it. Alex knew the team at Eagle who liked to party and had sent special invites to the group. From analysts to principles and some very special admins were on his VIP list. It was VIP for a simple reason that made sure what stays at the office, truly stays at the office and what happens afterward was unique, kept quiet, and rules did not apply. It meant that no one had titles, or big bank accounts and that the group was uniquely tied to one another through a bond, not like a special pass to an IG or Snap account, rather a true understanding of trusted partners. Alex called it "EL-E-VATE or E8 for short," and enjoyed telling people his unusual rites of passage.

Of course, the first rule was you must work at Eagle Investments. Second, there can be less than eight persons to an invite, but never more than 8. The other rules concerned gender, tenure, title, and respect. The most challenging rule was similar to a rite of passage and involved sensitive information that made each member uniquely vulnerable. The responses varied from confessions, to secrets, eye-opening truths, or desires that were never shared beyond this group. However, to play it safe and not damage any marriages or partnerships, the person's key must be about money. After all, this was a group of bankers.

Alex was an extra lively character at heart. He went to college to please others and studied economics at the University of Chicago on a

Presidential scholarship. He was an excellent writer and passed almost every test involving essay writing, economics, statistics, or hierarchical word problems. In his junior year, he studied and passed the GMAT with a 785 (perfect score was 800). He remembered the entire test and could recall the few errors he made. This was a high enough score to get him into the top five b-schools including Harvard, Stanford, Northwestern, and UPenn (Wharton). He knew his days in the Midwest were numbered and did not want to simply go to another brand name school in Chicago (Univ of Chicago, Booth MBA program), so no application for NU/Kellogg.

Then, there was Harvard at the top and Wharton in Philly. These two schools had history and prestige and would be an honor to attend. Finally, there was Stanford and a quiet application to UC Berkeley (Haas). His father went to Wharton and believed that the schools in the west were always second tier to the Ivy's. To his credit, he was accepted to all the schools he applied to, and it was time for some college campus tours. B-school was very different from undergrad in that the program's reputation was paramount to the degree and the likely job offers that followed. The trips to Boston and Philadelphia were amazing and included the traditional campus tour and dedicated time in each city to take in all the sites. The west coast trip took a bit more coordination with a direct flight on Friday afternoon from O'Hare into SFO. Alex rented a car, drove to Palo Alto, and stayed a few miles from the Stanford campus. On Saturday, he met up with his tour group at 8am and saw all the campus highlights and a fun walk through of the stadium. The guide took them to a special VIP box and name-dropped some popular alumni seats, including Condoleezza Rice, Elon Musk, and Jennifer Connelly. Interestingly, both Elon and Jennifer were successful dropouts.

The tour ended at 11am sharp and Alex rushed to his rental car, added fast driving to cover 50 miles to Berkeley, and grabbed a bite to eat before his 1pm tour.

The campus was massive and spread across 1200 acres, with rolling hills, and over 50,000 students. By 4pm, he was exhausted and ready for some rest time at the hotel. He was staying at the Grand Hyatt near SFO and was at the bar just before Happy Hour closed for his favorite bourbon. Looking back over the day, he remembered two important things. The first was that for a boy who grew up in the Midwest and dreamed of attending graduate school on either the west or east coast was a big deal. His family was affluent. However, they had never traveled to the west coast as a family. Both options were far from home and would require a relocation of mind and body. This was a big part of his growth and Alex knew he had to move nearly 1000 miles away and the options of 1 or 2 time zones (EST or PST). That night, he realized it was not about the east or west coast decision. Rather, his gut told him it was either Harvard or Stanford. As he chewed a few more bites of his filet, he wondered whether he was the type who liked structure and well-defined pathways such as Harvard, or the more entrepreneurial and creatively demanding side of Stanford. He took an early flight back to Chicago and was home Sunday evening by dinner. His parents were anxious to hear about his trip and learn the news that he was going to California in the Fall.

Jack's path through Stanford Graduate School of Business was as straight and narrow. He excelled in every class, was a leader amongst his peers, and graduated at the top.

He joined Goldman Sachs after business school and participated in investment banking and mergers & acquisitions. Goldman, Morgan Stanley and JPMorgan Chase were the top investment banks with the inside track on deal flow. In his first 3 years, Alex worked on over a dozen deals and was making a reputation with the partners. His favorite was Steve Anderson, who was in his early 40's and "owned" his corner office on 555 California Street. Steve drove a red Ferrari, had season tickets to the Giants and the 49ers, and swam every morning at the gym. He wore cufflinks daily, started every meeting on time, and ended each with action items and assignments. Steve ruled Goldman's new business on the west coast and would win any and all top banker awards.

～

The spoils became less and less for the folks who had been at Goldman since their IPO, and the shared rewards were unfair to winners like Steve. He held a small, invite only, lunchtime party at Nightbird, from his Michelin favorites. Alex was one of only 7 guests and very honored to be part of the festivity. The food was outrageously good, and the presentation was divine. Alex wondered if this was just commonplace dining once you've made it. Towards the end of the meal, Steve stood up and made a short speech. He said, "I wanted to thank my core team who have made my job much easier through dedication and excellent work. Banking is a profession that centers around money, which can be a benefit and sometimes be a distraction. Knowing that I am in the right competition is enough to keep me happy and I've been fortunate to win more battles than most. I also know that the last few years have been a struggle across Goldman's portfolio, and there has been a shift in how deals are played out. There are fewer IPO's and more "murders and acquisitions," in the Silicon Valley trenches. A handful of LPs have asked me to start a new firm and move to Menlo Park." Steve raised his glass to the small crowd and said, "I wish continued success to each of you. Know that you are always welcome in my home and a part of my family." They all raised their glasses and drank one last time for their hero. The drive back to the office was like heading back to a job rather than a profession. It was 2pm on a Friday in downtown San Francisco and felt like the world had ended. Alex knew Steve's admin and went over to see her. "So, Rebecca, how are we going to survive now?"

"I'm pretty happy."

"I'm confused. This place will never be the same without the master."

"Yes, I agree," she said. "That's why I'm joining him on Monday!"

"Seriously," replied Alex. Rebecca had been Steve's admin for over a dozen years and knew his every move and mannerisms. No event, meeting, transaction, or significant calendar date was planned without Rebecca's guidance. She was his right hand in getting things done, and

Alex finally realized this was happening. Steve and Rebecca were leaving, and the lunch was only his top insiders. What would it take to follow Steve? Alex was a bit nervous to ask Rebecca for help and tried anyway.

"I'm guessing you are the brains behind the new operation," He grinned. "Maybe Steve will need more folks to grind through deal flow and business plans?"

"I'm gonna say yes, but only because Steve has a new set of limited partners who want him to bring them a quick return on their investments."

"You mean like every high wealth person wants more for their money?"

"No, I mean these are impatient clients. I have already arranged 5 events next month for Steve and they include more work than one event at GS."

"Oic, I'm starting to see a pattern here."

"Yes Alex, I can't say too much, but you might call next week, and I can fill you in a bit more."

That was the golden reply and Alex could not wait till the weekend to push into the following week. The timeline was more like a month and Alex was employee #8, his favorite number. Eagle Investments was a new venture firm in an already crowded community on Sand Hill Road. Steve set up shop with himself as the managing director, two general partners, three analysts, Rebecca, and Alex for prospecting new deals. The office was gorgeous and would double in size by year-end. For many reasons, they opened a second office in San Francisco just a few blocks from their old stomping grounds in the Embarcadero buildings. The office was on the 22nd floor with a few of the Bay Bridge across to the East Bay and the Oakland Hills. Their routine was always Mondays in Menlo Park, Tuesdays and Wednesdays on the road, Thursday check-in from either office or Fridays left open. It was a perfect schedule.

The Elevate team had been summoned and the SF coordinates were delivered. Parking was always a challenge in the city and Uber was the right choice. Alex arrived early at the restaurant and went to the large table. Most of the team was seated when Alex got a text from Jack that read,

"On my way, be there in less than 5."

Alex responded, "KK."

Looking around the table, Jack was the most senior in title, but this crowd was less about authority and more about fun and when outside the office, it was much more fun. Most of this team had spent less than a year together, which in banking terms is equivalent to 10 years. They all put in long hours and the chance to get out and have fun was always important. It was an Asian fusion night, and the food was served family style, with dishes flying left and right.

Alex said, "This is a bit like left-right-center," and they all smiled as they often played this game after bonuses were delivered. About halfway through the meal, one of the associates asked Alex, "Many thanks for this outrageous meal. Does this mean we are working the weekend?" he smiled.

"No, on the contrary," said Alex. "As you know, when Steve opened Eagle, there were enough limited partners to pull in $100m for our first fund. Steve hired me to find new deals. However, most of the challenge was not having enough deep pockets to fund a deal through exit. We needed more funds to compete for the bigger deals and tonight, we are celebrating the early closing of our second fund."

Jack had heard a whisper that new money was coming, but it was held closely amongst the partners and the CFO. "This is great news," said Jack. He raised his sake cup, and said, "I think I may know just where to put the new money."

"You will get your chance soon enough," Alex smiled back. "In fact, Steve mentioned you are on the calendar for a partner presentation soon."

"Hey, let's keep the work talk to a minimum here," joked Jack.

"Ok," said Alex. "But hear me on this one: the new money is largely from a single investor, and I'd like you to meet with him."

"I'd be happy to meet with him whenever or wherever you'd like," said Jack.

"It's happening sooner than you might expect."

"Ok, that sounds ok too."

"How about after dinner?"

"You mean tonight?"

"Yes. You will be joining me afterward and meet our new investor. For now, let's enjoy more food as this group deserves all the credit," Alex said proudly.

When they stepped outside, the air was cool and crisp. They said their goodbyes and Alex and Jack walked separately for about a block, stopping to call an Uber.

"We're heading to the B&W," said Alex.

As they got into their Uber, Alex filled him in on some key details about Simon, his money, his family (and loss), and his passions. When they got to the address, they stood at the curve and Jack remembered being unable to enter without a car.

"Don't we need a car to get in?" said Jack.

"Yes, but Uber's are not allowed. Sit tight," said Alex.

He was texting and waiting for a response. His phone lit up with Will be at the curb in 3min. A black Mercedes S drove up and they hoped for a very short ride. Jack knew the routine and welcomed the tuxedo lady at the end of the tunnel. They entered the B&W and headed to the front of a crowded bar. As Alex turned around, a beautiful waitress was heading directly towards him.

"Simon asked that you join him if you are ready," said Ava.

Alex smiled and said awkwardly, "yes, we are ready now." Ava glanced at Jack and nodded for him to join. They walked past the tables and booths to a doorway at the back which led to a private room large enough to host 20 people, a pool table, and a private bar. It was a special B&W #2. Ava said, "Please make yourself comfortable and I'll let Simon know you have arrived." Jack caught himself staring at Ava's lips and remembering her lovely scent. Tonight, she wore a tuxedo crop top jacket with no blouse and a short skirt. Her long legs were bare down to a sexy pair of stiletto heels. The two men made their way over to a table and before they could sit down, Simon blurted out, "Welcome gentlemen. I hope you came here to enjoy yourselves!" Alex smiled, headed straight to a handshake with Simon, and said,

"It's great to see you again. This is one of our favorite bars in San Francisco. I'm impressed you know about it." Alex knew it was mostly invite only and he only knew about it through Steve A.

"You mean because it is by invitation only?" said Simon.

"Sorry, Simon, it makes sense that you would know Steve and his connections."

"No, I only met Steve through your introductions a month ago."

"Ok, I'm still very impressed that our favorite bar is where you invited us to meet up."

"I think you know I like things that begin with B's like building, boats and boobs. Well, I also like booze and have an import/export business that allows me to pass very expensive alcohol through the SF Pier. I can put it in cargo trucks and rattle across the country, or bring it here to the B&W. Besides. I own the bar too," Simon smiled with pride.

"Now that makes a lot of sense," said Alex.

"So, let's drink and have some fun," Simon said. He walked over to the bartender and counted with his fingers one, two, three, as if to request item after item. He returned to the table and the wonderful night began. Their drinks arrived from Ava and soon more ladies arrived at their table. Jack thought this must have been one of the finger swags at the bartender. Each man had his new friend, and the conversations about each other's past became increasingly significant. Alex knew there would be an easy fit with Jack who was talented, competitive, and in the perfect zone for compassion as Simon walked him through his years of entrepreneurship and brief parenthood. The drinks were flowing, and Simon pointed Alex to another side room.

He said, "You might take your guest to see what's in that room." Alex left with his friend and the two heavy hitters left alone.

Simon said to Jack, "So, I hear you have a way of making money?"

"Well, I guess that is true. My passion is science and technology and thinking of ways to help people."

"Maybe you were meant to be a doctor?"

"No, I want to help thousands of doctors so they can help millions of people."

"That's a big ask."

"Yes, but we are at a time when so many exciting ideas are emerging, and I want to bring them together to form new and exciting areas to help sick people."

"I guess you heard about my investment into Eagle. I read the investment thesis and your background. You are one of the primary reasons I invested, and I too hope you will bring new technologies to help others."

Alex returned as the two men continued getting to know one another. He pressured Jack to get his girl into the private room, but Ava was still distracting him. Simon asked if it was ok to share some cocaine and the three drew some lines and then headed to the pool table. Simon set the rack and handed a stick to Jack. "Ready to play some Cutthroat?"

"Absolutely," said Jack, before a loud and explosive break. He sank the 10 ball and after surveying the table announced. I'll take 1 thru 5. He sank another 5 balls with ease and then a very difficult bank shot awaited. He walked around the table and squatted down several times to make up his mental shot lines. He returned to the cue ball and struck it with enough force to make three banks before heading to the 7 ball which naturally glided to the pocket.

"So, I see you've played the game," said Simon.

"I love to play pool," said Jack. "It is a challenge that allows you to think for a moment and then execute a plan. What could be better than that?"

"Letting others shoot the ball would be a good start," said Alex.

"Sorry gents, you were right to let me play a few shots and enjoy the board. He gently hit the cue to the center of the felt and handed his stick to Simon. Take your time. The balls are in your favor."

"I think I should have had a bit more coke," said Simon. The three managed a few games and then returned to their table. Simon left for a bathroom stop, Alex was groping his newfound friend and Jack was anxious for time with Ava. This was his chance to speak with her and when she returned, he quickly got out of his chair, went straight to her, and said, "I'm sorry to say we are leaving soon, and I wanted to spend more time with you."

"I'd like that too," said Ava.

"Maybe we can meet again soon."

It was nearing midnight and time to call it a night. Alex and Jack said their goodbyes to Simon and made their way to the lobby. The "house" Mercedes awaited their hung-over selves and carried them to their respective addresses.

CHAPTER
FOURTEEN
AVA'S YOUTH

AVA SPENT her childhood in Oakland, an East Bay city overshadowed by the splendors of San Francisco and the majestic Oakland Hills. Though marred by pockets of low-income communities and limited opportunities, Oakland was home.

Her parents worked minimum-wage jobs, striving to provide for their family of five. As the youngest of three children, Ava's world orbited around her mother's loving care and a firm relationship. Her room, decorated with traces of happiness and joy, was a temple of dreams and hopes where her imagination could take flight, and she could envision a wonder-filled life.

In addition to taking care of her creativity, Ava's mother taught her the importance of faith. They shared morning and evening prayers, forging a connection with each other and the spiritual realm. These prayers and their relationship with God were the pillars of their relationship, providing guidance and strength as they navigated life's challenges.

As Ava entered her teenage years, her body underwent remarkable changes. She grew tall and graceful, blessed with long legs from her American Indian father and her mother's elegant shoulders. It was a winning genetic combination. Her slender yet strong physique lent itself to demanding sports like gymnastics, swimming, and track. At just 12, she executed a flawless double backflip. Yet excellence came with challenges. Swimming, for instance, required her to brave the pre-dawn chill to reach the YMCA pool during winter.

Ava found her true calling on the track in the 400m sprint, a race she seemed born to excel in. In middle school, she demonstrated her extraordinary talent by winning not one but three races—the 200m, 400m, and 800m—in a tri-meet held in her hometown of Oakland.

By her freshman year of high school, she left gymnastics to focus on dance. Her teacher recognized her athleticism and exceptional grace. She saw in Ava the potential for a talented and captivating performer on stage. Over the years, Ava's dedication paid off. By her junior year, she had become Northern California's fastest 1500m swimmer. She also consistently broke the 50-second barrier in the 400m sprint and secured starring roles in multiple dance performances.

As her senior year began, Ava weighed six athletic scholarships from prestigious institutions, including UC Berkeley, Stanford, UCLA, and USC. These opportunities marked a critical moment in her life. Though drawn to art and dance, the allure of the full-ride scholarships was undeniable.

She embarked on campus visits to help her decide, finding Berkely and Stanford relatively straightforward. But USC captivated her. Nestled in gritty LA neighborhoods, the campus pulsed with vibrant energy, its imposing brick buildings asserting their presence.

Towards the end of the tour, Ava and her father were brought to the track stadium, where they received a surprising revelation. The host proudly declared that USC could compete in the Olympics and rank among the top 10 nations if it were a country. This statement added another layer of intrigue to the USC experience, further complicating Ava's decision-making process.

"I understand one of you is on a track scholarship, and we have a special guest for you today," the host said, ushering Ava and her father inside the stadium. On the track, a few athletes were training.

Ava's father spotted her first - Allyson Felix, the legendary sprinter, gliding around the far turn, warming up for her 400-meter sprints. Ava's eyes were now fixed on Allyson's every move as she changed her course and headed back towards the tour group.

She approached Ava. "You're Ava Lewis, right? From state finals?"

Ava's heart raced, and she replied, almost in disbelief, "Wow… you're Allyson Felix!"

Allyson nodded and said, "Yes, the USC team would love to have you as a Trojan. They have some of the best coaches for middle distance, and they'll help you become the best runner you can be. I need to get back to my practice, but the next time you come down, let me know, and we can link up and train together."

On the drive home, Ava buzzed about USC's track and arts. The decision felt effortless—it was the Oakland of SoCal.

The next day, Ava received a direct message from Allyson, reminding her of her unique talent and the power of God's grace. Allyson encouraged her to accept her purpose in this world, also keeping in mind that there would be challenges and great achievements ahead. It was a message of support, to remind her of the balancing act that Ava was about to journey upon, and a promise that Allyson would always be there for her.

Ava was genuinely touched by the kind words of her new friend and mentor. She had initially joined Allyson's Instagram, intending to merely follow the legend, not expecting Allyson to ever engage. However, the unexpected connection left a lasting impact on her.

During a cozy New Year's Eve family gathering, Ava made a significant announcement to her parents: she wanted to attend USC as an art major and relocate to Los Angeles in the fall with a track scholarship. It marked a pivotal moment that aligned her passion for athletics and the creative arts.

Ava threw herself into track that spring, drawing inspiration from legends like Carl Lewis and Allyson. She secured CCS titles in the

200m and 400m sprints. Ava's form on the track was impeccable, and she glided with the grace of a supremely gifted athlete.

After clinching the California title in two events, Ava was ready to prove herself in college.

As a USC freshman, Ava thrived academically, immersing herself in classes that nurtured her creative instincts. She delved into the works of the masters, honed her craft through painting and sculpture, and even explored the realms of language, teaching herself about poetry and creative writing. Ava was like a sponge, absorbing everything related to the study of love, compassion, and the complexities of the human heart.

Her commitment to her creative passions led her to make significant changes in her life. She decided to cut out all digital distractions, from TV to dance music and instead became obsessed with reading and writing. Most of her time was now dedicated to the artistry of the written word.

As spring unfolded, Ava was determined to find a balance that allowed her to keep her creative flame alive while excelling on the track. She had become a testament to the harmonious coexistence of her two great loves—the challenges and rigor of track and the boundless, dynamic spirit of art.

Track workouts at USC proved to be more grueling than Ava had anticipated, far removed from her days in Oakland. She thrived under pressure when she could deliver, and USC pushed her to the limits of her comfort zone. The training regimen bordered on the militant, with drills becoming progressively harder and more demanding as the season opener drew nearer.

Ava constantly felt her legs teetering on the fine line between peak performance and the need for rest to allow her muscles to recover. In high school, she had grown accustomed to rigorous workouts, pushing herself through 400-meter laps, gradually increasing the intensity until nothing was left in the tank. However, USC introduced a weekly ordeal called "Pussycat-Hellcat" drill every Tuesday. It was designed to break athletes down early in the week before Saturday's race.

This grueling drill involved men's and women's squads, with whistle-blowing coaches monitoring each second. The first 5 or 6 laps were at 75% speed, but soon they were pushed to 80-90% capacity by lap 10. Subsequently, every lap was expected to fall within the 90-100% range, though the coaches understood that 100% was too much for training. The highest throttle was 95%; anyone exceeding it would need to stop the drill.

The team found themselves drained by these demanding drills. A single whistle signaled "go," two whistles meant "slow down," but the triple whistle indicating the end of practice never came. Falling short of completing a lap meant being on track to miss Saturday's competition, earning the dreaded "pussycat" label. The coach was willing to see his team of "tomcats" diminish if it meant preventing top runners from competing.

During the grueling pussycat-hellcat drills, superstar athletes sometimes appeared, showing off their skills on the field. Coaches would often tease the team, pointing out the presence of luminaries like Michael Norman or Allyson Felix jogging alongside Sydney McLaughlin, leaving them breathless.

Each athlete on the USC track team had to find that delicate balance between giving their all and holding back. These "terrible Tuesdays" persisted from February through May, pushing the team to their limits. Ava was no stranger to hard work and was born naturally able to shift between gears when needed.

After her freshman year, she introduced a new "fourth gear" gear that meant going flat out, a relentless drive to outperform everyone else. She rarely used this fourth gear in training but relied on it during some of the most challenging tri-meets, particularly in the regional competitions. Whether it was called fourth gear, FG, or just "freaking great," Ava's ability to kick it up a notch was awe-inspiring. Her father, who made the six-hour drive to watch, would shout, "Go get your gear now!" when she turned on the final curve of the 400m. Ava could hear her father's voice among the cheering crowd, spurring her to unleash her breathtaking stride and bring home the gold.

It was an impressive start, and she planned to continually improve her performance each year.

As Ava's sophomore year began, there was a feeling of excitement, anticipation, and anxiety. Her academic pursuits were going well, and she relished the opportunity to expand her love for art and dance. However, her workouts became increasingly demanding, pushing her to new stress levels and intensity. To cope with the physical toll, she started undergoing hydro and massage therapies to keep her muscles in top condition. Hot and cold baths effectively controlled lactic acid and managed joint pains. Ava also regularly visited the chiropractor for back issues and eventually added deep-tissue massage to her therapy regimen. It was all part of the extreme conditioning required of a track athlete; a side of the sport rarely discussed but essential for success.

Midway through her second track season, Ava participated in a regional meet where she competed in the 200m, 400m, and 800m preliminaries. This meant racing five or six times daily, leaving her more exhausted than usual by Sunday. She devoted the morning to stretching and various hot-and-cold therapies for her ankles. In this demanding competition, she secured a second-place finish in the 800m, claimed victory in the 400m, and faced the 200m final at 3 p.m. The 200m required a swift start and a strong push on the turn.

Ava had lane 3 for the race, giving her a clear view of most of her competitors as they lined up. When the starting gun fired, the women burst out of their blocks with determination. After the first 100 meters, they all emerged from the turn with appropriate staggers, positioning themselves for the final sprint.

Ava pumped her arms and accelerated as she rounded the turn, her goal to reach full speed about three-quarters of the way through the race. But disaster struck when she heard a terrible click near her feet. She immediately pulled up, limping and unable to put weight on her right leg. It was devastating as she lay helpless on the track, realizing she had severely torn her right Achilles tendon.

That evening, when she called her parents, Ava felt like she had lost a vital part of herself and couldn't fathom a life without track. Her parents provided much-needed comfort and support, driving to Los Angeles the following day. They spent the weekend ensuring their beloved daughter was okay and helping her adjust to crutches and a knee scooter. They also scheduled her surgery before the summer break, and she would undergo her recovery in Oakland.

The following summer was unforgettable, filled with one-legged activities and a profound shift in dreams.

Ava had to transition from being a world-class athlete to contemplating a career as a professional dancer. She joined a local dance club to aid in her recovery, primarily to observe and engage in stretching exercises. It served as a therapeutic way for her to heal, channeling her energy into the world of dance as she embarked on this new chapter of her life.

PART THREE

FIFTEEN

FIVE SAINTS

THERE HAD BEEN VERY few advancements or discoveries in the field of autism. However, recent studies showed a rise in the number of afflicted children. Evidence suggested a 16% increase in the incidence rate of autism spectrum disorder (ASD) over the past 2 years. ASD was also 4 times more likely in boys than girls. Interestingly, when one twin has autism, there is a 76% chance the other will also be diagnosed. But Jack and Robbie were different. They were born from incredible loving parents who wished for them daily through endless prayers. They shared DNA and extremely good looks. However, only Robbie had the gift of autism.

Every day, Jack was fascinated with his brother. From as early as he remembered, his little twin brother was amazing. Jack was older by about 12 hours, but the world thought Robbie was his little brother. Because of their physical appearance and the offset of their sizes, it wasn't always clear that they were twins. One thing was for sure: Robbie was a saint. His place on this earth was truly to bring his gift of love and kindness to others.

There was an unusual gift that this group of kids possessed, and Jack wanted to know more about how they had such a unique group communication and ability to learn and grow as if they were wired in the same manner. They clearly had better sensory systems allowing more data to enter their brain and a peaceful ability to focus on what information was true versus noise. When speaking, Jack never had to repeat himself. It was always clear and right the first time. Sure, this was academic material, but what about if he tried philosophy or religion. Would the team enjoy Aristotle or the Gospels? He knew this group had a far greater ability to comprehend information and group sessions soon became rich with happiness. Each team member enjoyed the group with more and more enthusiasm. They feed off one another and "elevated each other's game."

By the end of his volunteer term, the group included Robbie and 4 boys, each of whom had been at every one of Jack's recitations. Before Jack left that summer, he started a club that included three students from the clinic, his brother the savant, and a one other misfit with extreme capabilities. He called the club, "The Upside Down Idiots." After all he thought to himself, who needed another genius club. One of the simple challenges was that the group did not like working "online," and preferred group sessions. Even though they seldom physically interacted in the group, their minds were always active. To avoid being called "The Silent Think Tank," Jack started each session with a finger-snapping routine and made sure each team member had their own act. He was their "smart" leader and perhaps their best friend in life. Interestingly, the group would remain together for many, many years to come.

This extraordinary group warranted a name that resonated with their uniqueness. Something more profound than "Fabulous Five" or a typical superhero reference. Individually remarkable, together they were an even more formidable force. Their names—Robbie, Luke, Michael, Joseph, and Paul—held deep significance. They were sent to this world with a distinct purpose and immeasurable value. Their minds were exceptional, and their hearts boundless. They were destined not only to save lives but also to forever alter perceptions of autism. Jack recognized their exceptional nature and proposed they be named after Saints.

It was their final session for the summer, and Jack had gathered the group for a special occasion. There were no more books to read or sessions to conduct. This was a simple ceremony. Simple, yet the most heartfelt gesture from their kindest leader. Soon, they would celebrate and praise each other leaving behind their common pasts for their anointed futures.

The first to be anointed was his brother, Saint Robbie. At 15, he was slender, curly dark hair cascading down his shoulders. His warm, captivating gaze could hold one's attention for hours. Jack affectionately teased him about his intense stare, and Robbie would respond with a tilted head and a smile. Jack approached Robbie, placing a necklace with a metal name piece around his neck. It read; "Saint Joseph, son of Jack, father to Jesus, carpenter, patron of a happy death." As he kissed Robbie's forehead, Jack spoke:

"To my loving brother, may we never be far apart, and our hearts always beat as one."

Jack then turned to Paul, the youngest of the group, just past eleven years old. With his hair falling to his shoulders, he aimed to appear more mature, though it sometimes left him looking like a girl. Alongside ASD, he grappled with epilepsy and endured frequent seizures. Paul was the ideal subject for studying neurobehavioral conditions, with enough charisma to intrigue most doctors. Jack placed a necklace around his neck and kissed his forehead, saying: "Saint Paul, the apostle, the author, the Pope. Your joy is spreading your love and kindness as Jesus did before you."

Next was Luke, a 13-year-old with an affinity for boats and the ocean, akin to Jack. His favorite pastime involved watching boats entering the harbor, estimating their length, and committing their names to memory. It was as if he'd been a ship captain in a previous life, navigating the seas by the night sky. Jack anointed him as "Saint Erasmus of Formia" or Saint Elmo, the patron saint of sailors, and added with a touch of humor, "Oddly, he was the reliever of intestinal ailments and women's pain in labor. You provide the guiding light of St. Elmo's fire to sailors lost in stormy seas."

Finally, the oldest members, Michael, and Joseph, at 16 and 17, were nearly adults. They stood taller than Jack, their older-brotherly stature occasionally allowing them to look down at him. These two were inseparable, affectionately known as "M&J" and eventually just "MJ." Jack addressed them as a pair. "I want you both to know how proud I am of your talents and charm. You've shown exceptional leadership to our team, and everyone appreciates your role. However, it's time for your anointing, and I'm very proud to speak with each of you."

Addressing Michael first, Jack expressed admiration for his talents and key role in watching over the group. He called him "Saint Michael the Archangel," the protector and guardian against danger and sickness. As he presented Michael with his necklace, Michael's smile radiated warmth.

Then Jack reached for the last necklace and walked over to Joseph. The last and perfect saint. He was the eldest of the bunch and understood his responsibility as their leader. Standing nearly 6'3", Joseph could be a gentle giant, or a serious threat as required. Fortunately, he never needed to exercise his strength with most of his time spent in the hospital. As they entered the court, he and Michael shared a magic handshake like NBA players. It was their way of letting others know they were connected to the outside world, even if neither could shoot a basketball.

Jack spoke: "It is my pleasure to know Joseph. He has been given the physical presence which commands respect and carries the burden as our lead soldier. However, as we all know, his real gift is to be the most loving and kind of all of us. Scripture tells us that Saint Joseph married Mary and was the father of Jesus. In the Fabulous Five, he will be our protector, guide, and father figure."

Jack looped the necklace over Joseph's head and gently touched his forehead. He then returned to the center of the group and continued.

"I know that I am still too young to appreciate the wonder of this group. I hope that by some miracle of faith, we may always be together, and our friendship and love will endure. I am blessed to know each of you, and it is my honor to visit with you as often as possible."

As the team smiled back at Jack, each member was experiencing their anointment as if a true ceremony had occurred in front of an audience. The energy was overwhelming and more memorable than they could imagine.

CHAPTER
SIXTEEN

AVA PASSION WORK

AVA KEPT A VERY tight schedule of activities from Monday through Thursday with a business-like approach to each day. Her mornings began with Parisian coffee from a press and fresh cream. This was the calmest part of her day; she would enjoy the aroma of her mixture, the peacefulness of a Zen dining area, and a reminder of why each day was important. Ava was deliberate in her simple morning ritual of special coffee, focus of her mind and body and understanding that whatever transpired during the coming day would be a journey worth living and remembering.

The days early in the week seemed destined for more chaos. On Mondays and Tuesdays, she would be fully dressed by the time coffee was ready and as Wednesday or Thursday came along, she was still in lingerie. The curse of the western calendar and obsessive clock weakened her approach. But let's be real here, this was a very busy woman with countless demands on her spirit and she was far ahead of most.

She was showered, dressed, made up, coffee brewed, and Zen charged by 7am most days. The front end of the week was a routine. Her day bag was prepared for either dance, yoga or Muay Thai. Ava's dress was classy professional style with typical fashion from Vogue for late twenties professional women. Her commute to work was about 2 or 3 miles, usually an Uber to save the heels. She worked for an import/export mogul who leased a very large property in the China Basin district. The owner was a high-wealth, Singaporean family who had renovated over 200,000 sq-ft of office space including a spacious lobby and 2 floors looking out to the bay.

For most, import/export meant some form of money laundering. However, this property dealt with many forms of legitimate art and there was far too much of a following to have anything crooked. Ava's boss was a blend between an art collector and a curator. His name was Philipe and although born in France, he did most of his training in New York. He was a very stylish dresser, an excellent art historian, and knew how to host major events. This was one of Ava's most exciting parts of the job as it included everything, she adored including art, food, exotic art critiques, and of course those who came to buy. The gallery held a party for one of their collections every quarter and invited a few hundred guests. Besides being one of the loveliest hosts, Ava's job was to steer the money to the artwork. Philipe paid her a modest commission, but the thrill for her was bringing together the artist work and the buyer. Other than creating her own work, which she someday hoped would be in a gallery, she loved the sell.

After one of their best gallery showings, Philipe ran the numbers and paid the staff for their hard work and dismissed them with praise. He singled out Ava for a short chat and handed her an envelope with her earnings. It felt heavier than usual and made her excited to open. Philipe told her, "As you know, tonight was one of our best evenings. We sold over 90% of the collection and more than $2.5 million in sales, which puts $25,000 in your pocket. More importantly, the owners have asked us to come to Singapore and help procure the next collection, which includes trips to Indonesia, Thailand, and Vietnam. "Get your passport ready girl. We are going first class to Asia," said Philipe.

CHAPTER
SEVENTEEN
FIVEOGRAPHY

THE SAINTS BECAME friends in their early teenage years. The initial bonds were formed in their reading circles and expanded to everyday journeys across all areas around Seattle. There was a small age gap of about five years (from oldest to youngest), but the team was a very tight fraternity of souls. The Saints' fiveography included a mixture of heights, dates, colors, schools, and a short story about their lives.

Paul: Paul Simpson, tiny, blue-green eyes, shared left-handedness with Robbie

Birthday:Jan 31, 1994, the youngest (2 years younger than Robbie), Aquarius

Fav Color:Blue

Music:Harmonica, guitar, violin, Peter, Paul & Mary

Story:Paul was always closest to Robbie due to their physical size. It was nice to have each other and no need to remind them of their height. He always wanted to go to Vegas and loved the Bellagio water show. As a Michelin restaurant connoisseur, he was the first to review and approve dinner menus. Paul Allen was his hero.

~

Luke: Animated, musical.
   Birthday:Aug 22, 1993, Leo
   Fav Color:Red, Rainbow
   Instrument:Piano, Trumpet
   Story:He joked about joining Jack on a trip to the moon. Loved music from the 1960-70s like Elton John, Peter, Paul, and Mary.

~

Joseph: The eldest saint
   Birthday:March 22, 1989, Aries
   Fav Color:Cranberry red
   Instrument:Percussion, drums
   Odd Phrase: Stick and Bindle
   Story:Joseph and Michael were the strongest of the bunch. Joseph was first through the gates of any adventure and kept a close watch over his flock forever. His passion was sports cars, engines, and anything that made things faster. As he grew older, like Michael, he grew to like more unique and powerful engines that traveled into space and was destined to be a pilot or astronaut. Mix in a little physics and he was set for one of the university labs at Caltech, or MIT.

~

Michael: Attracted to space, stars, gravity, sailing around the world.
   Birthday:June 10, 1990, Gemini
   Fav Color:Black, with stars
   Music:Piano, George Michael, and Queen
   His Story:Was the most likely to leave Washington State. He had the brains to be a physicist or astronaut. The path forward should

include stars, planets, and the universe. His school choices included the ivies like Harvard, Princeton & Yale, techies like Berkeley, Cal Tech, MIT, and top brands like Stanford, University of Chicago. Michael loved to drive, and road trips were his favorite.

Robbie: Robert (Robbie) Joseph. The leader. Creative.

Birthday:Feb 28, 1992, Pisces

Fav Color:Blue

Fav Band:The Stone Poneys, featuring Linda Ronstadt

Word Choice:Understood vs Overstood.

Instrument:Piano, and the forgotten Oboe

Story:Youngest of the Mohr family, born hours after his twin brother. Since childhood, Robbie was destined to be near a hospital, in a good way. His goal was to become a physician and likely a pediatrician. He also wanted to be closer to his brother and went to UC Berkeley for his undergrad, which was initially remote and eventually, he would settle in California.

PART FOUR

EIGHTEEN

OYSTER PEARL TWO

FOR A CITY of over 7 million people, San Francisco was one of the easiest big cities to navigate. Besides the iconic cable cars, Lyft and Uber vehicles were now sharing the road with autonomous cars. Cruise Automation convinced the city officials to provide a trusted route from the south (near SFO) to the toll booth at the Golden Gate Bridge. They had a fleet of over 15,000 vehicles fetched from any phone (using their app) and provided inner city transportation for typically around $5. Jack remembers being in a hurry to get from his home in Pacific Heights to Union Square - it was only a two-mile walk or drive and yet, he had less than 10 minutes to get to his lunch appointment. He pulled up the Cruise app on his iPhone and within 45 seconds, a white Chevy Bolt pulled up to his curb and the passenger window automatically rolled down. A woman's voice came over the car and his phone welcoming him to his ride. He jumped in the back seat and as soon as he clipped on his seat belt, the car pulled away from the curb and on his way. His lunch appointment was inside the Westin St Francis and parking would have been ridiculous. Instead, he managed the trip in 8 minutes (according to his trip details on the app) and he was heading to the lobby before his noon appointment.

Jack really liked to be on time and made his way to the restaurant on the 2nd floor. It was a business lunch on a Thursday which typically meant meeting a startup founder with expectations for funding. Either Sandra or another office staff would typically arrange these visits, and the challenge was always determining who the lucky party was for lunch.

Today, Jack was less prepared than usual and had only briefly read about the company. The founder was an MD who, after a successful but short career as a neurologist, decided to team with a research group to see if they could create lifestyle devices to help those with debilitating neurological disorders better keep up with the GenX, Millennials and others. His name was Dr. Keith Stevens, and his business plan was short, well-written and very much to the point. It was less than 5 pages, covering the full spectrum of who, what, and why his company should receive funding. Stevens was likely in his late 40's, early fifties and Jack was just over 25. Between bites of lunch, they provided each other insights to both the entrepreneurial idea and the various paths that could be envisioned toward success. The doc clearly knew both science and patients. However, he lacked any background in running a startup or operational skills in product development.

He was seeking a $2m seed round to complete some patents, gather requirements for a device, and advance a few experiments which were at first glance, game changers. Jack was impressed with how easily Stevens articulated his way through his plan and how he covered the various risks with objective, medical school-like methodical reasoning. Jack provided a few visuals including herding cats and the best-made plans of mice and men. Keeping new entrepreneurs grounded was essential. Keith was a cross between a very intelligent doctor and a mid-life, wannabe entrepreneur. His idea was novel and worth a deeper dive with the investment team. Jack closed out with follow-up items and the chance to meet with him at the office the following week.

NINETEEN

PARTNER PRIVILEGES

THERE WERE five limited partners in Eagle Investments. They included Steve Anderson, Andy Weinman, BJ Williamson, Ian Felton & Todd Goldberg.

After Jacks' investment in "Newco, his first deal," a note appeared on his desk. It was a fancy envelope that looked far more formal that he was used to seeing at work. He carefully opened the seal and pulled out a single sheet of paper with a handwritten note. It read," Congratulations on your first deal. Let's celebrate with the partners. Best Regards, Steve." Hmmm, Jack thought, how nice to receive from his boss, but what does it mean…? He walked over to Sandra O's desk and showed her the note. Sandra was Steve's Administrative Assistant and knew all the group's inner workings. She looked up to Jack and said, "How wonderful! Your first deal is complete, and the group wants to show off." Jack glanced back at her and said, "I haven't made any money for the firm yet, is it really time to celebrate…?" Oh, don't worry, she said, "your part of a very select group and the writing is on the wall that you will be successful here. I will update you on the group dinner and fill you in on some specialty items beforehand."

Jack knew there were privileges with being a partner, but he really didn't have any details. As a Limited Partner in the firm, you were invited to invest a minimum of $5M and up to $100M of liquid assets. The money went into a "sidecar" fund, took a portion of each deal in their syndicate, and had minor preferences that allowed for internal flexibility. In other words, a partner within the firm can increase or lessen their ownership by "buying or selling" amongst other team member investors. This also put their skin in the game and made for good looks with their other limited partners outside the firm.

The Eagle comprised one managing director, 4 seasoned general partners and one new general partner. Jack was offered a partner position and asked to stay in the business flow as an EIR. However, he put in a "partner size chuck of $5M " when he joined the firm. It was the largest investment from his net assets and certainly his riskiest deal. He discussed the investment at length with his lawyer and decided that although it represented over 30% of his portfolio, he could afford to risk this amount at such an early stage in his career.

Steve Anderson was originally from Philadelphia and attended UPenn with some executive leadership courses from Stanford. His favorite football team was the Eagles and when he moved to California, he would listen to the Eagles band. Naturally when it came time to set up his new firm, the naming was easy. Steve was very successful at Goldman and when he spun off on his own, he brought a rich network and deal flow. He was the perfect managing director with that fine balance of class and greed to drive a successful venture capital firm.

Monday mornings were the deal flow meetings and a chance for the partners to assemble as a group. Before each session, the guys discuss their weekend travels to exotic whereabouts and miscellaneous purchases. Earlier in the week, the most seasoned GP at 47, Andy Weinman, announced he was buying a small coastal property in the Mediterranean. He said they had looked along the coasts of Spain, France and Italy and finally decided on Monaco. He casually mentioned that the address was in Monaco. However, the property was in nearby France. Andy owned a yacht and wanted to be sure he could have direct beach access with deep waters for his liking. The house had 7 bedrooms, 5 bathrooms, 2 kitchens and a downstairs wine cellar that stored over 300 bottles. The property was on 5 acres and sounded like a fantastic investment. Ben J. Williamson (aka "BJ") asked if the villa came with any staff housing to keep the riff raff away during the off-season. Jack thought he was joking until Ben mentioned a recent case of one of his good friends who had their summer home in Italy rented out to an Airbnb scam where the property was falsely rented for several weeks. Although nothing in the house was damaged, it was upsetting. It sounds like even the rich get taken advantage of Jack thought briefly. Andy handed Ben a flier for the Monaco Yacht Show and said, "you should come visit this September, maybe it's time for you to buy a bigger boat." Thanks, replied Ben, I'll add it to my calendar.

Jack wondered about the wealth of his new partner peers and thought the answers to his questions would certainly come out through conversations. The amount of money spent on homes, cars, boats, and vacations was outrageous. During a coffee break, Jack overheard one of these colleagues approving the architecture bid on a second home remodel in Tahoe for over $2M and another working on a land investment deal in Napa (to get closer to the grapes) for nearly $12M. After the first 2 months on the job, he learned that money was just reward and the real pleasure was spending it. He also noticed that "everyone" had some sort of club membership and he needed to get into some sort of sport or exercise routine. It was on his to-do list and perhaps a way to meet new people.

Sandra sent a group email inviting everyone to a special dinner to celebrate Jack's first deal. She called it the first of many new deals to come and that Steve had asked that the partners join him at The Hakkasan for dinner on Thursday evening. Drinks starting at 6. San Francisco has several top-shelf restaurants, which was near the top of the list. It was located on Kearny Street just a few blocks from the financial district. The group met in a private dining room where the drinks flowed. Jack arrived early and walked over to greet Andy.

"This is a wonderful place," he gestured.

"It's one of Steve's favorite clubs," Andy replied.

"This is a club? It feels more like an exotic Chinese restaurant."

"It's much more than food. Let's see how the night goes."

Jack knew the team had excellent taste. BJ and others soon joined, along with Sandra with some small packages. She laid them down on the front table, wished everyone a wonderful evening, and then went. The room had a soft glow of gold from the lighting and was surrounded by gloss black columns and iridescent blue shimmering from the table trim. It was some sort of Chinese-sheik look and felt like a classy club environment. The waiters wore black tuxedos with white shirts and blue Lapis buttons. Jack took an extra look as his favorite stone was Lapis. He noticed the buttons and cufflinks as the stones were carefully set in gold trim. The male staff were all well-groomed and the women wore their hair up. The woman's dress was also a tuxedo pant and vest, although the blouse was very feminine and unbuttoned more than halfway down. A classy and sexy look.

At about 6:15pm, Steve entered, greeting each partner with a welcome smile. He was clearly in his element and enjoyed the small talk with the team. Jack was enjoying a salt-n-pepper squid appetizer and watching as he approached.

"Great to have you join us and hope you are enjoying the evening," Steve added.

"Of course, this place is wonderful," said Jack.

"Oh, you will love this place when I'm through, just sit tight."

Steve then went into some more business small talk about how nice it was to have fresh new blood on the team and a new perspective. He liked Jack's approach to finding new deals and was looking forward to his contributions. As he walked away, he gave the waiter a finger roll to suggest the start of the evening. The table was set, and it was time to have the guys sit down. It was a large round table for six with a large spinning centerpiece. As the team members came to their chairs, the last two spots were for Jack and the main event host, Steve. Fortunately, they were not together, and Jack found himself safely between Andy the elder, and Todd the brilliant maestro from the East Coast office. Andy and BJ were from Stanford and often shared stories from their past. Finally, they were all seated for dinner and the powerful team was assembled. The waiter from the bar entered and refreshed everyone's drinks. As the drinks were delivered to each partner, Steve would watch like a proud leader of his crew. He looked back over his left shoulder and immediately the female waitress glided over his side and whispered in his ear. She left the room and returned with dish after dish of elegant food and several helpers to bring small servings to be placed on the "lazy Susan," roundabout. Steve would announce the food. "Please enjoy the prawns. Hope you like the duck, and here comes my favorite, Brazilian lobster."

The team knew the menu was fantastic and Steve's taste was impeccable. They were enjoying the starters and some dim sum extras. Jack loved Chinese food, but this was over-the-top delicious. He looked around the table and wondered if his teammates had stories to tell about travels to mainland China. As the young kid of the bunch, he could keep his curiosity to himself and wait for the right time to ask or simply wait for another time.

Then Steve announced, "Hey, this is great food and wonderful company. I want to thank each of you, especially our newest member, for coming this evening." He went on to address Jack's newest deal and praise the elements of the team, the timing of the firm's investment and the hopes for upside in the many portfolio exits. The team had heard the speech before; however, this time Steve added a few words of sincerity regarding the hope for medical breakthroughs that would also help the world. It was a speech for the team and some extra warmth they could take home to their partners. He then stood up and walked over to the table to the gift bag left by Sandra. He returned to his seat, placed each gift on the centerpiece, and rotated it around until each partner had their gift.

"In addition to our latest investment led by Jack's team, I want to present each of you with a small token of appreciation. As you know, Eagle's second fund returned over 34% to our shareholders and the proceeds were dispersed last month. I am very pleased and proud of each of you and look forward to the next 5-years and success of Eagle Fund III. Let's enjoy tonight and enjoy the spoils." He raised his glass and announced, "Cheers."

The partners retrieved their gifts one by one, anticipating perhaps a fine watch or a gold iWatch. Jack was no exception. He first opened the card, reading the thoughtful words. The wrapping held a framed piece of art. Expecting a tech gadget, Jack was taken aback. He examined the artwork— an early drawing by Pablo Picasso from 1958. His heart skipped a beat. Andy, noticing Jack's surprise, raised his sea compass and quipped, "Hey Jack, come visit me on the coast of Spain, and we'll find out where your masterpiece came from." The jest was clear, but Jack sensed the team's influence on the gift. Turning the piece over, he discovered a gallery card tucked into the frame. Later, he would find out that this small drawing was an original worth over $95,000. It was evident that Sandra had delved into his appreciation for art and his passion for significant contributions to medical advancements. She had made some astute calls, including consulting Jack's enthusiastic sister, who had suggested the major influencers in his life, Picasso, Matisse, and Mondrian.

So, this is how it was when you've made it to the big leagues. Work hard, play hard and enjoy the spoils. Jack felt a bit undeserving, yet he also knew that Steve had done his homework and was taking a calculated risk on Jack. He bet that treating his newest "partner" like a major contributor would pay off. It was certainly working. And being generous was expected within the venture bunch, however, this was very genuine, and Jack felt he needed to say something. He flipped the piece over to view it once again. The boys were chirping away at their spoils and a little gap opened. Jack spoke up. "Thank you all for having me here with you this year. Working with you is a privilege, and I hope I can deliver on the promise."

Steve interrupted, "You've already proved yourself to us and we welcome you to the group. Sorry it's such a tiny drawing, next time, let's get a full-size painting!" The group had a good laugh, and Jack realized this was just how they rolled, and he had better get used to it quickly.

"Agreed," Jack said, raising his glass.

TWENTY

22ND FLOOR

THE MAIN COURSES WERE DELIVERED, each dish an indescribable delicacy. Jack felt good at the partner table and thought, "this is easy to get used to." Finally, the dessert tray was presented including a sweet pudding-like dish. Jack noticed that the lights in the room were dimming little-by-little over the last 10 minutes and realized later it was all part of the show. Steve carefully pushed the tray around along with a small white shot glass to each partner.

He raised his glass, smiled, and announced, "Again, it is my privilege to work with you guys and I hope for more success. May the Eagles soar!"

Each toasted and threw back their bourbon shots.

As Jack placed his shot glass on the table, he felt a gentle touch on his left shoulder and a woman's breast rub across his right shoulder as a long, slender arm reached out to refill his glass. He looked around the circle, and standing behind each partner was a beautiful Asian woman. Each gorgeous model wore an evening dress and stiletto heels. The room lighting was now dark in the surroundings and the glow from the center lighting bounced off the faces of these ladies.

Steve offered his final toast, "Enjoy the evening."

One-by-one, the partners stood to leave with their new "partners."

Jack slowly turned to take in the full beauty of his date. She was almost 6' tall in heels with long black hair and bright red lipstick. He reached his hands to join hers and walked to the edge of the room where the glass wall overlooked San Francisco.

"The city looks beautiful," he said. She stepped closer to him and slid her left leg forward gently rubbing against his thigh.

"You must be the new Eagle we heard about. How do you like the team?"

"They are an amazing bunch of guys and really know their investment shit." He let language slip a bit, but she just smiled back.

"I think you must be smart, too, if you're with them."

"Thanks. I am getting used to their style and the wonders of this city."

She tilted her head. "Where are you from?"

"I'm from Seattle."

"And do you like it here?" She was caressing his hands and although Jack was looking at her face, he could not resist glancing at her body lines as she entangled herself into him.

"I do. It's my new favorite city."

"Let me show you around." She turned and led him out of the room, holding onto his hand. His view was wonderful as he watched her tiny waist and hips move inside the silky gown. They headed to the elevator and as she pressed the 22nd floor, Jack said, "Ah, that's my favorite number."

She looked over her shoulder, giving him a coy look. "Oh, good. I like it too."

The twenty-second floor was the top floor and the doors opened to a large foyer. She walked him to the double doors and waived the card key across the gold fixture. She entered the room first and Jack passed her gazing at the oversized entrance. Like the restaurant, the room was mostly black with marble floors and dark pillars with plenty of gold trim. The difference was that blue was replaced with red and the effect was stunning.

It was the Presidential Suite, and Jack felt very presidential.

"Would you like a drink, Jack?" she asked while strolling towards the bar.

"I'd love one," he replied. "So, it seems like you know me, but I don't know you..."

"Oh, sorry, that's true. My name is Leila."

"And you work at the Hakkasan?"

She shook her head. "No, I work at a club downtown. We know Sandra and she takes good care of Steve's team."

"Oh, I see."

Standing behind the bar, she lifted an eyebrow. "What can I fix for you?"

"A bourbon is fine."

Leila poured two drinks in crystal drinking glasses and presented them to Jack. "Follow me," she said and walked him to the window. "We're a bit higher now. What do you think?"

"It's really lovely from here."

She tapped his glass gently and asked, "What would you like to do tonight? Would you like me to give you a massage?" Leila held her drink in one hand and slowly rubbed Jack's shoulder with the other. Then she placed the drink on the window ledge freeing up the other hand to explore his chest.

Before he could respond, she was working both hands across his chest, down to his stomach and then back up to his head where she used her fingers to comb the back of his head. She used this grip to gently pull him forward, while leaning into him to whisper in his ear.

"Mmmmm, you still feel stressed," she said with a slight accent. "Let me take care of you."

Jack forgot about the lovely San Francisco skyline and immersed himself in this woman's lovely touch, smell, and soft voice.

"Ok," he finally breathed. "I'd love that."

Leila pulled his hand and walked him to the entrance of the

bedroom. Of course, it was a huge room. Jack noticed the bed, the lighting, and the beautiful artwork on the walls. He couldn't help himself and said, "Wow, these are really gorgeous." He gestured to the wall.

~

"Of course, we are at Top-of-the-Mark."

She gently pushed him towards the bed and then disappeared into the bathroom. On her way, she looked back at him and pulled her heels off, first the left and then the right. As she came to the doorway, she reached around to the zipper on the gown, and when she pulled it off, she stood there with a sexy, sheer black bra and thong panties. Jack was seated on the bed trying to get his shoes off and was careful not to take his eyes off her. Even without heels, she was very tall, with a beautiful ass that the thong outlined perfectly.

After Leila ran the tub water and lit candles around the bathroom, she returned wearing a bathrobe. Jack's gaze never left her as she walked over to the remote control. Everything she did was perfect, as was the music and scent of candles were now drifting into the bedroom.

"Let me put on some music for us," she said.

She approached Jack, who was now down to his boxers and patiently waiting for what was coming next. Pausing near the edge of the bed, Leila dropped her robe, revealing her naked self. She leaned over him slowly, so close her perky breasts rubbed his stomach as she reached around him and slowly pushed down on his boxers.

Leila moved slowly down with her face following closely as his shaft appeared. She softly blew on his cock and then raised one hand from below to gently slide up his thigh and cup his balls. As his shorts came off, her lips softly kissed the sides of his cock, carefully avoiding his tip.

Carefully, she finished removing his boxers, and after Jack stepped out of each leg, he was led into the bathroom. This time, there was no thong, just a lovely, sexy ass that begged to be trapped and kissed. Leila entered the bath first and submerged her body up to her neck.

Jack looked down from above and enjoyed the view from her beautiful face, her lovely tits and in a blurry depth of water, her naked pussy.

The tub was long and narrow, and he stepped into the opposite end. Leila moved swiftly with both hands on his legs. She wrapped his legs around her and had her feet and toes up against his butt cheeks. Jack's head was perfectly fit to the edge of the tub with a towel under his neck. Her hands worked their way up from his feet to his knees and thighs.

She ran her hands over his entire body, admiring the taut muscles and hard angles of his form. Every caress left a burning sensation on his skin, and her softly spoken compliments only amplified the pleasure running through him.

The remaining time in the bath had waves of excitement and then rest as she would tease him with pleasure from his body and hers.

"Do you like that, Jack?"

He could only nod in response, as the sensations were so intense that even words failed him.

She rubbed her wet nipples across his face, turned her body to almost "plug herself in" and then pulled away. Jack was hard during the foreplay and was never sure how much submarine activities would happen.

At last, Leila murmured, "Maybe we should continue this on the bed."

She stood up and Jack took a first look at her. She was stunning. She was shaved but left a very small "V" patch that he wanted nothing more than to touch. Leila shrugged into her robe and Jack followed, wrapping himself with a towel. She pulled down the covers on the bed and asked Jack to come and lie down. He lay face down on soft cotton sheets and goose-down pillows. She then put a silk sheet over him and pulled it down to his waist.

Leila started the massage at his neck with some passion oils, two-hands rubbing from one side to the other and used a specialty massage on the arms. Each arm was treated specially and ended with finger pops. She completed the back, moved the sheet, and addressed both legs from feet to hips. Jack knew it was "flip" time and was anxious to see her face again.

His breath hitched when she leaned over, whispering in his ear, "Why don't you turn over."

As Jack turned over, the room became blurred; all he could see was Leila kneeling beside him. She reached behind her head and let down her hair. Then she draped the silk sheet over him covering the fun parts and began slowly rubbing away from his neck and down his shoulders.

He barely resisted grabbing her and pulling her in.

She worked both limbs and then straddled him, her ass resting just above his cock and only separated by a silk sheet. She put her arms to his sides and then pushed back carefully sliding herself across him, touching every lovely gentle part until he was exposed and her face just in front of him. She gave the tip of his cock a kiss. As she continued with her mouth, her hands joined the party.

One below near his balls and one above on his shaft.

The artificial romance was just what Jack needed. His life was nearly 100% work and left very little for playtime, especially with a sexy woman. Leila brought him new excitement and emotions that helped him explore more than his normal self. Before the night ended, she managed several positions from missionary to cowgirl and his favorite —doggy style.

He stood at the bedside and drove into her lovely pussy from behind, his fingers splayed over her perfect ass. She was more than willing to grind away and as she turned her head around; she could see he was pleased. As Jack released, he let out a burst of orgasmic excitement, including a few "Oh my gods," "Ah, that was lovely," and "Uhmmmmm."

Spent, he collapsed on the bed, closing his eyes until Leila returned with a warm, scented washcloth and cleaned him up.

Back at work, everyone acts normal, except of course for Alex. He needed to know every detail from the partner party and grab coffee with Jack. "Ok, let's talk about last night," said Alex.

"What goes on, on the 22nd floor, stays on the 22nd floor," Jack replied with a grin.

"Not okay," Alex groaned. "You need to give me a few juicy details."

"Let's say it was more than amazing and fulfills all your sexual fantasies. For several hours, you will forget everything and be treated like a king with the passion of your concubine. It's an evening you will never want to end."

Alex sighed. "I knew it would be amazing. I gotta get to that partner table."

CHAPTER
TWENTY-ONE
AVA SPECIAL

AVA WAS one of the easiest palindromes.

Detartrated was the most complex in English and saippuakivikauppias perhaps the longest word in Finnish, which translated to soap stone seller. And how did any of this matter except to a group of crazy intellects driven by a leader who kept records of odd boat names?

It makes perfect sense if you are an endless reader and you naturally stumble into these words, numbers or sequences and see the joy in it. A palindromic sequence is one where the letters may be read forward or backwards with the same effect.

The short examples are Ava, Dad, Mom, or Wow, then peep, noon or toot and then we move to madam, radar, level, and you get the idea.

If we advance to phrases, we might say "Step on no pets" or "Was it a car or a cat I saw?"

Ava was special in so many ways and now even as a palindrome.

TWENTY-TWO

LA MAISON DE CONFIDENTIELLE

EAGLE INVESTMENTS OPERATED on five floors in the downtown financial district. The first two were administrative, the next two for management and the top floor for executives. Men mostly operated the firm—as many venture firms in the city were somewhat biased towards men. The top floors were about 90% men, and the bottom floors were filled with lovely interns and secretaries. It was common for the secretaries who shared the workload of a few general partners to make $250,000. They were sometimes the most valuable part of the team and ensured everything in the office went according to plan.

Jack was still a newbie, used a shared resource, and made it a point never to date at work.

Today was a good day and time for some celebration. Jack wanted to go out and have some fun. He remembered the night out with the partners and his special guest on the 22nd floor—he thought of it often — so he texted Leila.

"Hello, it's Jack. We met last month at the Presidential Suite. Are you available tonight?"

Just after he sent the note, he wondered if the timing was right for him to message her. He hadn't spoken to her since their special night.

He barely knew her and wondered if she had some relationship with Steve (Anderson). Then he received a response.

"Hey, you, of course I'm available. You need to call the Huntington Club and ask for the House of Secrets."

"Thx, I will call and hope to see you," he responded, a wave of excitement coming over him. He called ahead and asked for directions. The "Club" was downtown and located on the top floor of the Beverly Building. He jumped in an Uber and went straight to the lobby as soon as he arrived.

It was a large commercial lobby with a night watchman behind a large desk. Jack approached and asked about the Huntington Club and was sent to the elevator and directed to the 27th floor. When the elevator reached the top floor, the doors opened to a dark lobby with an open doorway to the club.

A woman in a silver cocktail dress stood at the entrance. Jack walked over to her and asked about the House of Secrets, and she told him about the "invite only," policy and hoped he might know someone from the club. Jack pulled eight hundred dollars from his wallet and accurately described Leila. Smiling, the woman in the cocktail dress discreetly took his money and brought him further into a private area. She had him sit down and asked if he would like a drink. Jack ordered a Manhattan and enjoyed the view of the club watching several lovely ladies pass by.

When the woman returned with his drink, she asked Jack to follow her to the elevator. He felt strange, as if being asked to leave, but then she said, "Leila sent for you. Please follow me."

This felt better. "I was hoping I might see her again."

Above the 27th floor was the penthouse suite, which was card access only and a quick trip. The elevator doors opened into what looked like a new club from the House of Secrets. As Jack entered the room, his escort wished him well and returned to the elevator. He stood for a moment in silence and then Leila appeared. She came over and hugged him, kissing him softly on the cheek.

He was already excited and suddenly all the memories from the 22nd floor returned.

"I'm so glad you came," said Leila. "I've missed you."

"Mmmmm, I'm happy to see you again."

Grabbing his hand, she led him into a nearby suite. "Welcome to La Maison de Confidentielle."

Jack knew a little French and put the House of Secrets together with La Maison. He was captivated by whatever was happening and learned to go with it. Leila brought him to the bar and offered to top off his drink, so he smiled and handed his drink for a refill. He was enjoying her sexy look as she poured his drink and her outfit: a short skirt and silky, see-through blouse—one of his favorite looks.

"Since this is your first time, I should fill you in on a few things," she said. "You may be a beginner at this."

"Okay…" His voice trailed off.

"Only a few people know about La Maison, and we want to keep it that way. We specialize in fantasy, sensation, and pleasure. We also like to visit extreme pleasures for some of our men. Our evenings will explore many new areas of eroticism and physical limits that draw out some of your hidden desires.

Jack started seeing Shades of Grey and thoughts of whips and chains. "I think you may be right, I'm new at this, but I'd like to know more."

She smiled. "Let me introduce you to your new senses."

Leila was a very kind teacher. She started with a massage to heighten his senses, starting with his hands, where she pulled and popped his fingertips, and decided tonight she would explore a new area of sensation. Leila walked him to an exotic chair that looked like Ava's artwork. It was made of metal that included leather straps for bondage.

Once he was secured, she blindfolded him and began her chair dance. She rubbed across all of him and drove him slightly crazy. Without his sight, his senses were twice normal. She pushed her breasts into his face, and he could feel her nipples. He wanted to grab her and pulled at the straps, wondering if she was fully naked.

When she lowered herself onto his lap, he was already hard.

The next hour would bring him to nearly climax, but he managed to keep his juices inside his clothes. She finally removed his blindfold and straps so they could move to the bed. In some cases, the second time for sex is all about mental excitement and then a letdown.

With Leila, however, it was even more pleasurable than their first time together.

Afterwards, he was exhausted and had to drag himself into his Uber to try and get home.

PART FIVE

CHAPTER
TWENTY-THREE
BABY ANGIE

SIMON DROVE a white Ferrari Portofino which he proudly selected while on vacation in Italy. He used to say there was only one sports car brand and nothing else compared to the Ferrari. His car had a twin-turbo V8 that produced over 600 horsepower and a top speed of 200 miles per hour. The most popular Ferrari colors were red or yellow, so Simon selected white. The seats were tan, and several accent pieces and brake calipers were red to support the Ferrari's need for speed. It was a hardtop convertible and with a push of a button, a carbon fiber black top emerged and sealed the car into a gorgeous luxury coupe.

Simon was average in height standing just over 5ft 10in and weighed in at a trim 175 lbs. On a good day, he could be Simon Cowell with jet-black hair and a cocky swagger with emphasis on both his walk and head jesters. He learned early on that the time to make an impression was in every second of life. There was no time to suddenly (paddle) shift gears and be the man you always wanted to be, rather to go get it right now.

As a self-made millionaire, perhaps the swagger was justified. Simon grew up in Southern California as a military brat and only child. He spent most of his childhood in military housing on or near Point Loma Naval Base, rightfully known as "common." His father entered the Navy as a junior seaman who never made it past petty officer ranks and his mother worked in retail to make ends meet. They were a very attractive couple with low aspirations for ladder climbing and most of their interest lay in hanging out near the beach or visiting Mexico for food and fun. At least that was what Simon recalled about the trips to Tijuana. His parents would be sure to have a babysitter take care of Simon on weekends away and they would always return with some cheap trinkets to keep Simon entertained. Later, Simon would learn that most of their trips were to visit small towns near Tijuana known for purified drugs ranging from marijuana to extreme hallucinogens.

As Simon recalls, there was life before age 16, and then afterwards. The previous part was mostly an average childhood concerning friends, schooling, and activities. He was never one for team sports, however, he did like to run, bike and swim. His father was a somewhat talented surfer, and this had Simon in the ocean and on the end of his surfboard when he was very young. The key difference between Simon and his father was that Simon flew on the water as he swam. Watching him glide through the water like a fish was a joy. His Dad joked that he had 3 or 4 lungs and could out swim anyone in Mission Bay (their local surf).

Turning 16 was the true beginning of Simon's life and his freedom. He bought his first truck and started a house painting business with brushes, extended ladder, sander, and plenty of spackle. He made flyers and posted them all over town. His ad read:

Expert House Painting Service
Exterior: $1000-$3000 / Interior: $250/room
Most Jobs Completed in 2-3 Days

He started the business as soon as summer started in late May and quickly started making easy money. He started with back-2-back jobs and as the calendar filled up, he started overlapping work where he would prep one house in the morning and paint the next in the after-noon. By mid-June, he had completed his first 8 houses and had another 6 in the order backlog. His specialty was exterior painting for single-story homes and less interesting were the interior jobs which took too long and eventually he raised his prices to discourage indoor jobs. In early August, he tapered down his business to get ready for school. However, he kept new bookings that would be ok with week-end-only work. After expenses, he had earned over $30,000 and could make around $5,000/mo. until the cool weather started. In his second year of painting, he took on an extra worker and set a goal to make over $100,000 yearly. Simon enjoyed the rising value of his bank account and was diligent in his savings. His daily life consisted of high school studies, some form of cardiovascular training including swim, bike or running fitness, and then his business planning for the future. He knew painting was a means to an end and that he would quit after age 18 and be off to college or a backup plan to join the military. College was a big step up for Simon with no family influences, and his anxiety outweighed his excitement. He was certainly competitive in everything he attempted and this coming year he decided to create the "destiny challenge." The destiny was for him, and the challenges were made up of three elements including: time, money, and rank (taken from the military). And just like most of his pursuits, these three chal-lenges came in layers.

Time had three segments: from now till Christmas, January till June, and everything after high school graduation. The first stage was mostly focused on meeting deadlines and applying for college. The Jan-Jun period was to determine what other exciting or exotic careers he would consider (besides college), and the last period was time for the rest of his life and how he would see himself years later.

The money challenges were simply quantitative challenges to reach new heights in numerical value. At age seventeen and a half, Simon had a bank account worth $165,000. Most of his friends had a few thousand dollars and most of that came from their parents. By Christmas he would achieve $180k, and by graduation up to $225k. He wanted to push to a cool $250,000, but he knew the work was only weekends and holidays, and expanding the team was the only way to pump this up. So, Simon sharpened his pencil and decided to hire 2 more part time helpers through the Christmas season and see if they could be a part of the team during the year. He revised his goals to $190k by Jan 1 and $250k by June 1st. If you're reading this book, you know Simon exceeded his money goals.

The final category was rank and had a slightly different meaning to Simon. His father lived the life in rank and file, which drove Simon crazy. The boundaries were set up to keep you growing in a slow methodical path and for his family, it meant achievements that were not obtainable. It was time to create a new set of ranks that would eventually make him an Admiral, but not in the Navy way. Simon knew he was gifted with powerful lungs to out swim or even out paint almost anyone. He could push himself to the limit and struggle with exhaustion. He also knew that setting his personal goals would always outweigh any arbitrary bar set by academia or the military. But he would keep one element of military rank in his mix: to grow his sphere of influence amongst his peers and rise above the rest in stature. Simon liked the term stature over status as he recalled a lesson in church. It was from Luke 2:52 and read; And Jesus grew in wisdom and stature, and with favor with God and man, which meant that as you follow Jesus' growth pattern, you" find that the elements work together perfectly, and you will become more like Him. In the end, Simon changed rank to stature, and it became his internal motto to be one of the highest statures. He left wisdom off the goal sheet as it reminded him of some sort of test or wise guy quiz that he might not be successful at passing.

In April of his senior year, Simon received acceptance from 8 colleges and the Navy. He got his first commercial painting job for a large multi-unit apartment complex (worth over $45,000) and had 5 people working for him. He would graduate high school with honors, a bank account closer to $300k, and attend San Diego State majoring in business. He lived on campus his first year, then had to decide in his second year to pay nearly $10,000 for housing, or to buy his first condo and get roommates to help pay the rent. He went shopping for a 2 bedroom, 2 bath condominium and determined that he could put down 30% for a $300,000 condo and have payments of $2000 per month and with 2 or 3 roommates he would actually save money vs campus housing. Before his sophomore year, he bought his first condo, had 3 condos, and had a net worth approaching $1 million when he graduated. After graduation, Simon took his family to the business class festivities, including mostly cheap liquor and snacks. As they posed for a family picture, Professor Mathews offered to take their photo.

He told the family, "You know your son is one of my best students. He is a pleasure to have in my class and I know he will become a great businessman."

"Your words are very kind, and we thank you for helping him on his journey," Simon's mom replied.

He took a handful of pics and handed Simon his phone. "Please know you are welcome on campus anytime," said the professor.

"I really enjoyed your finance classes and the excitement we had learning about money," grinned Simon. "I plan to use all my teachings in business and finance to work smart and play hard."

For graduation, Simon planned a field trip with the boys from work. His painter crew as always available for a road trip, which was fully sponsored. They loaded up the truck and headed to Las Vegas. It was a 5 hour drive and they arrived just before midnight into the Bellagio. Simon paid for everyone to have their own room and handed each of his crew $1000.

"You guys know how much you have meant to me over the past 5 years," Simon said. "I will always remember this time in my life as we built a great business, made some good money, and now can enjoy the spoils. Here is some play money to enjoy yourselves. If you're up for it, there are a few more exciting events in the morning, so let's meet for breakfast around 10am." They all knew it would be worth showing up as long as they were sober.

The next day, Simon hosted events including exotic car racing, skydiving in squirrel suites, and a steak dinner at Andiamo's. Their eyes widened as they glanced down the menu in anticipation of the best meal ever. Simon ordered first and set the bar high for the finest steak on the menu.

"Ok, this is my last speech to you guys," Simon grinned. "If you remember nothing else, I hope you will recall the freedom of flight, the speed of high horsepower, the juiciest of steaks, and best of all, how rare these times spent together are." They all raised their wine glasses and toasted to a great weekend in Vegas. Simon knew this was also the end of an era with his paint crew and his time to expand his horizons was quickly approaching. He also knew that you must stand on sturdy shoulders to get a greater view of what's ahead and he had a solid crew that loved working together.

Over the next 8 years, Simon worked a few jobs in industry to help support his true hobby in real estate. He played the part to fit in with the corporate life and was excellent and stayed in front of his work and easily passed up his peers. His first job was with a conglomerate called Perkin Elmer. They made large industrial and laboratory equipment for healthcare diagnostic and analytical devices for food and pharmaceuticals. Simon liked the enormous workforce and reminded him of his dad working for the Navy. It took a small army to get things done, which fit perfectly with his plan for his future.

Simon was an early riser from his days as a surfer. He was up at 5am, coffee'd up, paper read and into his car by half past five. He finished most of work by noon and went to the gym for a lunch break. His routines included a 5-mile run, a 2-mile swim, or an all-calisthenic workout of push-ups, pull-ups, sit-ups and stair climbing. Then back to work for a couple hours and home by 4pm. The weekday evenings were spent planning, reading, and reviewing his real estate business or what Simon called his Real Business. At age 25, he grew his portfolio to have a dozen single-family homes, a 12-unit apartment complex, and a large storage property. His secondary income was larger than what his primary job pays, and it was all due to his hard work and dedication. For his thirtieth birthday, he bought a 5-bedroom home in Del Mar. It was over 3,000 sq ft with the rear of the house sitting on the beach. His new routine in the morning included swimming or surfing in the ocean. He could walk down a flight of stairs with his coffee and flips and be in the water in moments. Simon was living large, and this home was a perfect way of expanding his world. It was time to spend some of his savings to fill up the place with high-end furniture, a couple of luxury cars in his 3 car garage and start some collections. Exotic watches were an easy beginning, but Simon knew that retail shopping was not for him. When he bought his AMG G-Wagon, he drove to Los Angeles and enjoyed negotiating for a heavily modified car with only 5 miles.

Apparently, the owner backed out of financing and Simon knew he could beat any salesperson to the punch regarding deposits versus purchasing. The car typically sold for $250k and with custom options (mix of carbon fiber and matte black, engine tuning, tinting, and one-of-a-kind rims) was worth well over $300k. Los Angeles was filled with high-wealth individuals from movie stars to sports heroes and then there was Simon who showed up in a quad cab pickup. After a test drive with speeds up to 90 miles/hr down city streets, it was time to make a deal. Vehicles like this did not have a sticker value, rather a street value and Simon decided he wanted it. The premium options cost the dealer less than half the value, and they easily made 15% on the vehicle. After some mental math, he decided he would pay no more than $275k. Simon figured their breakeven was just above $250k but knew the LA market was hot and they would hold out for $300k. After a 20-minute "discussion," it was time to walk away. He looked down at his Rolex Daytona watch as if to have another appointment, and then walked back to his pickup and drove back to San Diego. The drive seemed longer than before, and he couldn't stop thinking about driving the G-Wagon. It's just a car, he thought. Then, he recalled the three elements of time, money, and stature. How would Simon define himself? Up till now, he was supremely confident, his plan was working, and he was happy. He pulled into his garage, entered his gorgeous living room with an ocean view, and ordered his favorite UberEATS.

The next day, he received a call from an unknown number and "213" area code. Simon answered and the voice said, "Hello, this is Roger Williamson from Mercedes of Los Angeles. Is this Simon Bilteau?"

"Yes," replied Simon.

"I understand you visited the dealership and were looking at the G-wagon. It is one of the nicest upgrade versions of this vehicle and stands out well in a crowd. We have just received an offer for the car and wanted to let you know it may no longer be for sale."

"So why are you calling me?"

"Well, I understand you showed great interest in the car, yet you never offered a counteroffer to the asking price."

"That's true; however, I do have a number in mind,"

"Let me make this call easy for both of us. The car is yours and delivered to your doorstep for $280,000."

"I'll pay cash for $275,000."

"Excellent you have your car. We can work out the bank details and I'll have the car detailed and shipped."

Simon got his G-wagon! After he hung up the phone, he went to his nearly empty garage and imagined how nice it would look with his new ride.

At 32, Simon's wife Teresa, was pregnant in the first six months of marriage. They were a happy couple with a new baby daughter, a home filled with love and true friendship as husband and wife. Simon managed his workaholic lifestyle to a manageable 8 hrs per day and invested in his family. They added a puppy to watch over baby Angie. The house quickly filled with family photos with two boys, Simon, the dog, and two girls, Teresa and Angie, in every imaginable pose, fashion, and expression.

When Angie was 18 months old, she began crying more than usual; comforting her was impossible. She was eating and pooping ok, but she would close her eyes and start crying out of nowhere. After a week of no way to calm her down, they visited their pediatrician.

The doctor was very loving and looked into Angie's eyes with his flashlight, then rubbed her temples, under her chin, and even behind her ears. He was extremely gentle, and Angie thought he was sweet to be so caring to him. He did his routine with the stethoscope, pressed with 2-fingers at her belly, and down to her toes. He asked a multitude of questions about the crying episodes, her diet, her sleep patterns, and any other activity that might create discomfort. Simon mentioned one scary moment when she started crying in the bath. She put her head underwater to feel better, and Simon quickly grabbed her. The doctor acknowledged the events and decided to see a specialist. This was unexpected.

California had three Neonatal ICUs including UCLA, Stanford, and Fresno. In the associated surrounding areas were specialists who cared for infant issues from birth through age two. Over the next month, Angie was seen by five doctors including thorough evaluations, testing, imaging, and finally, a doctor who decided to perform genetic testing of each parent. Angie's condition seemed to worsen as the crying was being replaced with vomiting and an awkward sort of sadness as if she was beginning to understand that she was sick. The following doctor visit changed their lives forever. While in the office lobby awaiting their visit, she looked up to her father as if to say please help me stop this pain. Simon's face filled with pain and sadness, and he pulled Angie up to his chest to comfort her. The doctor shared that Angie was suffering from issues in her brain that were causing her to cry and vomit and that the next symptoms would include nausea, irritability and even depression.

"What is causing this," Simon asked.

"I'd like to have Dr. Somojian see Angie. He specializes in pediatric neurology and understands the nervous system better than anyone. I'll make a referral for you to see him tomorrow."

"Is there a need to see him quickly?" said Simon.

"Angie is showing some signs of progression and I don't want to wait."

"Doctor, can you explain why we had the genetic testing performed on me and my wife?"

"Normally, it is a protocol for conditions where kids are undiagnosed, and we screen for any genetic disorders that may give us clues to the situation."

"And did you find anything?"

"Yes, I'm afraid we did. The science in these findings is still early. However, you and your wife have markers that suggest a genetic predisposition for certain cancers. We will have you discuss your results further with someone who can suggest a plan moving forward."

"Are you saying our genes are the cause of Angie's pain and suffering?"

"I'm sorry this is a lot to take in during a single visit. We want what's best for your daughter, which means another evaluation, and then we can discuss your concern. Please understand that we have many variables here and determining cause and effect is tricky."

As they got back in the car and drove back to San Diego, there was no joy. So much for money and stature. This was about life's timing clock or lack thereof. It was the longest 24 hours until they returned to see another specialist. In the following days, Simon would learn that his daughter had brain cancer and his wife's genetic makeup was likely the underlying cause of Angie's sickness.

Angie never reached her 2-year birthday with her months in and out of hospitals and exotic clinics known for cancer miracles. No parent is ever ready for this sort of ending to a young life and the emotional toil is extreme. Simon and Teresa spent many days and nights that were smashed together keeping their daughter at the apex of brilliant doctors and nurses from some of the most renowned medical intuitions. Together, they had run hundreds of tests, inserted more than enough needles and tubes into a baby who was no more than 15 lbs. and who learned to walk in hospital hallways.

They buried her in a very small family funeral. Simon & Teresa would never have children again. It would be too soon for them ever to hear the word glioblastomas or make their way back to normalcy and the topic of children. They remained happily married and Simon would forever wonder about genetic testing and the power of the human DNA structure.

CHAPTER
TWENTY-FOUR

HANK YO

WHEN SIMON TURNED 35, he felt the need for change in his business dealings and explored some new ideas, including bitcoin, cannabis, and alcohol. Also known as Simon's wild ABC's and these new ventures meant it was time to set up some new rules, especially for protection or distance between his name and the business dealings. He set up several LLC's and a new business partner named Hank Yo to help with his discreet transactions. His investments varied from owning the entire business as with his bitcoin server farms in Oregon (about a mile from Facebook's data center), to a part ownership in a cannabis crop near Salinas, California. Simon's chief marijuana manager was named Juan Capania and he was in charge of growing, cutting, and preparing the product for shipment including seeds, buds, leaves and a few local recipes that combined the harvested weed with other plants such as chamomile, basil, and garlic. The farm produced and shipped more weed to California, Nevada, and Colorado than the nearest grower. Ounces became pounds and pounds became tons - that was 2000 pounds of weed sold by the ounce for between $150-$200 wholesale. An ounce would produce over 75 joints, so the math was astounding. A ton of weed produced over 2.4 million joints. Selling a ton by the ounce is almost $5m and by the joint is closer to $10m. To make things less obvious, Simon named the Salinas crops "Central Valley Harvest," and did his best to blend in with the lettuce and artichoke crops. Getting field workers to pick lettuce was easy. Getting workers to pick weed was more than challenging and required cameras and penalties to keep everyone honest. To be fair, Juan paid his workers a premium to work for him and they all respected his leadership.

The final ABC was alcohol and Simon had no interest in growing grapes or trying to compete in the wine trade. Like others, he liked fine wine and the drinking part of the business. But pulling together an estate for growing grapes and waiting for years for the harvest to mature was not for him. He was also not ready to make it the ABCD's, cause the obvious path to discreet riches was drugs.

Simon spent several years looking into growing specific grapes for harvesting with a target for Chardonnay or Cabernet Sauvignon. Owning a vineyard and potentially a tasting room was $2-$4m upfront investment with high risk on return. Although glamorous, it was not near the upside potential in pot or bitcoin, and he was about to pass on the idea when a new proposition came to him.

Simon had met Hank Yo in Macau during one of his exotic drips to southern China. Besides the glitz and glamor of the new casinos, there was enormous space to house or hide bitcoin mining operations. To be successful, these farms took mostly energy to power the fast computers, and a trusted boss to manage security, including safety measures and deterrents.

The Greater Bay Area (GBA) region of southern China included areas within the Guangdong province including Shenzhen, Dongguan, Guangzhou, and Macau. In major cities, a westerner would feel comfortable with food, shelter, and drink (not water). However, the landscape in southern China between the city hubs was riddled with some of the poorest lives, challenging foods to eat, or places to live. Some of the outdoor shops along the drive would sell odd looking things to eat, clothing accessories such as hats or boots, and mechanical shops to help repair bikes or scooters. Several vendors lived on their bikes with extended trailers to carry basics such as cardboard or other miscellaneous items that would be excellent currency during bartering.

The city of Macau has roots back to the early Qin dynasty in 200 BC, however, did not develop as a major settlement until the 1500's when it was a Portuguese colony. As a coastal city in China with key export of silk to Japan and was later leveraged for the lucrative trade of opium. In December of 1999, Macau was transferred back to China (after 442 years of Portuguese rule) and soon became the casino capital of China – or the "Las Vegas of the East." Casino gambling is illegal in China and Hong Kong giving Macau a legal monopoly on the industry. This 12 square-mile area is the most densely populated region in the world. The region is well known for holidays, festivals, and events with the Macau Grand Prix as one of the main attractions and the Lunar Chinese New Year as the most important traditional festival. The local food mixes Cantonese-Portuguese fusion cuisine with spices such as turmeric, coconut milk, and cinnamon to enhance African chicken, chili shrimp and salt cod.

Hank was from the mainland and owned properties in Shenzhen, Macau, and a condo in Hong Kong. Since most of his business was in social settings, he always made himself available when it made sense. He met Simon while gambling or drinking between the JW Marriott and the Ritz Carlton. Simon enjoyed the high rollers tables with Baccarat, Pai Gow, and Texas Hold'em. However, it was at the Blackjack table where the two spent their later evenings and got to know each other. Their conversations ranged from business and pleasure topics to fast cars and high-stakes poker with $50,000 minimum buy-in. Chasing 21 and watching cards flip was even more fun after 2 or 3 in the morning. Alcohol was flowing and the chip stacks were growing.

"How are the things at the farms?" asked Simon. "I assume the crops are coming along."

"We are doing very well with our first year, and may want to plant more for next year," said Hank. This code meant more land or more buildings and power.

"Any expansion issues?" asked Simon.

"No, but it might be wise to pick a new area, so we are not so concentrated."

"I'll leave that up to you and just let me know the timing and funding requirements." Then Simon was back to his cards and flipping chips.

Late breakfast in Macau was always lovely. Food service was 24/7 and since many folks were tourists, there was never any real time of day. It was whatever time. Simon thought it might be midday and time for some protein to soak up the liquids. He took his buffet treats to his table and waved for fresh coffee. Interestingly, the black coffee in Macau was amazing. Hank joined him at the table and quickly put out his cigarette as Simon hated the smoke. As they both sipped their strong coffee, Hank asked, "Anything special for today," he left the doors wide open.

"I'm good," said Simon. "I may try some time at the pool or even a massage later."

"You will enjoy the poolside cabana. Let me know if you have any preferences for your masseuse," said Hank.

"I'd like to try a tall drink of water today," Simon smiled.

"Let me take care of some details for you," said Hank. He knew how to please businessmen and for Simon, he would pull out all the stops. Discreetly, he immediately sent a couple of texts and started his search.

"By the way," said Simon. "Have you done much in import/export?" This was a very loaded question and Hank responded casually.

"Yes, I've worked on both sides of that trade. Do you have something in mind?"

"How about red wine?" Simon asked.

"You want some red wine?" responded Hank.

"No, sorry, have you worked with importing red wine to China?" replied Simon. "I've noticed amazing food and strong liquor, but the wine selection is terrible."

"That's because rice wine will never compare to grape wine and the 4-5 week cargo ride is brutal on the cases of wine. Some have tried shipping by the barrel, but that means some sort of aftermarket bottling and labeling which starts to sound more like a business than quick import/export trade."

"I just completed reviewing several business plans to grow tons of grapes in California and commit to the risky proposition of an annual crop subject to growing challenges including weather, disease, and other natural disasters. Cash is all upfront and earnings are annual and lumpy. So instead, I wonder why not set up an import/export business and play these odds. Even at a glance, the risk/return looks much better."

"Did you want to run some numbers while you are in town?" said Hank.

"No, I need your help asking around if we can have good sales and then perhaps the harder question is, what should we import back from China to the US?"

"You mean wholesale goods like jewelry or branded clothing?" said Hank. "Or do you want to go straight to the jugular and push lithium-ion batteries?"

"Keep those ideas flowing and we can talk more at dinner," said Simon. "I'm gonna digest my food and look closer at the pool amenities." The two shook hands, Simon headed towards the pool, and Hank finished his premier pick for the cabana. She was called Mia and would be the ideal drink of water with a model-like appearance and over 5 feet, 8 inches tall. Hank texted her the details and knew she would make his cabana experience unforgettable.

Mia made her way down to the poolside and found Simon's cabana. She approached him and said that Hank had asked her to stop by. As she reached up to draw the screen closed, Simon enjoyed the view through her coverup. She turned to him and removed her gown with only panties left on her gorgeous body. She reached into her purse, pulled out her phone, selected her playlist, and walked to him. She knelt down to remove his flips and then positioned his body across the bed. She asked Simon if he would like a nuru massage and he nodded. The next hour was lovely. Lying next to the pool, I heard the splish splash of hotel guests while being secluded in his private cabana room with exquisite music. This was magical and included an orgasmic happy ending.

Simon and Hank met up after dinner at one of Simon's favorite casinos. Hank told Simon he looked very refreshed and ready for some successful poker. He reminded him to follow Feng Shui principles and that he was destined for more richness. Simon flew home the following day with renewed excitement and a prosperous trip to China.

Simon sends Hank a text reading, "Let's start with some Cabernet imports. Maybe a container run to start."

"Agreed. Let me know when you are ready and I'll secure demand for the cases," said Hank. The math for bottles, cases, pallets, and a 20′ container was new to these two. However, their first run was sold in less than a week. They tried a few varieties of Cab then expanded to other grapes. Hank became the Wine Shop of southern China and grew a small idea into a very profitable and expanding business. They eventually added walnuts to the mix and began the craze for China to eventually outgrow the US.

CHAPTER
TWENTY-FIVE
5-FIVE-5

THERE WAS a five-year age separation between the youngest (Paul) and oldest Saint (Joseph) with Robbie directly in the center. The Saints first met in the ages 12–17-year bubble with Robbie at 14, and the age of responsibility. While Jack still honed his entrepreneurial skills in middle school, Robbie could not get enough information about science and medicine, specifically anatomy, biology, cardiology, endocrinology, neurology, physiology, and some chemistry to support pharmacology. Most of the "ology" subjects were connected and reviewing the material in parallel was common for Robbie.

The Mohr family breakfasts were mostly attended during the week as long as the girls didn't have early sports practice. Julia prepared a full spread of eggs, bacon, and even pancakes this morning for 6. The kitchen was a buzz with serving, self-serving, and a rotating refrigerator door to meet everyone's needs. Tom and Robbie patiently sat, watching all the activities, and receiving a morsel or two as the commotion continued. The buzz lasted less than 15 minutes, and then there was a rush to the cars. Gianna and Amara switched off driving each other to high school. Julia drove Jack and Robbie to middle school, and Tom typically never stayed for breakfast and was out the door with his coffee.

Today was the exception and he enjoyed it when everyone was together. When Julia returned, she cleaned the kitchen. She approached Robbie's small library table with careful curiosity. There were over a dozen books with half left open and stacked in what could be some order. She knew how powerful the boys could read and that a stack or two of books was commonplace. In the center of the books was a spiral notebook with handwritten notes and colorful diagrams. Robbie was a brilliant student and also a very accomplished artist. His medical notebook could easily be published as advanced crib notes for premed students in college. Julia wondered how Robbie and Jack managed to go to school with a curriculum that although they were in the accelerated groups, they must be bored knowing they were both likely more advanced than any of their teachers. For these two, middle school was more of an activity to enjoy the social aspects - or more directly, the chance to meet girls. The wonders of that eighth-grade first kiss and the tingling physical excitement that followed. The Mohr boys were very special.

As the school year went on, Jack kept his plate full of academic, music, and sports challenges, while Robbie focused on extending his expert knowledge of the human body into healthcare and medicine. He realized that an applied part of his learning was missing and dissecting frogs in school was not helpful. Somehow, he needed to get involved in a hospital and the search began for opportunities. After school, Jack went to his sports and Robbie returned to the library. He searched everything online from Tacoma General Hospital. He narrowed the list for young adults to include community service hours, typically reserved for blood donor teams or light janitorial work. Yuk. Of the two, perhaps there was a path in the blood team to learn more than what he read in the textbooks. On the ride home, Julia asked the boys about their day and received a request to visit the hospital later in the week. Robbie had applied online and had a call back in the "blood team." "That's fantastic," said Jack. "They are about to hire the best premed student on the planet."

"But you are only fourteen," said Julia. "What will you be doing for them?"

"It's nothing Mom," said Robbie. "I'm guessing I will be washing test tubes or mopping floors. I just want to get a bit closer to the action." Coming from a 14-year-old was kinda crazy. After a short visit with the hiring staff, Robbie was given a temporary badge so he could start his shift as soon as possible. The blood team worked 24/7 and soon Robbie would understand the term "lifeblood." He took the Saturday morning shift and spent half a day watching phlebotomists draw their blood samples one after another. Robbie was allowed to watch, but his only interface was to carry the blood sample to nearby storage. He learned that a pint of blood, or one unit was at the core of all surgeries. Tacoma General had its own blood bank supply to support its internal demand, and managing type A, B, AB, and O was critical. There was the basic information about "how much" blood was in storage and eventually, Robbie learned about blood types (based on antigens), RH factors (+/-), contamination & cleaning. The team members were called blood technicians or immunohematology technologists and were all college graduates. For what seemed like a mediocre job, Robbie enjoyed every minute. Although his hands-on role was limited, he soaked up every conversation and discussion about healthcare. He discovered that the blood team was also the center of activities in the hospital. And by activities, it was really about scheduling patient needs for planned and unplanned surgeries. They lived on a mix of paper-driven accounting and digital inventory recordings to show an "anytime status," of the blood reserves. The operation was clean, efficient, and one of the most organized in the hospital. Robbie noticed a few blood bags marked "For Lab Use Only," and questioned the marking. "Who uses the blood for lab use…?" said Robbie.

"The Biomedical Engineering team at University of Washington uses the blood for their graduate students to support experiments," said one of the technicians.

"Most of the work is done using pig or cow blood, but we also provide them with blood that typically has some disorder in its readings. Some of their experiments work with saline, blood plasma, or whole blood. The mechanical or filtration studies use all sorts of fluids, but the bioinformatics guys like the rich red blood cells. It's only a pint or two for the love of science."

∿

After hearing this, Robbie smiled and knew he would enjoy this job. He would carve out time after school and the next several Saturdays to be on the blood team. During the off hours, he studied the core of red blood cells (RBC's), platelet-rich plasma (PRP), and efforts to use blood in regenerative therapies. He found himself at the intersection of tactical use, aka the blood bank, and strategic value in graduate research and development. Who knew blood would have such an impact on his early life.

Robbie was also the first to meet the four Saints. It was break time during his Saturday shift, which meant a trip to find some lousy food in the cafeteria. Robbie bought a sandwich, opened his backpack to a few textbooks, and started reading. He held the sandwich in one hand and read three overlapping books at once. His first encounter with Paul went something like this.

"Are you really reading all those books at once," said Paul.

"Yes, it's not that difficult," replied Robbie.

"Maybe for you."

"So, I should tell you that the three books are very similar and reading each simultaneously is easier than it looks."

"But you look about my age," said Paul.

"I'm fourteen. How old are you?" replied Robbie.

"I just turned twelve," said Paul. He was small for his age and Robbie looked very young too. "Do you work here?"

"I work with the blood team," said Robbie. "I'm on my lunch break now. How about you?"

"We hang out here on Saturday's."

"Do you like coming to hospitals?" Robbie smiled.

"It's just the best place to get together and learn."

"Do you take classes here?" questioned Robbie.

"No, it's just a bunch of us who like to read."

At first, Robbie pictured a junior book club and a crazy place to hang out in a hospital. Then Paul asked him a few questions about his lunchtime reading.

"I'm assuming you're not a vampire and reading about blood for work, is that right?" said Paul.

"Yes, I want to know much more about blood and better understand its full potential."

"Have you read works by Drew or Blundell?"

"I don't recognize those names," said Robbie.

"Drew pioneered blood storage and Blundell performed the first human-to-human blood transfusion."

This was no casual chat with a 12-year-old. There was something extraordinary here. "I'm not sure how you came up with those references, but you might be into the same academic readings that I enjoy. I wonder if you also read about other sciences?"

"Yes, of course. Our group reads just about everything in science, history, and engineering. You're welcome to join us anytime!"

It was after lunch and Robbie's shift ended at 2pm - a 5 hour shift. That was the first 5.

Robbie made his lunchtime overlap with the "readers" in the following weeks far more prevalent. They exchanged ideas, subjects, interests and even removing things with no interest. The readers went well beyond blood and followed Robbie's lead into the various sciences that made for an ideal medical foundation, to the newer topics of providing better healthcare. They would often use the forum to spin up an idea for review and then grab associated textbooks, internet reviews and any expertise for their open session.

Although the group was larger, the core team of Robbie, Paul, Luke, Michael, and Joseph became increasingly connected. The second 5 were in place.

CHAPTER
TWENTY-SIX
GO THE SPOILS

SIMON LOVED everything about southern California, but it was no match for lure to San Francisco. Before he bought the B&W Bar, he looked at properties for over 3 years and made his business commute to the Bay Area every month or two. This included stays in elegant hotels and restaurants from San Jose up to Marin, and it meant spending time on the bay for a ferry ride, then even better. He learned the ports and eventually how to manage the docking of "Go the Spoils."

Simon was a gracious host and wanted everyone to enjoy a night on the San Francisco Bay - no special occasion, just a "Simon Holiday." His boat was a 147-foot superyacht with 4 sprawling decks, five staterooms, movie theater, and plenty of room to entertain over fifty guests. To the victor, go the spoils.

In the main entertainment area, like center stage, was a piano keyboard and a fresh upstart musician playing early 70s music. It was like a combination of "La La Land" and the soundtrack from Guardians of the Galaxy. It reminded Jack of the movie "Nice Guys" where two bubblehead detectives crash a party in a Hollywood mansion with 70's music, drugs and a bar with mermaids swimming in the background. He played an electric keyboard with percussion and the music sounded really good.

~

"If you like Pina Coladas and getting caught in the rain," he sang.

The crowd responded, "if you're not into yoga, if you half-a-brain… write to me and escape."

~

The alcohol flowed, and the dance floor was less than half full. Jack was near the back sipping Jack-n-Ginger. The music vibe was a bit old for him, but he liked the mood on the boat and felt very comfortable just relaxing. The artist finished his set and then said there would be a short break to sit tight for a special treat.

As Jack looked out from the boat, he realized just how much he loved being on the water. The trip had taken them into the San Francisco Bay and in the distance was the shimmering of city lights. He recalled being on the bay near (name place near SEA) on nights when the sky lit up, including colors such as green, purple, and rose. He thought this was one of the first times when a man-made skyline could majestically compete with side effects of the Aurora Borealis. In the distance, he saw Simon dressed immaculately and wearing his signature mask. He mingled with the crowd, leaving smiles behind in his wake.

When the piano man returned, the stage had changed with a center floor space and guitar to accompany him. He began the melody, and everyone raised their glass to Sade as she entered the stage to "By Your Side." Jack had heard a rumor about Simon's party's and his "spare no expense" attitude. It was hard to believe Sade was singing right in front of him. As the song continued, a gold pole dropped slowly from the ceiling into a plate on the floor. A lovely woman appeared slowly spinning from the pole. It is a slow song, and the dancer perfectly synced with Sade. Once half-filled, the room was now jam-packed, and Jack had to stand to keep his eye on the show. It was incredible. He was less than 30 feet from this epic singer and yet, he kept his eyes on the dancer. She was captivating, sexy, and elegant all-in-one. She wore an outfit that started with a Brazilian bikini and then added several straps to connect from her ankles, wrists, and her neck. She wore a gold feather mask with straps tied in back of her head and then woven into a headpiece that held her long brown hair. Her body was long, slender, and flexible. The soft lighting from the night sky bounced off her light brown skin and shimmering gold flare. Her routine included a bicycle leg kick where she looked out to the crowd and teased the audience with her outstretched toes. Twirling slowly around the pole, she held her legs together and kept the "juicy views" to a minimum. It was a class act; she was just the background dancer.

As she spun, the gold straps flew by as if she was a sparkling ball with a sexy center at her butt.

"Oh yum." Jack thought to himself. This woman was hot. She looked like a blend of a track star and a model with a tiny, decorated waist. She had an exquisite body. Her outfit hid nothing, and every line looked lovely. Sade did a 3-song set and both Sade and the dancer bowed and then left the stage to a long, loud applause. It was time for a refill and Jack headed over to the bar.

"Wow, that was an awesome show!" He said. "You must love working for Simon."

"Yup, he takes care of his people," said the bartender.

"I really liked the dancer. Is there any way to get backstage?'

"Sure, just look over there" he pointed to the helipad.

Sade was being escorted back to shore by helicopter. Jack understood that the superstar had to leave the boat but wanted to ask more about her. He wondered how the party would continue beyond Sade and if there might be another dance set. Somewhat frustrated, Jack scanned the room and suddenly realized it was filled with power names. His eyes caught Steph and Ayesha Curry, along with Mark Zuckerberg and Priscilla Chan and he began to wonder if this was a fundraising event. What was Simon's ulterior motive tonight and why was Jack invited? It was certainly time for a drink refill and some tasty hors d'oeuvres. Bacon-wrapped anything sounded good or perhaps some lettuce-wrapped beef - Jack was reeling off his mental wish list when Ava appeared. She was also grabbing a treat and heading back for a wardrobe change. As she passed him, he could smell her scent and almost recognize her, but it all happened too fast. With his mini plate full, he moved to a nearby table and watched the pianist return to the stage. He began playing The Tony Rich Project and Ava returned to the stage. This time she included pointe shoes and mixed several pirouettes into the routine. Jack was captivated and could not take his eyes off her, until someone blocked his view.

"Are you enjoying yourself?" Simon asked.

"Just how many helicopter visits are you planning tonight?" Jack smiled.

"Sade is one-of-a-kind; sometimes you must think outside the normal to get what you want. She prefers pure entertainment and keeps her private life to herself. So, we made it simple for her to sing her songs and then jam. Besides, folks in this room will book her for their private gigs many times. It's a win-win in my house."

"I'm just not sure why I'm here?" said Jack.

"Because you deserve to be here. I know your path ahead and am bringing you into the mix early to prepare you for fortune and fame. You should just relax and be as social as you see fit. No one here is selling tonight and there is no big check written at the end! You're safe," said Simon.

Jack glanced around Simon and Ava was still performing. Simon also turned around and said, "Isn't she lovely," as in character with Stevie Wonder.

"You really know how to class up a superyacht party," said Jack.

"Let me know if you need anything special," said Simon. Jack knew he meant some form of sex, drugs or other boating entertainment rituals, but his mind was still distracted.

"I'm enjoying the scenery immensely and hope to take it all in," said Jack looking out across the shoreline.

"Enjoy my friend," said Simon.

CHAPTER
TWENTY-SEVEN
AVA'S PLACE

ON SUNDAY, Jack received a text reading, "Hope you liked my dance. It was fun to see you on the boat yesterday."

Jack had put the name in his phone as "B&W Hottie" and was pleased she texted him. Of course, he remembered the beautiful dancer and finally realized the woman behind the feather mask was the lovely waitress from the club.

Excited, Jack replied, "Oh I had no idea that you were such a lovely dancer," and trying to play it cool texted, "Hope to see you again soon,"

"Yes, me too," Ava responded with 3 winking heart emojis.

Ava lived in the industrial part of the city of San Francisco's industrial district. Though there was plenty of homelessness and graffiti, crime was rare in the city. Her building sat centered on the block, with a converted metal garage door and an adjoining passage door to the side. There was minimal street parking and after 5pm, you were not likely to park without finding a lot nearby.

The building was tall and must have been four or five stories high. Metal walls rose abruptly from the street to a broken fire escape, detached at the last floor. The street door likely once led to a small retail space, with an interior window and countertop left of the door, and a second locked entrance to the right.

Ava, a third-year art student at the Academy of Art University, swung open the door to reveal a first floor that looked as large as a gymnasium. Massive metal beans supported the second and third-floor mezzanines, spaced broadly enough to easily convert the "apartment" into a dozen condominiums. Dark, stone-like flooring covered the concrete slab floor.

The vast room was purposefully left rustic and filled with artwork, eclectic furniture, and plants. Plants were everywhere, from mature trees to bamboo growing nearly five floors high. Crisscrossing vines created a jungle feeling.

A long stairway against the rear wall leads up to two huge suites on the second-floor mezzanine. The first suite was Ava's "daily" room, which included a queen-sized bed, a few long couches, some exercise mats, a large dresser, and chair. The TV was like a silhouette on the wall, unused unless there was an occasional reason to turn it on for a movie. Ava preferred listening to music over watching TV.

On the back was a spacious bathroom with a large sink, toilet, bidet, and a shower with a dark wooden bench inside for relaxing amid the steam. It was big enough for two shower heads, but Ava felt if two people showered together, they should share everything.

An enormous walk-in closet separated the two bedrooms and mostly acted as a staging room. Entering the second room brought an immediate sense of peacefulness and wonder. The colors were warm and dark, and Ava had as much wood in this room as her wood shop downstairs. The only metal in the room was the dance pole and the light fixtures. There was even a small refrigerator hidden in a wooden chest.

The second bath was even more beautiful than the first. The floors and walls were made of dark stone patterns and the centerpiece was a large built-in bathtub for two. Ava had room for several dozen candles around the edges and still plenty of room for wine glasses and more. More glass shower doors and two black sinks were below a full mirrored wall. Lighting was beautiful and subtle throughout.

The balance of the first floor held a large walk-in closet, a small but modest open kitchen, the seating area with fountain, and Ava's studio. The closet was near the back wall and easy access to the stairs. Ava believed that bedrooms and closets should not be together and only a few articles of clothing would be near the bedroom or bath.

Sharing about a third of the first floor was her art studio. A thin steel wall separated the dining and living areas from the art and metal work. The walls ran up the beams to the second floor with an open ceiling to the roof. On one of the walls was some sort of graffiti that was tastefully and yet only partially covered up by Ava's artistic flare.

The door to her studio was the size of a small wall and hung from roller rails. It was likely left from some sort of garage and now converted as a doorway separating reality from fantasy.

Inside were three or four large, open room-like areas containing Ava's work in progress. Her style was still being defined and included unique mixed media with elements of light, glass, ceramic and metal overlays.

In the first area was the building blocks and mechanisms to bend and weld the underlying framework of the art pieces. Most of her work started with what might look like common shapes, such as a table or chair, and then dramatically transformed. Her chair series, known as "The Chair Dance," included a collection of exotic and intricate chairs that varied from amazingly comfortable to an S&M party for one.

One chair had smooth, clean lines with hinged joints. Black anodized metal and leather patches placed where the person would sit created a high-end look. Her collection also included a chrome chair that bent into a glory-hole position, a chair that carefully stretched the body parts, a chair for getting wet, and a chair for three (Thailand favorite).

Later, Jack would discover and enjoy the experiences of the chairs.

CHAPTER
TWENTY-EIGHT

SHEER DELIGHT

HOPING to catch a glimpse of the waitress again, Jack returned to the Black & White Bar. He contemplated whether to text her and ask if she'd be there. After drafting a few versions in his mind, he finally sent a simple message:

"Any chance you're working tonight? It would be fun to see you."

"Great to hear from you. I'm here till midnight. Maybe you can come by." A winking emoji followed.

"Let me finish a few things at work, and I'll be over around 9," he responded, excitement bubbling at the hoped-for response.

After a quick shower and shave, Jack donned a stylish dark shirt with a subtle wave-like pattern mixing blue and black hues—a step away from his usual stuffy business attire. Hoping to embrace the San Francisco lifestyle, he left a few buttons undone to showcase his fit chest from his swimming habit. He resembled a GQ model tonight, and the timing couldn't have been better.

Arriving at the packed, high-energy club, Jack sat at the bar, deliberately positioning himself with a clear view of the crowd and waitstaff area. The clock had just struck nine, and he couldn't help but wonder why the place was so packed on a Thursday night. Leaning against the bar, he extended his arm slightly, signaling he was ready for a drink. The Patek Philippe watch on his left wrist glistened as he waited.

Jack recalled dating trivia: 16% of singles know if they want a second date, and over 68% love follow-up texts. It made him ponder his situation with the beautiful waitress whose name he still did not know. Did they have chemistry? Would they discover common interests beyond raw physical attraction?

The tattooed bartender approached, and for a moment, Jack contemplated getting a subtle tattoo, like a Chinese symbol for "warrior." He ordered a Jack-n-Ginger and took a few sips. His excitement had slightly overwhelmed him, and he let the alcohol help regain his confidence.

Jack's gaze wandered up to the array of bottles behind the bar, and he found solace in their distraction. He read the labels meticulously as if evaluating an artist's canvas. The Jack-n-Ginger, combined with the bottle distraction, was working magic, gradually shifting his mood from haste and restlessness to a more patient, wait-and-see mindset. Jack knew he tended to operate at extremes, but tonight, he was finding the balance that allowed him to slow down, relax, and savor the room's ambiance.

Jack savored his second drink when he noticed her entering the room—it was her. She must have been working in other parts of the bar, as he constantly checked his view to spot her. Currently, she was tending to a table on the far side. Jack considered sending her a text but realized her outfit had no room for a cell phone.

She was dressed in a see-through white skirt that cascaded to the floor. It featured a daring slit that ran down the entire length of her leg, and as she moved, glimpses from her upper thigh to the tops of her black stiletto heels were displayed. Her upper attire consisted of a tiny black vest blouse—collared on top, tapering down to her mid-waist, with a gap revealing her enticing waist and belly button. Her flat stomach was delightful, and the vest, like her skirt and bra, added to the sheer allure. Jack felt like he had Superman's X-ray vision as he discerned the outline of her nipples through the sheer fabric.

She caught Jack's eye as she gracefully strolled across the room and offered him a warm smile before continuing to deliver her drinks. However, this time, she circled back and approached his side of the bar. As she drew nearer, Jack turned to face her. He appreciated her from head to toe, and the bar's perfect lighting seemed to elevate her from a flowing silhouette to a sheer princess.

Reaching a gap beside Jack, she leaned in to signal the bartender. "I'll take this one back with me," she said.

"He's all yours."

The scent of sweet ginger wafted from her as she reached for his drink. Her other hand lightly touched his lower back as she whispered, "Let me take care of you tonight."

Jack was relishing the evening he had been eagerly anticipating. Although the B&W Bar was bustling with patrons, it felt like they were the only two in the room. She seated him at a booth and smiled and delivered his first real drink.

"Let me close out my tables and meet you in the lobby in 5 minutes," she said.

"I'm ready when you are." He felt his response was a bit dorky and wished he could have been more romantic, but his nervousness was getting the best of him. With an empty table, it was time to leave.

The B&W lobby was unlike any other waiting area. On one side were the wild and vibrant nightclub doors, and a mysterious set of elevators on the other. Typically, people passed through this room in a matter of seconds. But tonight, Jack found himself waiting alone, constantly glancing at his phone. Then, the door opened, and she entered. Jack marveled at how effortlessly she exuded sexiness in her street clothes —heels, tight jeans, and a purse strapped across her blouse.

As she drew closer, she slipped her arm under his and pulled him close to whisper, "I've wanted to go out with you for a while now. Do you have any rooftop spots in mind?"

The city offered a multitude of nighttime pleasures, including the club scene, Michelin-starred restaurants, foodie bars, and, for locals, selective rooftop bars that showcased the night sky. Jack was still basking in the warmth of her whisper and wasn't thinking too clearly. They emerged from the parking garage; their phones filled with possibilities.

"We can also just grab something light. Do you like sushi?" she inquired.

"Mmmm, that sounds perfect."

She knew several nighttime spots known for good food and secure parking, given that San Francisco had a reputation for car theft and vandalism. They found parking, and Jack appreciated every gesture, from opening her car door to requesting a table for two. She cared for him as if they had been dating for ages. She shared her favorite sushi rolls with Jack and inquired whether he preferred mild or spicy dishes. Jack was up for trying almost anything and encouraged her to order for them. Three beautifully crafted sushi rolls arrived at their table, adorned with delightful crunchy toppings.

"I want you to try this one first." She reached for the middle roll with her chopsticks and offered Jack a small bite. A smile graced her beautiful face as she placed it on his tongue.

He chewed once and swallowed. "Oh my god, this is delicious."

"It's my favorite," she said.

They continued to feed each other sushi, and Jack was entranced by every feature of her face. He savored how she opened her mouth for sushi and couldn't help but imagine kissing her lips. Her tongue rolling over her lips with a seductive smile invited him into her world. She asked if they wanted more when the food was almost gone, igniting excitement in Jack's thoughts.

"I'm okay if you are," he eagerly replied.

She smiled, tucking a strand of hair behind her ear. "So, you seem like a sweet guy, and I think I can trust you."

"Yes, I hope so," Jack replied, a hint of nervousness still lingering.

"I live in a warehouse apartment nearby. We can stop by."

He nodded, standing up to follow her out.

Jack gripped the steering wheel tightly as they drove to her place, realizing the neighborhood wasn't quite suitable for his Lexus. She guided him to a public garage around the block.

"Your car is safe here," she assured him.

They walked to her warehouse apartment, and Jack found the entry different from what he had imagined—more industrial and less feminine.

She explained, "It's a converted warehouse from the 1930s. I think they used to manufacture parts for either shipping or the railroad. They added a front lobby for security, hoping to keep out unwanted guests. My landlord is a World War II veteran and wants to keep the building as-is for as long as he's alive.

The lobby felt like a mini-museum, with century-old pictures on the wall depicting the Navy Pier from years gone by. Jack wasn't sure what to make of the place, but he knew he'd follow her anywhere.

She opened the inner door, revealing her studio. "Please come in. I'm going to make some tea."

Jack was amazed by the spaciousness of her apartment, a rarity in crowded San Francisco. It seemed large enough for several families to live comfortably. As he entered the kitchen, he couldn't contain his admiration.

"This place is incredible. I can't imagine having all this space to myself."

"When I first moved here, the previous tenant was an artist and a painter. He fell on hard times and left some stuff behind when he moved out." She pointed to the wall. "That's his work."

Jack gazed at the stylish graffiti art titled "Nobody Knows" by the Tony Rich Project. "I'm afraid I don't know this song."

"It's a melancholic love song," she explained, shrugging. "He might have struggled with relationships and used his art to express his emotions. He left behind a dozen paintings, each filled with images of love and compassion. When you look at his artwork, you realize there was much more going on with the artist than what he painted."

Jack looked around the room, noticing numerous art pieces, ranging from canvas paintings to sculptures. There were also metal-formed furniture pieces, including exotic tables and several chairs.

"Did he work with metal as well?" Jack inquired.

"No, those are my pieces," she replied. "Art is my true passion, and I'm currently studying at the Academy of Art University to explore various art styles before pursuing my own."

Jack chuckled awkwardly. "You must be quite skilled if you're working with metal like this."

A little smile tugged at her mouth. "I love working with metal, glass, stone, and wood."

"I'm genuinely impressed," he admitted. "You're not only an incredible dancer and a creative artist but also manage to work as a waitress."

"The B&W is just to pay the bills, and I usually make enough in tips to work three or four days a week. These are my newest creations." She gestured across the room. "It's called the 'Le Chair Series,' featuring solo and connected chairs, each with a unique form and shape. I used rustic metal, but the seating and lying areas are smooth and sensual."

They shared a mutual passion for their respective arts, and his deep love for science found a mysterious connection to her artistic soul. Jack glanced around the room, noticing more art pieces, including 3D glass creations that complemented the metalwork. He wondered how this stunning model-like beauty transformed into a metalworker with a leather jacket, face shield, and acetylene torch. He would explore more of her artwork upstairs, including a homemade bathtub. Notably absent were any electronic distractions like a TV or store-bought stereo.

She enjoyed music while creating her art but kept it simple with her iPhone playlist playing through wireless speakers.

They sipped tea and talked until well past 2 a.m. Knowing he had an early start on Friday, Jack finally decided it was time to leave and made the first move.

"I should head home soon," he began. "By the way, my name is Jack, and I'd love to know yours."

She extended her hand with a warm smile. "I'm Ava. It was a pleasure to finally meet you."

As Jack walked to his car, he couldn't deny the uniqueness of this evening. He had dated for years but never felt as connected and comfortable with a woman as with Ava. He considered the possibility of an alcohol-induced infatuation but hoped the feeling would persist beyond that night.

CHAPTER
TWENTY-NINE
GENOME PHENOMENON

THE FIELDS OF GENOMICS, the study of genetics, and the use of gene therapies have become commonplace for those with a need. The race to create a perfect human DNA strand or attempt to clone such a complex organism continues in the murky convergence of intellectual property and human capital. Thanks to 23&Me, Ancestry.com and others, there is an enormous database of persons across the world who submitted their DNA to determine their genetic makeup concerning family heritage. They use genotyping to identify matching genome strings to an ancestral database, and then, after some algorithmic number crunching, it will provide a 99% accurate result of where in the world your DNA came from. It is then up to you to build the ancestry tree for full details, although some test kit services include extensive background searches from 50,000-200,000 years ago. Consumers now can define to their social media audience what percentage German, Scandinavian or American Indian, just to name a few. At this stage, the non-obvious questions that arise in the estimated life space, biomarkers, or other indicators are typically discussed. After all, the data is rich in information on health and disease. Early in their go-to-market, 23andMe began testing for breast cancer, specifically looking for breast cancer gene mutations aka BRCA1 and BRCA2 mutations. For some women, this was helpful; for others, it was devastating as fun conversations about genetic ancestry were overwhelmed by genetic markers for cancer.

Unfortunately, it became obvious that DNA testing in whatever form was selected from simple saliva mail in strips to more advanced full blood screening, these were simply the inputs to various models that took the input data and provided a wide panel of results. The 23andMe database is around 15 million with AncestryDNA.com just above 22 million. Even if we add them together and round off to 40 million samples, the world population is just over 8 billion, so this is approximately 40m/8b = 0.005 or less than half of one percent (<0.2%) - and what should we use to calibrate the other 99.8% of the population. Statistically, these numbers, albeit over 15 million, are just a sample set. And yet, 23andMe (NASDAQ: ME) has a market cap approaching $1b with nearly $300 million in revenue.

Even if the top DNA sample companies doubled their installed base, it would approach 1% of the population or 80 million samples. There is an abundance of the population starving to assume that the data collected, and the individual samples are perfect sample size for making assumptions about ancestry and certain health-related decisions. Why is this acceptable? Because it beats the alternative, and a further identity makes it all worthwhile.

How about the new field of genetic embryologists who engage with couples wanting to know more about their potential offspring, and they want the detailed results of the test. Now, more than ever, additional requirements or genetic information may influence marriage or having a family. It's like having "DNA value," as currency with your partner.

Dr. Bruce Conklin, MD., a professor at UCSF School of Medicine, focuses on decoding and repairing genetic diseases. He refers to gene correction or targeted drug therapy, combined with patent-derived induced pluripotent stem cells (iPSCs) to model diseases in tissues. He is leveraging other scientists at the Innovative Genomics Institute to prepare large animal models and clinical-grade reagents to prepare for human clinical trials. His primary research is in genome surgery where he will combine precision advanced microscopy, gene editing, with select CRISPR/Cas9 combinations for optimal benefits.

Dr. M. Porteus, MD, PhD, Stanford faculty, and brilliant professor of definitive and curative medicine, may have been the first to demonstrate gene correction before gene editing. Matthew's research program continues to focus on developing genome editing by homologous recombination as curative therapy for children with genetic diseases but also has interests in the clonal dynamics of heterogeneous populations and the use of genome editing to better understand that affect children including infant leukemias and genetic diseases that affect the muscle.

UC Berkeley Professor Jennifer Doudna shares a common passion as Dr. Conklin including the Genomics Institute, and of course her pioneering work in CRISPR gene editing. A portion of which led to her 2020 Nobel Prize win and then a gauntlet of patents and patent lawsuits have snowballed such that everyone wants a piece of the CRISPR pie. Let's assume for this novel that the merits of CRISPR far outweigh the concern for ownership or profit. Jack needed to meet folks like Douda and Conklin and discover what was behind their research and how they envision a future where small changes make huge impacts. He wondered if these researchers were big thinkers for the common good or algorithm geniuses captivated by complex numbered strings.

Somehow, he needed to bring the Saints into the mix and ask more important questions about this new genome phenome. Jack sent Robbie a Snap to this extent and requested a group chat. Code word was "Who is Gene Crispr Kelly" - just enough to cause some confusion on the internet. The group chat was set for next week and everyone knew their assignments. Jack set the Zoom call for 5pm hoping to grab everyone's calendar spot. He received their acceptances and despite a few exceptions, the Saint made other arrangements to support this call. Jack believed in being prompt and started the call a minute or two early and they group were all present before start time. They each used their camera and the matrix of familiar faces made everyone even more excited to begin. Jack laid the framework with his usual 120% completeness and then posed the question for the team.

"For the past 25 years, determining a person's genetic makeup, aka, their genome was a complex mathematical feat that can be obtained when combined with superior compute power and algorithms. There are even commercial "sales" on full genome mapping. State-of-the-art folks like Illumina offer WGS (whole-genome sequencing) as a website offering. So, let's put that topic in the win column for science. And, if folks now have access to their genetic makeup, plus rich databases that show critical markers about one's future health, then we have valid concerns to address."

Gene editing is one of the greatest achievements in genomics since the development and isolation of the full human genome. The timing of these discoveries makes perfect sense along the research timeline and computer power convergence. In a recent study, over 53% of Americans could not name their four grandparents. There is an insatiable desire to know more about our history including names, personal stories, and eventually medical histories or markers which may lead to future healthcare predictions. And here begins the major shift between patients seeking medical advice and direction from professionals or specialists versus taking matters into their own hands, getting test results, and then taking courses of action that may result in extremes, such as breast removal surgery based on positive BRCA testing from an online resource such as 23andMe - recall this database represents far less than 1% of the population.

However, it is also true that the total patient population is small when a drug passes through Phase 1, 2, 3, and 4 clinical trials. Pfizer's

Phase 3 clinical trials for the Covid vaccine was 46,331 persons and considered an accurate sample across 153 sites (including US). These trials were largely watched due to the impact of the pandemic, and this sort of scrutiny is not likely to occur again soon. However, there are a few corollaries to our current state.

CHAPTER
THIRTY

COLORFUL DREAMS

JACK RECALLS DREAMING in vivid color. Vast landscapes with shades of greens, browns, and blues. He remembers boat rides with colors and sea mist across the many surfaces. Jack had a few dream compartments where he could recall and pull previous memories into his dream. Most are with Robbie and the Saints and now Ava. His combination of confidence and happiness recently created a few episodes of lucid dreaming.

The first was after too many beers with Alex and the team. It was just supposed to be a drink after work but had quickly turned into all sorts of dares and wild conversations around sexual behaviors. Glory hole roulette, karaoke strip tease, embarrassing threesomes, and the Alex-sexual brainteasers.

Nothing was off-limits, but then the idea of being flexible enough to self-suck and the potential for surgery to remove a rib was introduced. This visual led to facial twerks and a lengthy discussion on how normal the conversation was. But the oddity stuck with Jack throughout the evening and into his dreams. He managed a lovely evening alone and was flexible enough to maneuver the job through his climax. There was no need for surgery.

When he awoke, he found himself with a little precum for his efforts and tangled up in sheets but nowhere near as flexible as his lucid state.

One of his most memorable LDs was an evening out with Ava.

In the dream, they had made plans to attend an invite-only gallery in SOMA. Jack dressed sharply with lapis cufflinks, his new favorite, and a dark blue suit. The distance was such that they could meet up at the event, so he arrived earlier than planned.

He browsed most of the first floor, taking in each painting and artist and remembering his challenges with brush and canvas. He looped back to the entry and found Ava just coming in. He welcomed her with a hug and kiss and almost forgot about the gallery, but she tugged him along, eager to see the exhibition. He looked at each painting again, only this time he had Ava's comments, which almost always provided underlying points in the art where true meanings were discovered.

Some freedoms of lucidness were remembering what you will and emphasizing what was in your heart's desire. Jack noticed, but never questioned, certain areas in the dream where hallways and rooms blended—or when they went from the gallery to Ava's place, as if to just turn a corner.

The lovely evening ended with Jack removing Ava's dress from the back, allowing it to fall flat, and watching her walk to the bed in her heels. She bent over to pull the sheets open and spun around to bounce lightly, lifting her feet upwards for him. Jack carefully unwrapped each glass slipper and then got out of his clothes in a lucid second.

He loved getting under the sheets with Ava like she was a new enchanted girlfriend filled with desire, romance, and passion.

She was a very giving partner, but Jack wanted to focus on her pleasure first. He moved down her with light kisses — from her lips to her shoulders, across her breasts and tummy, and then slowed down once he reached her trimmed bush. He would spend the next dream memory with senses of smell and taste, warmth and touches, and her body's slow rhythmic movements.

He continued a bit longer with gentle fingers and his tongue after she had orgasmed. There was a pause, and he rested his head on her like he was going to sleep, his face between her thighs. She moaned for him to come to her side. Then, it was her turn to drive him crazy with her hands and mouth. And after warming him up, she gently caressed his balls and sucked him. Ava loved to control him through his climax, and he exploded with cum and excitement.

She squeezed his butt playfully and then crawled up the sheets to his side.

"Oh, that was nice," he groaned, and Ava smiled.

"I hope you liked it; I did."

They snuggled a bit more and drifted off, the end of the lucid memory.

Finally, there were the anime dreams.

They were typically preceded by gaming with the Saints or a path from Pokémon cards. Jack and Robbie collected graded cards and enjoyed reviewing their collection when Jack was in town. They amassed over 300 graded PSA 10 cards with values from $100 to over $2000 per card. Most were over 20 years old and ornate with gold stamps, foil, and full art graphics. Robbie believed you could never look at these cards too often as they brought him fond memories of time with his brother. Pokémon anime was a bit cartoon-like as the artist needed to keep to the game, and 25 seasons means they were doing something right even at 8 fps.

Then, the leap was from Pokémon to graphic novels and manga series.

The brothers were voracious readers and consumed graphic pages as fast as their eyes and hands would move. They knew the brain stored traditional text differently than graphics and text and only slowed down when they came across colored pages. Their favorites had a few pages in front with full color, and they would start with these pages and then read traditionally from back to front in either

English or Japanese. Both Seattle and San Francisco had their local knock-off Comic Con events with freaky fans, and of course, their favorite part was cosplay. For the elite costume wearers, this was a dress rehearsal for San Diego.

Outfits ranged from superheroes to fantasy, with thrills and attractions to keep you wanting more. Some characters came straight out of gameplay. Maybe there were a few too many Spiderman and not enough Vampirellas or Boosettes, but they all looked like crazy adult fun. Jack particularly enjoyed an enhanced LD after their last Comic-Con visit, and mind-play included Ava as Snow White from SINo-ALICE and again as Emma Frost.

Apparently, he had a thing for her in white.

In his dream, he was on a boat, and Ava appeared on the deck in her white lace and satin Snow White outfit and weapon, the Greatsword of Corruption. She pointed her blade towards him and, in a sultry voice, commanded him to the back bedroom. He felt the need to change things as he turned and entered the room, a smile tugging his lips. Ava became Azur Lane as he turned around, and innocence took over. White bunny ears replaced Snow's headdress, and the long breaker sword disappeared. Now, Ava wore only a white bodysuit and stockings and playfully beckoned him closer.

"Welcome home, Commander. I've been waiting for you." She spoke as if performing in a hentai anime, her voice high-pitched and excited, as if she was already having sex with him. She turned around and placed one knee on the bed, showing Jack the cottontail attached to the bodysuit. "Are you ready to give me your orders?"

Jack had never been so aroused in his life.

If you could give a lucid dream, it would be given as the most precious of things. Imagine a Soylent Green setting with the world's most comfortable couch, 360 surround view, and instead of any dystopian overpopulation issues, it was a spa-like visit starting with cool, sparkling water to get the senses started. The room would be in various shades of color and slowly morph into photographs leading up to the dream state. A favorite playlist would be piped in; the last was a gummy on the side table.

~

Jack brings up the idea with the Saints in a video group call. He says it's a business waiting to happen and will cater to country club elitists who will pay for any path to extend happiness in their lives.

"There are so many appealing angles to this ideal therapy," Jack tells the Saints, his gaze imploring them to see the potential in his ideas. "If there were a 20% chance of success, I'd say it was a worthwhile investment."

Raising an eyebrow, Paul chuckles. "You're gonna bet the farm on dreams?"

"Why not promise to make dreams come true as well?" said Michael, his expression telling. The crowd is getting a bit juicy around the topic of lucid dreams and how close this sounds to television drama.

Jack shakes his head. "I'm not saying it's the smartest or innovative idea. It's just a narrow crack in the ice that may be connected to an iceberg."

"Let me go out on a limb or brain stem for a second." Robbie steeples his fingers to his lips. "No one has made a commercial killing anywhere near the dream state, and most people know Lucid as an electric vehicle that costs much more than a Tesla. So, let's break it down a bit. I can tell you my favorite ice cream, how I like my steak cooked, and which scooter is the best for getting across town, but how do I know my perfect lucid?"

Jack starts to speak, but Robbie continues, slowly lowering his hands from his mouth.

"What if a married guy wants to have a "lucid affair" with his secretary or bully wants to pop off at someone? On one hand, there are therapeutic effects. From a full psychological perspective, it's both enhancing and dangerous. On the other hand, we do many things to maintain our physical appearances from skin, hair, body shape, and all the many accessories, and yet, we seldom have outlets for our mentally aligned cells. Saying you would see your therapist was acceptable over time, like gender, or pronoun referral. This is like the investment in partial ownership of a luxury jet. It's an expensive habit for those who can't afford the real thing."

"Any other potshots from the gang, the door is wide open." Jack gives the group a ghost of a smile.

"I'm okay with the premise and think there is a need for this, but it's like renting scuba equipment in shark-infested waters," Michael says.

A moment of silence passed, and then Luke eloquently adds, "Or we could carefully limit the traffic, and find sanctuary for those in—"

"Okay, I kicked the hornet's nest with this one," Jack cuts in, a hint of frustration lacing his voice. "But we're not quite done with lucid dreaming, weightlessness, and EV launch modes. Let's keep enjoying our sleep, dreams, and building our enhanced memories.

Jack knows that visionary people see past the noise and confusion in the world. They can see past obstacles with their dedicated and clear vision of the future. Some see these paths with small steps and others with very large leaps. Most are independent thinkers and although they use elements of their surroundings to build their story, the key points are often so unique, the view can be seen as either far-fetched or simply amazing. But independent thinkers also know the power of creating a conducive environment that allow innovative ideas to grow and develop with nonstop passion to achieve what others have not.

Jack has several wall hangings near his office, including the seven natural wonders of the world, and events that marked significant breakthroughs in medicine, science and technology. One picture is dedicated to an algorithm to decipher enemy war communications. Another picture climate change and the final image expressed concern for population growth. Each is impactful in their own way, and even more important is the reminder of greatness.

Greatness comes from the daring and fearless, those who aren't afraid to take risks and share their vision with others, even if the path is still blurred.

There is nothing new about thinking big, but the idea of having bigger than normal thoughts to create larger-than-life achievements fuel Jack.

THE SAINTS WERE all living within about a 30-mile radius of Seattle. They were all in their early twenties, and no one had a partner yet, so there were no excuses for getting together. During one of their outings to Lake Elliot (near where Robbie & Jack are from), they planned a leisure walk to shore, carrying an oversized picnic blanket, lunch and some sports toys including frisbees and Waboba juggling balls. They knew the beach well as they visited almost every weekend in July and August. On this Saturday, the temperature was ideal, in the high 70s. The boys picked their spots and dropped camp for the day.

"Wow, I can't believe how gorgeous it is today," said Michael. After looking up and down the beach, he continued, "I think we are the only ones on the lake today."

"Nope, look straight ahead," announced Joseph. There was a boat far out.

"That doesn't count," replied Michael. "The people on that boat are testing the edge of the flat earth," he said smiling.

"Haha, you gotta be kidding," back to Joseph. "If they disappear, we will know the truth after all."

The boys knew the crazy conspiracies about the "Flat Earth" and often joked about the phrase ``is it round like a table or round like an apple? For a long time, many critical thinkers, historians, poets and philosophers believed the earth to be a flat disc shape. In the 4th century BC, Plato and Aristotle provided reasons to believe in the globe shape. Although word spread about this theory, nearly 1000 years later during the Middle Ages, it was thought that the earth resembled a wheel.

"Hey," Robbie yelled, "let's go for a walk around our spherical world," he grinned and waved in his direction.

As they headed off, they walked in a pack with a small enough distance between each other to hear any conversation. And as they walked, they talked and talked. One after the other, there was never a lull in the magic and mysteries that went on in their minds and transformed in their discussions. The beach brought them out in a way that made perfect sense. The crashing of the waves and the solitude of the shore allowed them to express themselves freely to one another. Today's various topics included Luke's interest in where pelicans sleep at night, Michaels unending imagination about sailing around the world, Joseph's creativity with the colors in the sky, Paul recalling lyrics that speak to their joy and togetherness and finally, Robbie reminding the team that they were children of God and that their days were fulfilled by a plan.

Their journey out was nearly a mile and Robbie signaled for them to turn around. The boys all wore sunscreen and hats to keep the ultraviolet away. They protected their eyes with polarized glasses with brands including Maui Jim's, Ray-Ban and Nike. As a casual observer might suggest, they looked very cool.

Michael sprinted ahead to create some distance. He had the frisbee ring and threw it sailing back just overhead of everyone. It floated for a bit and then crashed diagonally to the sand. The mini game began, and the group spread quickly to form a circle. It was organized chaos and between awkward throwing and lousy catching, no one really knew what they were doing. Perhaps the two lefties, Michael & Joseph, had better-throwing aim, but it didn't really matter. Robbie reminded them that it was never a contest with this group and just watching each other in play was enough.

They crashed down on blankets back at the picnic spot. Luke grabbed the speaker and connected his phone to music play.

"It's time for Elton," he shouted.

"Hey, let's try some Simon & Garfunkel or Beach Boys," said Robbie.

"Queen, I want some Queen Bohemian Rhapsody," chimed Michael.

"Ok, we're gonna take it back to the 60's with some Peter, Paul & Mary," Luke said. He played Leaving on a Jet Plane, and the team settled into this groove. They opened the basket of food and distributed sandwiches and chips. As the first song ended, Luke cranked the volume up and announced, "here's another favorite." The song came out, "Puff, the magic dragon lived by the sea...," and everyone made the gesture of raising a joint from their lips to the sky. They were all cool and hanging at a 60's outdoor gig wishing they had some tie dye wraps. From hammering to blowing in the wind, they enjoyed listening to these oldies.

"To close this set, I bring you the Wedding Song," said Luke. He stood and began waving his arms softly, whispering, "there is love, there is love," to the chorus.

"Thanks for playing my dad's favorite song," whispered Robbie.

As the afternoon ended, they piled into Michael's jeep and returned home. Robbie enjoyed the middle "hump" seat and couldn't help visually navigating the route through familiar streets. They were all a bit tired from the sun and exercise. Next, was dinner for those with an appetite and a Saturday evening to each his own. Luke and Paul were dropped off first, and then Robbie. Joseph, riding shotgun, jumped out to open the door for Robbie and grabbed the empty basket.

"Many thanks for bringing all the food and fixings for our trip. As always, you take good care of us," said Joseph.

"You know it's my pleasure and I only wish we had more Saturdays at the beach to enjoy." replied Robbie. "Someday, we will have our own beach and spend more time with warm sand between our toes, and delightful music in our ears."

"We'd love that all too much," said Joseph. From the car, Michael shouted, "I'm ok with every day being a Saturday, wearing flip flops, and hanging out."

"I already miss you guys," said Robbie. "Hope you enjoy the rest of the weekend and hope to see you on Monday."

Robbie grabbed the gear and headed up the front stairs to the porch. He turned and waved to "MJ" and made his way inside. He set down his belongings and rested on the couch. He brought his fingers to his temples and rubbed tiny circles. He used his other fingers to move around the sides of his skull looking for ways to massage the pain away. It was becoming a frequent occurrence of his headache pain and nothing simple would relieve the pain. He eventually made his way to the kitchen, prepared a simple Tylenol/Aleve cocktail, and choked down a few over-the-counter pills. Soon, there would be some minor relief. It was another quiet Saturday night, and it was time to play his favorite relaxing music and unwind. Robbie made his favorite chicken noodle soup from a box and salty crackers. The soup was comfort food and made his heart warm. Simple and yummy. Before bed, Robbie looked back on the glorious day with the boys and the joy of being together. Highlights of a warm sandy beach, his favorite Subway sandwich wrap, and social bonds of the Saints that claim the day. Sunday was near and he decided to share the updated news with Jack.

Julia and Tom attended the same church for over 35 years. It was the First Presbyterian Church of Reston with a congregation of nearly 300 people, an energetic choir, and full spectrum pipe organ. There were two services: a traditional service at 11am and a more progressive one at 9am. This Sunday, the Mohr group would get to church early and enjoy the youthful congregation, live music, and multimedia including digital photographs and short videos. Few folks recognized Jack visiting and praised his time in the church. On the drive home, they stopped for deli sandwiches and pasta salad. They would eventually end up on the backyard deck with a chance to relax before Jack's return flight. The food was really yummy, and Jack said, "I've always loved the routine of church and then fresh sandwiches from Pete's Deli. I remember getting my favorite pepper turkey on a fresh baguette and salad with my favorite fusilli noodles."

"After today, I regret that we don't always stop at the deli," said Tom. "Probably from being in a hurry to get to nowhere."

"No worries, Dad," said Robbie. "We are all anxious to get to the next event in our lives, and probably a good segway into my next chapter." Robbie sipped his lemonade and cleared his throat. "You all know about my challenges with AGS and more recently with my immune system showing signs of being compromised. Although my health is considered ok, I would prefer feeling more energetic. My doctors have me on an immunosuppressant cocktail which helps guard off a unique form of lupus, and I am looking into DNA/RNA gene editing therapies through my connections at Cal."

"How often are you seeing the doctors?" questioned Jack.

"I have local clinic blood draws. Doctor visits include Zoom calls every month, and visits to the clinic every quarter or so in Berkeley."

"When is your next appointment?" asked Jack. "I'd like to know more about the new therapies and what they hope for with your treatment. And full disclosure, our team at Seres is working with the folks at Innovative Genomics Institute (IGI), especially around gene editing and blood-based diseases. If there is anything I can do to assist in your care, I want to be front and center for support. Please let me know when you have your next meeting, and I will be there."

Robbie's care was from some of the finest researchers in the field of immune deficiencies and had experience through AIDS, Arthritis, Diabetes, and Lupus. This included invasions from viruses including HIV, SARS and Covid-19. As an immunocompromised patient, he was an ideal candidate for convalescent plasma transfusions as a potential path to rebuilding antibodies against a host of Robbie ailments. During his recent visit to the clinic, he sat with another dozen patients in their transfusion center. There was a mixture of chemo, blood cleansing, and plasma infusion patients getting through visits that lasted 1 to 4 hours. Robbie was currently ramping up from 1 unit to 2 units per visit. There was plenty of evidence that this therapy was helping victims of post-Covid care. However, this process had limited data on adults with AGS and it was safe to say the team was still experimenting with Robbie.

When Ava finished her competitive years in track and dancing, she was in the best shape of her life. She initially relied on her legs for strength and speed, then later for balance and grace. For the last 5 to 8 years, her body had more physical therapy, hot & cold baths, painkillers, weed, and the occasional corticosteroid injection to ease her pain from hips, knees, and ankles. Although she continued her routines with yoga and stretching, there seemed to be an issue with her energy and stamina. Luckily, physical intimacy with Jack was never a problem. However, the long days of waitressing in heels created a new sort of tiredness that she was not used to. She naturally had a slight iron deficiency and kept a strict supplement regimen to keep her strong through monthly cycles and demands from work. She worked 4 days at the B&W and did freelance dancing for high-wealth clients. The rest of her free time was split between Jack and her artwork, giving her little time to worry about herself.

Ava's diet started to suffer as she replaced one set of carbs for another and moved from diet cokes to energy drinks and other food substitutes. The daily cycle went from breakfast time with a light protein and lots of caffeine, to midday snacks with liquids filled with caffeine, taurine, glucuronolactone, guarana, ginseng, ginkgo biloba, l-carnitine and more sugars. She replaced the good from coffee and espresso with the bad from artificial sweeteners. Then into the evenings with alcohol or a combination of alcohol and energy drinks, depending on her energy levels. Her amazing ability to compete in sports at an extreme level meant she was filled with optimism, confidence and recently a declining sense of self-esteem. During a recent day off from work, Ava finished a new art piece, and although her work was always filled with her unique creativity, this one had no such energy. As she stood back and looked at the metal sculpture, where she wanted to portrait depth, it was flat, and where she wanted outward expressions of joy, they were replaced with sadness and depression. This was intended for some artists like van Gogh, but for Ava Lewis, it was a dark point and felt uncomfortable. She was reflecting on whether her day job, which was filled with the money elite, narcissist, and otherwise masculine power-hungry people was starting to influence her more than she realized.

She particularly liked Jack as he never played the arrogant card for money, intelligence or status. Ava threw a cover on the art piece and took an afternoon shower to restart the day, with a new purpose. She wore an outfit that immediately made her feel happy, sexy, and ready for a walk. She looked lovely in stretch pants, jogging shoes, and an oversized hoodie. Her favorite smoothie place was a short 3 blocks away and she loaded up on fruit and real sugar. When they asked her if she wanted an energy boost shot, she said "no," and ordered extra vitamin C for a change. It was late afternoon and she decided to check in with Jack and her text read, "Hoping you're having a great day," with extra emojis.

He was delighted to hear from her and quickly replied, "Work is going well with a few new excitements from the genius crew. I know it's your day off. Did you want to rest or maybe go out for dinner?" replied Jack. "I'm gonna stay in tonight, but I'd be happy to make you dinner at my place," with three red lip emojis. "Just let me know what I can bring and when to arrive," replied Jack. "White wine and any time after 7pm," she replied. She entered the kitchen and assembled the fixings for a Thai chicken dish with her special pad Thai stir fry. She seasoned and soaked the food for a couple of hours and managed a lovely 45 minute nap to carry her into the 6 o'clock hour. A quick second shower with extra bath moisturizer and scents. She wore a flowing skirt with a southwest Asian pattern, a bare tummy section, a sheer buttonless blouse, lovely jewelry accents around her neck, and earrings. Her hair was pulled back to get through the kitchen duties, and soon her place smelled of lovely chicken and vegetable stir fry. At seven, there was a light knock on the door, and Jack entered the "lobby." She greeted him with a kiss. She had a Cat Stevens playlist working and made the rounds to light several candles. Jack poured the wine, and their eyes met as he handed her a glass. "I'm so lucky to have you in my life," he whispered. "After your text, I couldn't wait for the day to end and the chance to come see you."

Ava smiled and said, "I'm glad you're here too. I've been kinda busy with silly work items and finally had a day to myself and wanted to share my time with you. I also wanted to catch up with you after your trip and time with the family."

"That might take another bottle of wine," Jack commented. "The short answer is that I need to spend more time with Robbie and get closer to some local therapies he is going through in the East Bay."

"If you're stepping in, it must be serious, and I hope you can help him."

"Robbie and I have had the intense bond of twinship, with a sibling relationship where love and kindness have always taken the front seat. However, a new twist of chaos may require a bit more sacrifice in time or schedule."

"Is there anything I can do to help?" asked Ava.

"I just need you to be aware, and I will keep you posted. For now, let's enjoy your lovely meal.

Tonight, Ava kept her health to herself and focused on Robbie. Her dinners were restaurant-class delicious with a progressive romance after every course. This night ended with a steam shower for Jack and the start of a neck massage. Ava was behind him, pressed her naked body into his back, and made sure his senses were excited from her nipples down to her vagina. She moved her fingers up into his scalp and massaged tiny circles of pleasure. He could only take so much and turned around to pull her down into the sheets. He returned the favor, and with her encouragement and tight hand squeezing, he spent extra time "Down at The Y." After her orgasm, she rolled Jack over to his back and began touching and kissing him starting from his legs and working up. As her tiny stomach slid across his, she started a sensual grind until he was inside her. She was warm and wet. She knew his timing, and just before his release, she twisted her back and rhythmically squeezed her pelvis to make him explode inside her.

Jack was up early and quietly down to the kitchen for some coffee. The sunlight beamed into her warehouse as if to guide the path to a new day. He quickly sipped his first cup and wrote Ava a love note before sneaking off to work. She slept in a bit longer and smiled after reading his note, "Please know that as I spend more time with my family, I want you to be a part of me."

CHAPTER
THIRTY-TWO
SAINT NEWCO

THE INITIAL NEWCO plan had the right intentions and targeted a medical breakthrough. Jack's first draft was in outline form and needed several gap fillers. He completed several group calls with the Saints to pull in their expertise. Most of the questions were not in the public domain, research, or practice. Some of Jack's queries dealt with chemistry, genetics, artificial intelligence, enormous databases, combined with a complex convergence path that required fast computers and even faster algorithms to support the platform. As he outlined the four key phases, the business names also transitioned from Newco to Saint Newco, into the first company name Seres, and then the code name for the exchange would be Herman (after Jack's first childhood cat).

~

Phase 1: Discovery

Seres celebrated its first year with, of course, a boat ride on San Francisco Bay. The team met at Pier 50 at 5pm and went to a charter boat named "Abundantia." By 5:30, everyone was accounted for and time to leave port. It was a perfect evening with very little wind and a clear sky. The yacht was gorgeous and would make a few passes around the bay with amazing shoreline views. A PA announcement came over: "please make your way to the main deck where we have a lovely buffet and short announcement."

"I'm so glad we are all together tonight to celebrate another major milestone," announced Jack. "As you all know, our company has the horsepower and brain trust to change the world. We have told our investors that our first stage would be about deep discovery, sharing of brilliant ideas, and the thesis that keeping our minds open to new, even unheard of approaches, would be acceptable. Throughout this past year, we have studied our brains, stretched the envelopes of reason, poked at new, elaborate theories of blockchain storage, genome sequencing, artificial intelligence probing, and survived a pandemic. We have started the early building blocks for our solution and tonight we introduce the Human Capital Exchange Platform, or codename Herman. and identified several partners who will help accelerate our progress. We will roll out our vision map on Monday and begin the product realization journey. Let us relish in our achievements and recharge our batteries to bring together a platform like no other that influences, improves, and empowers everyday people." Jack raised his glass to a crowd of smiles and elated team members. Robbie was one of his guests and played it rather cool around work folks. In almost every case, it was someone else directing questions towards him. He knew crazy math and data science and could converse with leadership and ease. But tonight, he also had a new piece of information to share with only Jack.

As the sunset on the bay, the boat made its way back to port. It was a mid-week celebration and time to draw things to a close. Jack and Robbie were last off the yacht and watched as almost everyone either Uber'd or took public transportation. The boys walked back towards town and could see Chase Center in the distance. "We might take in a

Warriors game this season," commented Jack. "We get a block of tickets at Eagle and maybe we can take in a Lakers or Suns game."

"I'd like that a lot," said Robbie. Let's shoot around and watch Steph light up some long 3's." They managed another 20 or 30 feet, and Robbie said, "I know we both managed through Covid with only minor symptoms after testing positive, but there is something you should know. In rare cases, Covid can trigger a disease known as AGS or Aicardi-Goutieres Syndrome, affecting the brain, spinal cord, and immune system. It is a genetic disease that targets young kids from birth to young adulthood. There are few onset cases for people in their mid-late twenties and I'm still learning about all the details. I've recently started an arthritis medication which shows promise in slowing the disease. Sorry to bring this to you now."

"I'm sorry about all this news and don't worry about timing,' said Jack. "I wanna help in any way I can. I guess I should get a blood test started too." Jack's mind suddenly raced with questions about family history, genetics, and twins. He wanted to quickly run tests and perform as many diagnostics as possible to resolve this issue. He also knew this was not just another problem to solve, rather it was Robbie, and his life now had a limited expectancy associated with it. He chose his words carefully and spoke, "I'm guessing you have had some time to process this news, but I want to get in front of this bastard and conquer it. No fricking AGS is gonna tear into our family." They headed to the closest bar and dropped a few Manhattans. Jack called the driver from Eagle to pick them up and a black Escalade gave them door-to-door service across the bay to Berkeley. Robbie shared with Jack that he was commuting to the UC Campus for work and health issues and got a small apartment. It was the college life he never fully experienced and now he appreciated the folks in his corner and now he had Jack's support too. It was nearly 11pm when he got dropped off and then Jack had the driver circle back to his condo. This was an eventful day to say the least. As Jack rested in bed, he told himself again, "there is no room for disease in my house."

Jack woke up early on Friday and was at work by 7am. Until now, the team had worked at an aggressive pass for research, but now it was time for development and execution. He was filled with piss and vinegar and wanted to review his assumptions, take a second look at the vision map, and then tighten up just about everything. It was double-time. He and Robbie were 26 years old.

Phase 2: A Better Exchange Platform

Cryptocurrencies have run their course in both the financial and technical market. Players were reaping the benefits of the exchange. Folks like Coinbase and Binance are constantly battling with the SEC around regulation to be considered a formal currency. Another exchange run by FTX went bankrupt, losing over $8m in customer funds, and over 100 debtors filing for the loss. In their case, they leveraged their future by buying failed companies, falsifying bank records and eventually becoming victims of class-action lawsuits by their investors. Coinbase's market capitalization is over $18b and Binance is nearly double at $36b. Regardless of whether these players ever get SEC approvals, they have created a market for currency exchange and active with contracts, currency exchange and a marketplace for NFT (non-fungible tokens).

The NASDAQ reported that the key technical contributors to the cryptocurrency business would be such players at IBM, Intel and nVidia. Jack knew several folks at these firms and remembered when nVidia was so small they had wine and cheese parties on Friday with Jensen Huang. Run a bit like a startup. The early days of graphics chips were filled with techies trying to solve basic graphic accelerations issues and making PCs seem more like video consoles. Years later, the graphics processor units (GPUs) chips became the underlying compute chip for advanced algorithms that solved issues in artificial intelligence and applications such as autonomous driving cars and crypto mining machines.

What Herman needed was at the core of crypto using the underlying blockchain methods to help store massive genome data. The distributed ledger technology was ideal for accuracy, scalability, and portability.

If the human genome has over 3 billion base pairs amounting to over 1.5 GB of data. Compare this to a piece of plastic with 16 unique digits, called a credit card. The first six digits categorize AMEX, Visa, MasterCard, and Discover. The next 5 digits are also allocated to AMEX, Visa, and MasterCard. There is also the CVV (card verification value) and security chip (for encryption) protection. We use these devices every day for purchases from $1 to over $10,000. Or, if you have established wealth over $1 million, you can get an AMEX Black card with no credit limit. And with this comes added responsibility and security which is not the purpose of this brief comparison. One of the challenges with Seres is finding or creating an exchange methodology that will support very large data sets, likely using blockchains SHA-256 hashing algorithms. Jack's instinct was that blockchain was more than capable and in his mind, he was setting up a 3 or 4 dimensional model with 1 dimension now understood. They would need to develop a new platform that would initially become a default exchange. A bit like Tesla charging stations to be sure the common person could enjoy travel vs the elitist who monitored their electric charges between each exotic trip destination. Early Model S drivers would make comments such as, "I wonder if there is a supercharger near our cabin in Tahoe, or there must be a Tesla-like AM/PM to support a quick cocktail or massage for the long drive." Seres would spend extensive hours ensuring they could satisfy their network of users for exchange.

Phase 3: MVP

Here is where the non-Tesla rubber meets the road. Defining a mean viable product (MVP) is crucial and Jack knew the team would both question and support whatever vision he prepared for this next phase. They were defining a unique language written with roots from financial, biological, and point-of-care inferences. Saint Newco had the ultimate challenge of converging massive elements of science, secure transactions from finance, and common man principles for a point-of-care service model. He needed to carefully turn his scientists from their love of data mining and analytics, to converged algorithms that can support the query of the current state (Anonymous 1, with issue), mixed with new variables (Anonymous N, solution set), and final state (Anonymous 1, no issue). Jack knew he was suggesting what sounded like "a cure," and he wanted to be careful how he worded the next set of MVP items. Clearly, their solution would include data center-like compute servers addressing a dynamic database of genome data as a baseline. Call this the data layer. Then, the fuel to make their engine run was to create an incredibly complex solution set which included a mix of known pathogens, harmful genetic markers (current and historic), and an iterative, predictive intelligence algorithm that ran trillions of compute cycles to analyze, suggest new genetic strings via modified CRISPR editing, and then run a lifecycle analysis. The MVP would determine the sickness, define the cure, generate the medicine, and then test it for future years.

Stage 4: GTM

The MVP will prove many parts of the system and verify Herman as a platform. The system consists of the backend processing functions (human capital database, advanced models, and AI diagnostics) and the portable application version for a smartphone. Beyond the challenges of analytical complexity, there was also the need to incorporate a trusted commerce layer, and the exchange map application (or the map app). The Seres transaction platform would be the first of its kind allowing basic elements of the human genome sequence or biological markers to be shared to interact and in some cases remove genetic, neurological, and/or psychological disorders.

The business plan had a chapter and verse on every business

portion. Jack was meticulous as an entrepreneur and as a board member. Saint Newco's plan of record had 1-2 years of development, a year of "trials," and revenues starting in the third year. A domestic launch would keep a few problems bound, although there was a strong interest in Canada and the UK - mostly for the ability to move around the FDA and HIPPA or Department of Health. Finally, the sheer amount of software development meant hiring a small army of talented coders and keeping them focused on a world-changing experience. The demand for AI/ML projects funded mostly from autonomous driving vehicle startups was daunting. However, the lure for Seres would be different. Jack would secure enough funding to pay his team handsomely and to make the experience of building the next medical miracle on a grand scale as only a handful of breakthrough drugs have ever achieved.

CHAPTER
THIRTY-THREE

JACK & AVA

JACK AND AVA had enormous attraction toward each other, and it was hard to find any fault in their love. For Jack, he was drawn to her from the start of their brief encounters at the B&W Bar. Her physical presence certainly struck him, but there was so much more as she became his lover and confidant. For Ava, she was not in the market for a partner when they met, and this made their magnetism even more attractive. She knew he was a class act when they met, but there was so much more to enjoy, and each new encounter brought more layers to their bonding.

There were also things not in common, like the obvious that Jack was not a native American Indian or that Ava was not very Canadian. However, they were a very cute couple, and the ancestral mix might just be fun. She was a runner, a dancer, and an artist. Jack was also a runner, an artist, and would always enjoy watching or sharing a dance with Ava.

Jack knew that his mind was a gift that included advanced memory functions, a constant curiosity to learn, and humbleness to know when a challenge is to be left a mystery. At times, organized chaos meant progress and chasing multidimensional complexities was better viewed from both sides now, like cloud illusions.

Ava looked at life with a unique and heavenly perspective. She embraced her days from the outside in and with cloud-like points of view. If you happened to catch her looking upwards, it was to smile as if to say thank you. When she visited Jack at Eagle Investments, she would often walk to the glass windows of his high-rise office and while so many people would look down upon San Francisco's landmarks, Ava would look up as if to be closer to the heavens. She said her trip around the world was getting closer every year as the rocketmen aka Jeff Bezos and Elon Musk were pushing for flights to occur every week in the near future.

"I can't imagine you in an astronaut suit," said Jack.

"Why not? I can handle a jumpsuit," she replied.

"I'm not worried about how good you will look. I'm just not ready for you to strap on to a rocket engine to blast off into space."

"I won't go until it is incredibly safe and has a 100% return rate," she smiled.

Jack ensured his life included time and closeness with the Saints to round out his universe. Robbie was a given as they chatted, DM's or spoke almost every day or two. As for the other five, this was a bit more of a challenge to gather the group. They maintained a few visit rituals including birthdays, graduations, and other significant events.

PART SIX

CHAPTER
THIRTY-FOUR
ROMANTIC WEEKEND

WHEN JACK WAS GROWING UP, his family often toured the islands off the coast of Seattle. The tourist magazines knew it as Puget Sound, San Juan and Victoria Islands, but locals knew the areas of interest for backcountry hikes, hidden lakes and majestic shorelines.

His parents often took the family on very exotic vacations, and they enjoyed the peace and serenity of the various secluded venues. Now, it was time for Jack to think of a special place for him and Ava. And for Ava, it had to be the best of the best. He did some research and found a list of the top romantic getaways in the Pacific Northwest. There was the Fairmont Olympic Hotel, the Four Seasons Hotel Seattle and the local favorites including the Hotel Bellwether and the Cave B Inn.

As he continued to read, he could not connect with any of the names or places and wondered if maybe the Seattle area was not quite right.

The next day while driving to work, he heard an advertisement for a land and sea cruise ship bundle that started in Los Angeles and ended in Seattle. The idea got him thinking about his romantic getaway and that he should mix it up. He remembered talking with Alex about his yacht excursions and how he often bragged that the best part of owning a fancy yacht was the exotic ports of call. Jack recalled a story from Alex about a special evening that included a lovely boat ride, an exquisite dinner, and a 5-star hotel stay. That was it. The plan started to unfold in his head, and he'd soon have the ideal getaway.

The rest of his workday was distracted while he pieced together several elements of the trip.

~

Later, he texted Ava for a chance to go out for dinner and she messaged him back two red lipstick emoji. Excellent, he thought and sent back the time and place. They met at a rooftop bar called El Techo in the Mission District, where they both liked the open air and the house tequila. Ava ordered a cranberry martini and Jack his favorite Cadillac margarita. They ordered "small plates", including sautéed meat, shrimp, and vegetables.

Ava was into her second bite when Jack spoke. "I have a great idea for a romantic weekend getaway for us."

"Really?" Ava responded, her eyes twinkling with childlike delight. A mischievous grin tugged at the corners of her mouth.

"I have an idea that brings our passions together for an unforgettable experience."

Ava's interest was clearly piqued. She leaned closer, her fingers tracing the rim of her glass. "Mmmm, I like this so far."

"I don't want to give away all the best parts, but it will include time on a yacht, eating at a 5-star restaurant and sleeping so close to the ocean that you can hear the waves as you sleep," said Jack.

Her grin broadened. "Mmmm, I'm listening."

"We leave from the San Francisco waterfront at noon on a Thursday. I'll help you with what to pack and we'll have a lovely stateroom with an enormous closet, huge bathroom, and amazing bed with a view of the ocean. We journey north and then enjoy the evening sunset in our room."

Ava frowned. "So when can I see the boat?"

Jack chuckled lightly. "There's more romance in keeping some parts as a surprise."

"Yes, and some of us want to see more details."

Jack hesitated. His desire to keep things a surprise clashed with Ava's curiosity. "Okay," he finally conceded, a resigned smile splitting his features. "Let me share some pics."

He pulled out his phone and flicked through images of the luxury yacht, walking through all the amenities. Jack walked her around the exterior, expansive decking, and what could easily be a ship for a large company party. It was certainly spacious. Then he moved to the interior with a bar and seating area on the main deck and then down the stairway to the lower deck, the Oceanview stateroom.

"Wait," she said. "Scroll back to the bed."

Jack had taken the pictures online and wished he had a video or more details for her. The room was gorgeous, with elegant details, and the large king bed accompanied it. This was not some fancy hotel room suite, rather a room designed for two to enjoy a glass of champagne, music, and time under the sheets. He only had two pictures of the bedroom, and they were enough for Ava to imagine what fun they could have with her as the centerpiece.

"I think we should go soon," she said.

Jack stepped out to call immediately. He returned with dates for travel just three weeks out.

The coming weeks were mostly filler at work compared to the excitement of their upcoming weekend excursion. Afterwork, Jack spent a few extra hours at the gym working on abs and biceps. He had an athletic body and it responded well to the tune-up. A good look for him was an unbuttoned beach shirt with a view of his 6-pack and V-shaped torso. Since his days of competition, he had sculpted an even better body in a model-like fashion. Robbie used to tease him and say, "it is your temple, and you need to worship it."

Ava's planning was slightly more focused on fashion as she needed a few items. She would make sure each day and every evening would be special. She wanted to show off new outfits, bikinis, and lingerie. Some candles, edibles, and vapes. Massage oil, shower lotion, and a few of her scented oils would turn him from mild to wild. Finally, she made a couple of playlists for different times. Ava knew how to care for Jack and the times after dinner were for her to take over the evening.

He Uber'd to her place late in the morning on the scheduled Thursday, and they headed to the marina. They each brought small roller suitcases and walked from the edge of the parking drop-off towards the end of the pier. The parking structure covered the port area, and they took in the view when they reached the end. It was amazing. The yacht looked like it went on forever and even the entry ramp was lovely. As they approached, their concierge greeted them by name and quickly had assistance to help with their luggage.

"We are delighted to have you on the Regent Nine. For the next few days, you will enjoy every inch of glorious, outfitted amenities and have private access. Our services will be behind the scenes per your request, and besides serving food around the clock, the entire ship is yours to enjoy as if it is yours."

Ava smiled and said, "This is even more beautiful than I imagined." She turned to Jack, said, "I want to see everything," and pulled him away. She circled the main deck and then up to the top where she could see across the San Francisco Bay. The furniture arrangements that constantly prioritized richness and comfort obscured the ship's controls. Even the upper deck felt like a luxury room.

"Wow, you can see the Golden Gate," Jack said.

"This is already my favorite trip ever!" said Ava. The ship was heading out of the port, directly towards the bridge, and to sea.

"Aye-aye captain," said Jack.

"Now, I know how you must feel."

"What do you mean?"

"I know how you must have loved being around boats growing up. I've been on a few outings and just felt like a passenger. Today, I feel like we are a part of a much bigger place. The ocean makes me feel free, and being with you makes me feel in love." It was the first time they had used the L-word.

"I know what you mean. There's a special feeling when the ocean surrounds you and this yacht makes it feel even nicer." Jack smiled. The love comment landed in his heart with warmth. "We have more to see, but I'm guessing you like this view." They glided under the bridge and headed to sea with a slow, gradual southern turn.

"Do you smell food," Jack asked.

"Mmmmm, yes," she said. "What's for lunch?"

They descended to the main galley and guided their way by the smell of cooking. Getting on the boat at noon meant some sort of early meal, but there was not a soul on board. They meandered around through a passageway and then to a dining area. There was a decorative buffet on the right and a table for two near the window. Fresh cut flowers on every surface. The smells were divine. The hot food was covered, and Ava removed the first lid.

"Oh my god, these are my favorite pot stickers."

Danial lifted the second lid and his lettuce-wrapped filet mignon cubes were still sizzling.

"This trip is gonna be fantastic," he said.

"Did you speak to someone before we came aboard—it seems like someone managed to get all of our favorites."

"And this is just lunch!" whispered Jack.

Their table looked out a large window towards the coastline. Music played from the Tony Rich Project, and somehow, they either had info from Jack's music or were incredibly lucky. Regardless, it was working. Jack looked at Ava as she moved her sexy heels to the music. He raised his champagne to hers and said, "I'm so lucky to be with you. I hope we have an amazing weekend getaway filled with loving unforgettable moments, delicious food and most importantly, time together. I love your smile, beautiful eyes, incredible body, and the magnetic spirit of Ava Lewis that I can never stop thinking about during the day in my dreams. This chance to be with you for a weekend is my new favorite!"

"Oh, thank you, Jack. I'm hoping this will be our best time ever too. Wait till you see me for dinner," Ava winked and softly chimed her glass to his. The white napkins touched her leg just beyond her skirt. It was a five-star beginning and lunch was officially complete.

"Can we see our room?" Ava asked.

"Oh, I think it's time to walk around and find the stateroom." Jack stood up, but Ava beat him and into her first stride to the exit. She was excited and watching her made Jack excited too. She acted like a guide, but only knew the direction was correct and had no idea how to find their room. They were on the lower level and made it to a lounge. It was as wide as the ship, with windows on the port and starboard.

Ava scanned the room and took in the artwork including paintings, sculptures and her favorite was a custom-made chair and table. As a struggling artist, she knew that somehow this piece made it to a superyacht, and she relished in the fact that she was going to rest her butt on the art.

She lowered herself in the chair and looked up at Jack. "I think I'll take this piece."

"Would you like the matching table?" Jack asked, and she smiled.

"Well, I'm here for the weekend. Let me think it over."

Jack thought she looked very natural in the artwork. Her naked arms rested on the piece and her legs crossed elegantly. He struggled to take his eyes off her but pulled himself to scan across the walls and see a well-hidden set of double doors. There were few instructions when he made the reservations, but there was one clear message. It read: "In the stateroom lounge, a mural of the SF evening skyline will be stretched over eight feet wide. The key to your room is located near the bottom right side of the Golden Gate Bridge. He felt his way across the mural area and found just enough of a button edge to push. It recessed slightly, then a click sounded.

The walls opened, and a massive room appeared, making Ava leap up from her chair.

"This is magical" she said.

Jack grinned. "The party starts now!"

∿

As far as they could see, the room stretched far and wide. The yacht was likely 120 feet long and 30 feet wide. As they looked across the room, it was probably 70 x 30 or 2100 sq ft - it was time for them to enjoy their Presidential suite. There was a lovely small dining area for six, a fireplace, bar, assorted couches for lounging or loving, two large bathrooms with double showers, an oversized hot tub style bath, and the all-important super king size bed. There were matching bedside tables, and a small couch at the base of the bed. The bed was centered at the far end of the room with soft and wide couches under the windows on each side of the suite.

Ava walked across the room and gracefully flopped her sexy body diagonally across the bed. She looked at the ornate ceiling with its gorgeous wood, mirrors, and tile. "I want to stay here forever."

As Jack walked along the sides of the room and enjoyed the views, he looked back to his love and said, "We only have it through Sunday, but I'm sure we can extend a few days or weeks," in his raw humor. "I'm really glad you like it. I love it too." He played with the soft switches on the wall to reveal lights, window shades and a hidden TV. He found the on right keys to scroll through the movie selections. The room had the latest films, and some of the content was still in theaters. "Not that it's important, but we do happen to have some nice movies in our room."

"Oh, that might be fun after dark. We can have the movies on the wall and the ocean in the window. I like my movies with champagne and strawberries," said Ava.

"I like your style," he said. "We should change into comfy clothes and take a quick nap."

"I'd love that," she said, wandering into the large bathroom. "Wow, I'm gonna get really used to this style." She looked around the double shower, hot tub bath, dual sink, and wall-to-wall mirrors and inside the closet with all the linens and then walked back out to her suitcase. She opened it, grabbed her toiletries and a cami, and returned to the bathroom. After a few quick clothing changes and a brush through her hair, she went to the walkway to ask, "Are you ready for some spoon time?"

"Gimme a minute." Jack got his act together with a quick freshen-up.

He joined Ava in bed and got to his favorite position with her body perfectly touching him from chest to toe. She gently backed into him and reached her arm backwards to pull his butt to her. Their legs interlocked and their sexy nap began. It was mid-afternoon with full sunshine, until Ava reached the bedside controls and lowered the window shades and the room softly darkened. They enjoyed their cave-like den and drifted off. When Jack awoke, Ava's hand rubbing was gently getting him excited. Before he knew it, she rolled over and mounted him with a soft and rhythmic grinding. He reached out his arms to cup her breasts and lifted his hips in sync with hers.

Their lovemaking was always mutually exciting, and Ava always knew the best timing. When his thrusting became more exciting, she interlocked their hands and spread their arms, bringing her face to his neck. She kissed him, murmuring gentle whispers. They both began moaning as he released with several strong thrusts. Ava collapsed into him and rested on his chest. Their bodies stayed connected for a while with a risk that Jack might head back to sleep.

Ava tapped his shoulders gently. "Hey, you, are you sleeping again?"

"No, love. Just resting."

"Ok," she said. "Maybe we should get some nutrition soon. Are you hungry or maybe thirsty?"

"Yes, to both," he said. "Let me check on where we should go." Jack pressed his favorite wall display and found the boat schedule. It was 4:30pm, and the boat was heading into Monterey Bay in the next hour. They would have the option for dinner on the ship, to head to shore, or both. Jack pressed the destination button, and a tourist menu for Monterey showed the aquarium, scuba diving, a 17-mile drive in Pebble Beach, and dinner spots along Cannery Row. He scrolled through several, then back to the top menu, and pressed the "On-Board Evening" button.

⌣

There was a full menu with almost everything imaginable. He named dropped Ava, "We have several options for this evening including an adventurous trip to shore and the Monterey Bay amenities, or we can stay on the ship surrounded by fine wine and dining with an amazing menu. You can ask for almost anything and the chef will prepare it for you including fish, beef, lamb, port, chicken and in just about any style —Cajun, French, Indian, Italian, Mediterranean, or Asian fusion."

Ava had brought a few special outfits for dinner and was excited to dress up. She didn't care whether they went out or stayed in, as long as she could show off to Jack.

"I'm torn. I want to explore the shore, but I like our yacht," she said. "Maybe we will stay here tonight and explore more on Saturday?"

"I agree," he said. "Tomorrow, we dock where there is a bit more nightlife and in SoCal. Let's plan to stay here and enjoy our private escape. I'll let the kitchen know we will be dining here."

They both opened their suitcases and put their belongings in the walk-in closet. For this weekend, they each brought special, new outfits to show off including clothes, jewelry, and Ava brought some candles, lotions, and scents for the bathroom.

"May I use the bathroom to get ready?" she asked.

"Of course, it's all yours." Jack made his way to the second bathroom and started his shower.

After a light shave and freshening up, he put on a dark blue suit with shirt and cufflinks. His cufflink collection was large, and he brought over a dozen on the trip. Most were gold or silver with a few having stones or diamonds. Tonight, he wore his favorite lapis stones in a silver setting. They were just ornate enough to make his shirt stand out perfect for dinner. Jack returned to the bathroom to touch up his face, hair, and one last glance with his suit coat. He looked sharp and ready for an evening out with a beautiful woman.

Ava zipped through her shower, shaving, and into her lace underwear quickly. The bathroom was spacious and made her feel like a queen. She was delighted that it would be hers to enjoy for the entire weekend and thought about sharing a shower or hot tub with Jack. It was a double shower arrangement with glass doors facing the room filled with mirrors. There was a long counter with dual sinks and a separate seating area with lighted mirrors and setup for hair and makeup.

She knew Jack had often seen her in black and white, so she would introduce him to burgundy and gray lace this evening. Her cocktail dress had gold spaghetti straps in front and an open back. The dress was thigh-high, and stockings was unnecessary with her golden skin. Her panties were see-through silver and matched her stiletto heels. She hoped the evening would end with her showing herself off in only heels and panties. Her long hair looked amazing flowing down her side. She opened the door and walked towards Jack.

"Hope you like this outfit. The color reminds me of all the creepy science projects you do with blood and guts." She smiled.

"You look much better than anything in science," he replied. She looked delicious, and Jack knew this woman was for keeps. He looked her up and down to ensure he took it all in and said, "I hope you will join me for a lovely dinner on our yacht."

"I'm all yours, and yes, I'd love to join you." Ava reached out to his arm, and they made their way across the room, through the secret doors and eventually to the main deck where they met the ship's captain.

Speaking with authority, the captain said, "I'm glad you will join us this evening. We have your table ready Mr. Mohr and Ms. Lewis." The dining area had been rearranged to host them with fire and ice roses, candles, and an open-air view (in one direction) to Monterey Bay.

Jack seated Ava and simultaneously a bottle of champagne arrived at their table. He described a few dishes that he recommended to Ava, and she nodded with a smile.

"How do you know what's on the menu," she said.

"I may have called ahead last week with some of our favorites." He grinned and raised his champagne glass. "Here's to us and a romantic weekend for two."

Focusing her gaze on him, Ava said, "I'm already having a wonderful time and know the next couple days will be filled with a lovely time with you." Their glasses touched and the evening was off to a sparkling start.

~

As promised, the food was exquisite, the presentation amazing, and the flavors ere out of this world. After dinner, Ava asked to take in the view up top. They looked across the night sky and the lights across the bay and knew they were in the most beautiful place in the world. The air was crisp, and the temperature was just starting to dip. Ava reached out to Jack's hand and guided him down as they returned to their amazing stateroom for the night.

She turned her head around while walking and whispered, "I hope you left some room for dessert?"

"I can always have more."

"I know you have a sweet tooth and like your sugar. This time, I'm your treat."

The sunshine carefully peaked into their room through the shade in the morning. Jack woke first, stood up from the bed, and approached the main galley. There were three papers for him to read, including the Wall Street Journal, the Los Angeles Times, and the San Francisco Chronicle. He grabbed one of each and a coffee. He sat and read his papers as the yacht continued southbound.

As he flipped through the paper, he read about worldly events, sports scores, new technologies, food, and recipes. These were all his favorite things. He read about a new Range Rover with new hybrid/electric technologies allowing for 51 mpg. Jack has his Lexus electric prototype and knew he would never return to a pure gas car and always liked the idea of a large SUV with good gas mileage. He snapped a photo of the article and returned to reading through the three papers. He raised his coffee cup in his left hand and two-fingers from his right hand and gestured to get coffee. He could not return empty-handed on this day.

Ava was rolling over in the sheets when he arrived. "How 'bout some coffee, love?" he said.

"Yes, perfect. I'm still debating on whether to get out of bed."

"Let me open the shade a bit for you and you'll enjoy the coastline." Jack walked her coffee to her bedside and then raised the shades to allow a beautiful view of the west coastline.

"Where are we going?" she asked.

"Somewhere between Santa Barbara, Los Angeles, and Long Beach. I think it depends on how much motor versus drift time. Santa Catalina is also one of our ports of call. After breakfast, we can speak with the captain and guide him on the route."

Ava knew Los Angeles from her days at USC, yet this reference to LA was nothing like her past. She knew this experience was letting her into the club where big money did make a difference in everyday life. Although Jack never let on much about his wealth, she had been with him long enough to know that although he wasn't a money-first type, he was destined to receive great rewards.

She said, "I like the idea of Santa Catalina Island or Long Beach."

"We can also do both if you like," he replied. "Let's plan to go to the beach on Santa Catalina after lunch." He walked over to the wall screen and entered on the touchpad, Santa Catalina after lunch and Long Beach arrived for dinner on shore. The captain made arrangements, including a quadricycle pickup on the island and escort to their private beach. They were treated as if on a honeymoon with every amenity possible. Similar or better treatment for their trip to shore with limousine at their dock and trip to dinner in posh Orange County.

They each enjoyed being on land and the rush of the club scene, but by nine, Ava was ready to retire early and said to Jack, "I'm really having a great time here, but I also went to enjoy our last night on the boat." That was an easy ask and what she really meant was "our boat," as she became more used to having a yacht.

"I agree. Let's get back to our boat," he said. They Uber'd to the port and were back on the yacht in less than 30 minutes.

"Let's put on some more comfortable clothes," said Ava, walking quickly downstairs. This time, she knew the hidden button on the Golden Gate Bridge and was into her walk-in closet searching for her velvet sweats. She stripped down and then into her jamy-sweats before

Jack could kick off his shoes. "I want a hot fudge sundae and bottle of red wine."

"Let me order it for you," said Jack and he spoke into his wall tablet interface asking for dessert and some liquid delights.

Ava was already on the bed and in full relax mode. "Did you want to watch a movie before bed?"

"Mmmm, now you're talkin'," said Jack.

They surfed through the menu several times and settled in on a romcom with Jennifer Aniston. The eight-foot screen descended from the ceiling and the two love birds ate ice cream and lay as close together as possible. Ava lifted the shades to see the lights in the harbor as the evening drifted into night. They reminisced on the day and the fun from Santa Catalina white sandy beaches, cocktails, and dinner at Joeys in Fashion Island, as the film continued. They stayed in bed until Sunday morning, and Jack had breakfast in their lobby.

He opened the double doors and a silver cart with covered plates and hot coffee awaited. Under dish one was eggs Benedict, dish two had pancakes, and dish three was fruit and yogurt. There was upright toast, butter, jam, cream, and sugar cubes. Jack rolled the cart into their room and let the aroma drift over to her. He ran his hand up her leg, across her ass, and then rubbed small circles on her back.

When she awoke, Ava smiled, her eyes still closed. "You're so sweet," she said. "A girl can get used to eating breakfast in bed."

He grinned. "Please do. I'd love to serve you anytime."

"Do you remember our long weekend in San Diego at the Coronado?" she asked with a little yawn. You got us a cottage on the beach, and we barely left the room."

"Of course, that was a favorite trip."

Finally, she opened her eyes. "Yes, but this is now my new favorite."

"Mmmm, I agree," he said.

CHAPTER
THIRTY-FIVE
COWGIRL BARBECUE

IN ADDITION to her wonderful spirit and spontaneity, Ava knew just how to please and tease a man. Her moments with Jack were always filled with love and joy and there were the times they spent in bed that neither wished would ever end. Ava recalls a Thursday evening visit to Jacks that began with a catered dinner. Jack's apartment was a high rise in the Russian Hill district where one of his favorite BBQ places served the best-pulled pork in the city. His favorite appetizer was slow-cooked chicken in a peppercorn soup. On this night, he ordered enough food for four including pork, tri tip, soup, mash potatoes, cornbread, chili, roasted corn on the cob, sauces, salads, and fixings.

When Ava arrived, she took in all the BBQ aromas and said, "Mmmmm, what are all these wonderful smells? You must have been cooking all day…"

"Uh no, not really," said Jack sheepishly. "But I promise, you'll love it." He spread the food across the dinner table and Ava's eyes grew wider.

"Did you invite others for dinner too?" she said.

"No love, it is always best to get extra food to munch on it all through the night. Please try the pork and an ear of corn." He brought out a couple oversized napkins and some bibs. As he tied Ava's around her neck, he basked in the closeness. "These are for precaution as it can get pretty messy with either the ribs or the corn."

Ava filled her plate and sat down with a smile. "This is more food than I can eat, but it all looks yummy."

"Certain nights, like tonight, are for enjoying every bit and enjoying the delicious calories. The barbecued food tastes like it has been cooking for days and the meat is juicy and tender." Jack had beer on ice and a few bottles of wine to open. "What can I get you to drink?"

She glanced up at him, her eyes twinkling. "Do you have any tequila?"

"Of course." And Jack walked back to the kitchen for backup. He brought a bottle of Tito's and some margarita mix and raised both to Ava. "We can do some shots, or I can make you a drink."

"Let's do both."

Jack poured two shots and placed one in front of Ava. "To us and having you over for my favorite barbecue."

"To us having more time for barbecue and drinks." She lifted her glass to touch his and they both threw their first shot back to start the evening. Closing her eyes, Ava moaned. "Mmmm, that's good, but I'd love a margarita over ice from my favorite bartender."

Jack zipped back for ice and the blender, fixed her a strong "Cadillac" margarita, quickly hand-delivered one, and poured a second for himself. This was an evening off to a fantastic start and only getting better with time. Ava carefully cut the corn kernels off the cob into a neat pile. She added some chili sauce, stirred with a fork, and took her first bite. Jack was loading up his fork with pork and mash. With his free hand, he buttered some cornbread before dipping it in a chili bowl.

"Mmmmm, this is perfect. Did you want to try some cornbread too?"

"I'll try a bit with butter,"

Jack dressed up a small bite and reached toward her sexy lips. As she mouthed his fork, she looked into his eyes. "This is quite a meal, especially for two."

"I always feel more like an outdoorsman or cowboy when there's a barbecue. I imagine a big open fire burning after a long day in the saddle. Feeling hungry and tired and knowing you need evening calories to refill the body for the next day." In his case, an extra-long workout at the gym with added cardio to burn enough for barbecue and fixings. Jack was about as far from a cowboy as Costner and Dancing with Wolves. He didn't own a pair of boots and would probably choose an outlaw hat from Clint Eastwood over any Stetson off the rack.

But it didn't matter as Ava would later get him a few outfits to help him with his cowboy fantasies.

There was a very large selection of restaurants in San Francisco. You could probably go out for dinner every night for five years without going to the same spot twice. Jack and Ava never drew lines around date nights on the calendar, but they managed over half their evenings out for food, music, or entertainment. They knew most of the rooftop bars, a handful of 5-star clubs, a few speakeasies, and a few dive bars with darts and billiards.

One day while at work and grinding through new deal flow material, Jack received a text that read, "Did you wanna take in some barbecue and Yellowstone tonight?" It was from Ava and her timing was excellent.

He was already excited to see her and replied, "That sounds perfect!" with a few extra smiling emojis. "I'll get the food and met you at my place around 7."

"I'll bring drinks and some fun! See you tonight," she responded a few seconds later.

The rest of the day went quickly, and Jack ordered the food for pickup on his drive home. He showered and tidied up the place, a bachelor dust & vacuum drill, emptied the trash, set the table, and arranged a few candles. Adding Yellowstone to an already wonderful night was the best trigger ever. Jack put on a western shirt with snap buttons, classy stitching, and some dress shoes with an alligator-like pattern.

He was on a path to being a SF cowboy.

Ava arrived with a couple of bags and lifted the heavy one to the counter. "Here's a good substitute for tequila."

Jack pulled out the whisky bottles including Makers 46 and 12-year-old Whistle Pig. "I see you brought your bourbons with you," he said, raising an eyebrow.

"I swear after every one of their fights," she pointed to the TV, where Kevin Costner's John Dutton was arguing with one of his TV sons, "they consume more whiskey than water."

Jack cast a grin at her. "It takes away all their pain from riding in a tough saddle all day."

"I want you to make me one of your signature Manhattans," she said.

"Let me get right on it." He returned to the refrigerator freezer, pulled out a couple of large ice contraptions, and walked to the sink. He ran water over the plastic molding and then pulled the halves open. Out popped a large round ice ball barely fitting into the cocktail glass. He walked over to the bar and put on a little show making up two Manhattans.

"Here you go." He handed her the first drink.

Ava sniffed the top and the aromas were powerful. It was definitely prairie-strong alcohol, and she took her first sip. "Mmmmmm, that's nice."

Jack lifted his drink to hers with a quick glass chime bump and then a large sip. He thought about the shift from Tequila (for Ava) to Bourbon (for himself) during cowboy night and smiled. They went about their meal and managed to try every portion across the table.

"How is it that you order so much food when we eat barbecue?" she said.

"I think it's part of the ambiance. I picture a feast is necessary for the crew to refill their bellies, get a good night's sleep, and to prepare for another day's ride."

She threw her head back and laughed, the sound warming Jack. "So, you're worried about us going on a trail ride tomorrow?"

"That would be great if we could find some horses."

"How about we watch some cowboy TV in bed," she said while carrying her dish to the kitchen. Jack brought a few dishes to the sink and then joined her in the bedroom, where he set up the show and started the episode while she used the bathroom.

"Okay to start the show?" he called out to her.

"Yes, I'll be right there!"

When she opened the door a few minutes later, Jack turned to the most beautiful sight. Ava was naked except for silk-lined, leather chaps. She stretched her long arm along the doorway, lifted one of her legs to a small bend, and then twisted her hips like she was on her stripper pole. His mouth went dry as he dragged his gaze over her.

"Well, Jack," she murmured, "I know you've had a long, hard day, but maybe I can relax some of your muscles." Slowly, she spun around for him, revealing her ass with chap straps between her cheeks.

As she walked over to the bed, Jack could hardly contain himself. She leaned in to give him a light kiss on the neck as her body and sexy chaps rubbed across him. She mounted him and said she would help him with his "snaps," and managed to remove all his clothing. Ava gave him a light massage and carefully worked herself from his shoulders to his toes. As he became aroused, she shifted into her cowgirl position and started her grind. She looked back at his face, and her mouth curved upward when she saw he was extremely pleased.

Reaching her hand back to his stomach, she increased her motion.

This was the mutually enjoyable position with fast timing required for Ava. Jack would try to outlast her, but it was impossible. She would arch her back and make cowgirl pleasure references to keep him on edge. Then she said she needed her stud to ride her, and she became more rhythmic, rubbing her lovely ass cheeks across his crotch with stronger and stronger motion. J ack would match her thrusting and listen to her voice as she climaxed. He could feel her release and her juices made him cum. Ava leaned back with her hands carefully holding him as he pulled out. She turned into him, her tummy pressing into his chest and her breasts touching his face.

Reluctantly, he pulled himself away from Ava and asked for her drink choice. He came back with two refreshed Manhattans and said, "Keep relaxing. You're gonna spend the night."

She reached out to her glass, swirled her fingertip around the contents and the ice cube ball, and then adjusted herself into her pillow, snuggled against him upright to take in some cowboys.

CHAPTER
THIRTY-SIX
FIELD TRIPPIN

JACK WONDERED if he might take the chance to bring one of the Saints down to visit him in San Francisco. He contacted the whole team with a group email and addressed the mail to Robbie, Joseph, Paul, Michael, and Luke. Within a few hours, he got a response from Joseph with the news. Robbie was sick. The email was vague but suggested that if anyone should be part of the invite, it should be Robbie and yet, this would be a heavy lift given the circumstances. Jack read the email and was sad he had not contacted the team more often. He took the surprise with mixed emotions. He knew they would understand his reply no matter how it read, but Jack wanted to be sincere.

He wrote back by starting with "my apologies," and tried to put in writing a way to express his neglect to the group. He mentioned his busy schedule and dedication to work, but the words did not justify his actions. After sending the note, he was ready to buy a plane ticket to Seattle and thought it was a token to such a group of intellects. This was a gut check, and he knew the right thing to do - he bought his ticket for the following day.

Jack arrived at SEA airport and grabbed an Uber to downtown. His -up email invited everyone to join him for lunch at the Palisade

Restaurant on Elliot Bay. He got a table with a view of the harbor. It was a lovely sunny day with light breeze. The boat slips were full. Jack scanned the name plates and grinned remembering his many favorites and the crazy connections between boat captain and their boat name. He had arrived a bit early at 11:30 a.m., and the lunch visit was for noon.

At exactly noon, Joseph, Paul, and Luke arrived together. The two youngsters followed Joseph by a few steps and walked towards Jack. He stood up quickly to greet them and hugged each before they sat down. Michael arrived a few minutes later and smiled as he approached the group.

"Sorry, I'm late," he said to the understanding crowd.

"No problem," replied Jack. "It is wonderful to see everyone again."

"Everyone except Robbie," Michael reminded them.

"Yes, I wish Robbie was here too," replied Jack.

"Maybe he can come next time," Paul remarked. He was the youngest and his thoughts were very well-intentioned.

Jack had planned the restaurant, the table, and even a starting speech to somehow address his feelings about Robbie's situation to the others. He started by reminding them of his great appreciation and love for each of them and how he felt their presence in him every day in San Francisco. He spoke about his efforts in medical research and hopes to make a difference, saying that any challenges he faced were always less significant than the hopes of one day impacting the world. Jack told the story of finding a new invention (aka Herman) and working to solve some amazing problems in science. As always, the team was captivated by his speaking and enjoyed every word from his mouth. Towards the end, he apologized for not staying close to them and reaching out with bad timing to find out the news about Robbie.

"That's ok, we understand," said Joseph from the voice of reason.

"No, I need to tell you that I am really sorry and hope there is some way to show you all that I messed up."

"We only found out recently about Robbie and you would not have had any warning. Please don't worry about us; we know you care for each of us, and we do you. We were delighted that you invited us all down to see you in San Francisco someday," said Joseph.

The words came heavy into Jack's heart as he knew there was much more to say, yet the team knew the situation was more significant than small lunchtime talk.

After lunch, Jack asked if they would like to walk on the pier. It was a short walk as Jack and Michael led the way. Elliot Bay was small enough to see across all sides with a channel leading out to the Sound. As the group walked, some questionable words about the adventure began to emerge. Although there was immense trust in any pathway along which they would follow Jack, their intellectual curiosity got the better of them. Finally, Paul said, "We wanted to thank you for the delicious lunch and amazing venue. Our stomachs are filled with extravagant blends of food and spirits. Our time with you is as valuable as time itself and we all want you to know how much we appreciate your visit."

"It is my pleasure to spend time with all of you and never let time or distance be our enemy," replied Jack. "I welcome this visit as we share common ground across all we do as individuals, and together there is even more powerful energy and love. Our walk has nearly ended, but I have a favor to ask."

They approached the end of the pier to find what looked like a fairly large party boat. Jack waved to the captain and exchanged words before turning around to the group.

"Gentleman, I hope you will join me on a small trip to see Robbie."

There was a unanimous set of smiles and young Luke spoke, "are we really going to see Robbie on the boat?"

"We all love the water and I wanted to bring us all together surrounded by friends and shorelines. Let's get on the boat and I'll share more in a few minutes. And yes, Luke, we will speak with Robbie shortly." replied Jack."

They boarded the boat and looked around with curiosity. Of course, it was chartered by Jack and looked amazing. The boat looked over 40 feet long with a lounge area for many more. There was a U-shaped seating area that quickly became the resting spots for the saints. Jack appeared from the lower cabin with a bottle of champagne and Martinelli's sparkling cider. He placed them on the center console with glasses and an ice bucket. He was the host with the most and a treat to be with tonight. As the boat purred from the dock, the team grabbed their glasses of sparkling juice and glanced at the midday sky.

Jack raised his glass and announced, "I want to thank you all for joining me and the chance to be together. After receiving your email about Robbie, I quickly investigated his care. As you may know, he has been seeing several specialists to determine the right course of action for his therapy. His diagnosis remains questionable regarding the right path to a cure; all we know is that his situation is complex. We are all intellectuals, optimists, and have more combined love for Robbie than any other resource. I want you to know my commitment to you is that we will have the best doctors and nurses in Robbie's corner as we get through this period. For over 25 years, he has been my best friend, my brother and means more to me than anything. The reason this event looks like a celebration is only half my idea.

Last week I called Robbie to learn more about his situation. I spent several hours discussing literally "everything" and when we were nearly complete, he asked me to meet with the group and share time surrounded by a beautiful setting, yummy food and the peace of the saltwater. He specifically asked that we dine in a classy place followed by a boat ride on the bay, bringing me to this finale." Jack reached into his pocket, pulled out a card, and read from Robbie's voice, "As you all know, I am not feeling well. In my recovery, some days are better than others as we experiment with chemicals, pharmaceuticals, and radiation. I have a rare disease known as AGS, which is inoperable and terminal. The doctors are analyzing my blood for how it responds similar to other autoimmune disease traits as this might explain some of the symptoms. Rest assured, there is hope and although it seems like I am heading for a perfect storm, it may be smooth sailing. As you drift on Robbie Bay, my beloved gang of true friends and enduring brother, let us hope or plan for a day together again on the beach with our feet in the warm sand and our hearts intertwined."

Jack handed the card to Michael to pass along the benches. Each took in the note. They returned their empty glasses to the center individually, and the afternoon had ended. Jack swirled his fingers to the captain to return to the pier. The mechanical wench rattled the anchor up to its base and the engines started their gentle roar. The boat circled slowly showing off the coastline and then centered on the point to return. When they disembarked, they watched as the boat pulled away and as the boat left the pier, Michael shouted to the team, "Hey look at the boat name!" The saints turned to see "Love is the Answer" on the nameplate. The pier walk was slower this time as the mood had shifted. Ahead of them were 3 limousines with drivers at their respective doors. Jack spoke, "I cannot say enough how much you all mean to me and Robbie. Please get home safe." Each saint agreed and as they greeted the drivers, each spoke to their respective saint for a direct ride home. Inside, each limo had an elegantly wrapped box for each saint. Michael and Luke shared a limo and Luke said, "This feels like Robbie's doing. I wonder what else could be added to this day?" Then Michael added, "I'm not sure I can open any more of my emotional boxes today."

Jack spent the night in a hotel in the Seattle area. Getting through today was rather easy compared to the coming days, and getting some rest was good. Jack needed a break, which meant a lovely steak dinner and some wine, maybe a lot of red wine. He ordered a medium rare filet and a bottle of Silver Oak Cabernet Sauvignon. He recalled Robbie telling him to always cut his steak with a slow calculated style as if it were elements of a masterpiece with a knife and fork as his sculpting tools. A perfect steak was a delight to cut and even better to chew and swallow. Jack went about his craft with deliberate attention to detail, and with precision the filet mignon reduced bit by bit until the last morsel was consumed. At the end, he placed the utensils on the plate, pulled back his wine glass to drain the juice and closed his eyes for a moment. He reflected on the day and special moments with the boys. They were the good part of a family that one always adored. Their minds were always churning with information and curiosity. Their questions were sincere and often the answers were heartwarming. Jack recalled Simon's query on the boat when he asked, "Before we were born, we lived and grew in water for months. In our current cycle, we start breathing by swallowing fluid and continue until it is time to leave the womb. I wonder what would happen if we transferred the baby to a bigger womb and safely provided nutrients to grow? Couldn't we live underwater or at least be amphibious creatures?"

"You're jealous of Mr. Limpet?" Michael grinned.

"Of course not," said Simon. "I just wonder if we could live a longer or healthier life underwater. We know animals live longer in water than land, so why not add another dimension to our lives? If you compare a mature distance runner to an elderly swimmer, the one soaked in water will look years younger and stronger. We may explore medical advancements by combining technology, lifestyles and environments to save lives."

"Ah," said Michael, "Now we've come full circle. We all want to help Robbie however we can, and your idea is well received."

Jack retired to his room with half a bottle of wine. He turned on some brain-dead TV and had a chance to disconnect from life. Sleep came easy. In the morning he took a quick shower, packed his bag and into the lobby for oatmeal and coffee before walking to the rental car. He pulled up his phone and entered the address for Tom Mohr.

It was a short and enjoyable drive to Reston. He pulled up in the driveway and his father was on the porch to greet him.

"Hello Son," said Tom. "It's lovely to have you home - welcome."

"It's really nice to be here," replied Jack. "I was on Robbie Bay yesterday with the Saints and enjoyed every minute of this Pacific Northwest clean air."

"Good for you. The Bay is beautiful this time of year," said Tom. "Would you like some coffee?"

"Yes please," Jack said with a smile. "I'd love some strong java."

It had been over a year since Jack was home (for the holidays) and they had some catching up to do. There were Amara and Gianna's ever-changing events and travels as they took on work-life challenges in and around Seattle. Amara was now into a 3 year relationship with her boyfriend. This was normally cause for celebration. However, with the Mohr daughters, there was always a plan and a calendar even for matters of love and courtship. Fortunately, Gianna was still in her adventurous mode, single and -spirited with no mention of settling down soon. She was a frequent visitor to Jack as she loved and enjoyed everything about San Francisco. Her trips always stretched the boundaries of a long weekend and leaving Monday by noon was commonplace. Gianna had an idea to taste new exotic food and meet at least a handful of people during every trip. Even her lodging was filled with adventure with Airbnb's lately in Sea Cliff, Cow Hollow and Pacific Heights.

As Tom filled their cups with a second round of coffee, he settled in on the couch opposite Jack. "I'm guessing you've connected with your brother?" Asked Tom.

"Yes, we were together last week at the clinic, of course not at his request." replied Jack. "I feel bad that you two have been making challenging decisions without my input. I know you are his elected caregiver, but I also want to have a say in his care. Robbie means too much to me to be on the sidelines and I want to be involved in his care."

Tom was expecting this response. He began, "Robbie's situation is like one of your investment decisions in that several variables affect his outcome, and the doctors on his investment committee are wondering which is the path to a successful outcome. Did I say that right?"

"Yes, Dad, your words are almost exact," replied Jack. "I guess there is some true overlap, but I wanna separate Robbie. When I visited him, he was his usual calm and collected self. But I also noted he was a bit more intense about each conversation as if to evaluate each sentence as a part of a strategy. When we were kids, he used to get into certain intense game modes, and I knew he was shifting gears towards an end goal. It was like moving from checkers to chess. I feel like we are entering a new phase where we are reminded of those who are healthy and without worry, and those who are sick and concerned for life's clock."

"I'm afraid there is one more layer that involves Robbie's audience," said Tom. "I know he speaks to you and me differently about his conditions and feelings. It's sometimes unconscious, but it makes our responsibility even greater as he decides who receives the truth about his situation and how he feels."

"Dad, we can only support his wishes," said Jack. "His mind is stronger than ours and until anything changes with those amazing brain cells, I think we are somewhat at his mercy."

"I cherish every day because I know that life is what we make of it," said Tom. "I savor time with family like I'm dining at a 5 star restaurant and ordering everything on the menu. I no longer have time to bring my emotions into arguments as there is no time to worry about such nonsense. I know that whatever happens during my day, was planned and I am going through it with joy and peacefulness. When your brother and I are together, time stops. I clear my life of distractions, reduce my concerns about whatever is in front of me, and make him my priority. There was a time as a parent when I watched over you two as if you were baby birds and could only survive on my every move. Leaving your side, meant taking a chance on literally anything that could happen. So, I always made the time away magically feel like seconds and never left your sides. Honestly, it was easy and mutual love made it work."

"But you need to take care of yourself," said Jack. "Your life is essential too and there is no getting time back on your life clock. I think we need a slight change to these arrangements and let me be more involved. Robbie will not agree to this, but I know it's what we all need; as of now, there are some new plans. Whenever Robbie is in California or any critical situation involving advanced care, I want to be involved or managing. I don't mean I have to be his driver to every appointment, but I will insist that I manage them. When I return, I will ask him to wear an Apple iWatch. I want this to be a supportive move and not a wrist bracelet - I don't want this to sound like police protection, but I want to know what's going on without asking for details."

"I want to agree but ask Robbie for acceptance," replied Tom.

"We will need him to agree, which may be a challenge," said Jack. "He will resist, and I will insist."

"Perhaps we can go for a walk," asked Tom. "You might need to fill up your memory banks with the fondness of your youth."

"It's an excellent idea, and I'm ready when you are," replied Jack.

The two men headed down the path from the house to a public trail connected to their neighborhood lake. The family dock was in good shape and just needed a boat to rest by its side. As they walked to the end of the dock, Jack looked across the water scanning the edges of the banks. "It always amazes me that the solitude of our lake can bring such internal happiness. I remember rowing our boat around the lake and looking for secret passages leading to an ocean escape. Robbie and I must have traveled every square meter to explore what seemed like brilliant new places. We smoked our first weed and many joints on this majestic lake since then. You could lie on your back from the bottom of the boat and just stare at the gorgeous blue sky for hours. As Don McLean wrote, Starry Starry night, Paint your palette blue and gray,"

"You know your brother still comes to the dock every few days," said Tom. "I'm sure it's more than just a wonderful imagination, a true feeling of friendship with nature. I've seen him sit at the edge dangling his feet watching his reflection and then fully reclining to assume the position of sky-watching. You two learned this from the boat adventures and have kept the fond memories front and center."

Jack took a few cell phone pictures before returning to the house. Tom was in his late sixties and kept in shape well enough to walk briskly with his son. "We made a simple lunch for ourselves in the kitchen," said Tom.

"I'd love something quick before I head back to the airport," replied Jack. "I plan to come back soon when Robbie is here, and we can enjoy some time together."

"Your Mom and I would like that," said Tom. "You know you are always welcome here."

Julia had made finger sandwiches and English tea. The company and setting reminded Jack of the peacefulness in the Mohr home and how they had kept a loving spirit alive within the home. Julia whispered to Alexa to play "Wedding Song,[1]" and the words flowed.

He is now to be among you
At the calling of your hearts;
Rest assured, this troubadour
Is acting on his part
The union of his spirits here
Has caused him to remain
For whenever two or more of you are
Gathered in His name there is love
There is love.

As the music played, Tom gazed out the window and remembered his family, his loving wife, and how true love was instilled in the everyday lives of his children.

"Many thanks for coming by the house today," said Tom. "I know you're at that peak in your career to produce phenomenal results and time away from the office is not easy. Your brother and I have settled into a pretty good set of lifestyles that overlap with minimal interference. I believe it is working and hope Robbie agrees."

"I'm sure that whatever challenges lie ahead, we will be better off as a threesome, and I appreciate your words of caution. I will be careful with my schedule. Let me head out and get to the airport. I took the early afternoon flight to arrive at SFO before dinner."

Jack drove his rental car back to SEA and boarded his Alaska Airlines flight. He reflected on the weekend and events that transpired since he met with Robbie 3 days ago. It was a successful trip, and he felt better about his support team. The next challenge was regrouping with Robbie, which could wait a few days. The elephant in the room was whether or not to use the Herman Exchange platform on Robbie. He was about as conflicted as anyone with equal reasons to pursue or not pursue with the familiar phrase regarding unintended consequences. As a far more important stopgap, he decided to plan the next road trip, this time to the Bay Area.

CHAPTER
THIRTY-SEVEN
SAY DO

JACK CO-WROTE the Seres business plan with Dr K. and a brilliant mathematician named Jeremy Torten (aka "JT"). The plan was brilliant in value, complexity, and timing. The world had survived the SARS virus, and any positive news in healthcare was relished. The elevator speech said, "We are creating a platform that will allow patients to discover important healthcare information about themselves and to make modifications that may greatly improve their future." Bringing the control of key information into one's own care, was instrumental in itself. However, this company aspired to put themselves in line with curing blood-based diseases. Jack would often gesture, "If LifeScan can put glucose meters in every Walgreens shelf to help monitor blood sugars, why can Seres put a point-of-care meter alongside which would provide a full blood panel assessment of your current and future likely diseases. No one is saying it can't be done. The solution has never been driven towards this end. It could be as simple as a blood analyzer accessory for the iPhone or Android with the data securely heading to the Seres Cloud (aka Herman). There were key building blocks for blood capture, analysis, bioinformatics, markers, gene editing, genome reconstruction, and human capital management.

As a very important sidebar, Jennifer Dounda was up and running with clinical trials combining strengths from UC Berkeley and UC San Francisco. Her goals were to leverage CRISPR-Cas9 against the horrible genetic disease called sickle-cell disease. The work included managing challenging variables including stem cells, bone marrow, and pre- and post-chemotherapy blood transfusions. Other teams at UCLA and Stanford are also performing gene editing trials and the Innovative Genome Institute (IGI) acted as a clearing house for bioinformatics and genomic activities.

Jack was a natural leader and would carry the CEO title to please the folks at Eagle. He put aside his banking and deal flow tasks for now and put 150% into the new deal. The team had raised initial funds to get through discovery, a framework for the exchange platform, and a 20-person team. For the MVP, the team would almost triple in size to 55 persons, across 3 locations, and a plan of record to be over 100 employees by year-end. The Series B funds were oversubscribed at $80m and would carry them through the middle of the Go-to-Market phase. At a high level, Jack managed all parts of the spend and delegated to key technical folks for their support. The early team was solid, and they managed their growth knowing they were building something special.

The team managed a few early breakthroughs, increasing everyone's confidence in their plan. One milestone of significance was combining the data path with their exchange compute engine. The proof of concept was to set up several data overlays that would filter, synchronize, and correlate specific genetic marker information from one subject (H1) to another (H2) or a group of subjects (G1). As a separate, parallel exercise, the subjects in Group 1 would be screened for unique genetic information that could act as replacement DNA strands. In most of the gene editing trials performed to date, the gene editing was performed within the subject's own DNA; however, Seres was looking to expand the editing to a much larger set. Dumbed down, now we can evaluate "Bob," across another Bob's, Tim's, Steve's or even Janice's. Bob has at least two differentiable sets of data including his strengths in his genetic code, and of course, his weaknesses, potential genetic markers and any other relevant information. Before the MVP phase, the team had created an environment for success that was plowing ahead and producing new data sets that would later become key elements for a patient application interface. This was a giant step in the right direction.

For every upwards positive momentum, there was also a downward step. There were now 4 development teams spread across US, Canada, UK, and Israel. The team in Israel would work on key server/cloud issues including hardware and software development. Canada took the lead on sensitive trial information where the boundaries between US & Canada were unclear. Finally, the UK team supported the User Interfaces and eventually the application. This left the US team to lead code integration and to prepare for Phase 4 Go-to-Market requirements.

As part of the recent $80m funding round, they allowed two strategic investors from the pharmaceutical and insurance segments to join in. Each stood to gain from the outcome of the work and the idea that a software company would be a major contributor to a medical outcome was exciting.

Plans of record are seldom worth the paper they are written on. Like the infamous "say do" ratio, referring to a CEO's deliverable of "doing" what they say. Jack knew that the valley was filled with whiz kids that blazed very wide trails, including the rise of giants such as Apple, Google, Meta, and nVidia, and the fall of Groupon, Theranos, and Yahoo. No plan had ever professed to create an exchange where a person's unique DNA could be traded as a valuable commodity in such a way as to improve the outcome of lives. This was far from selling internet search, advertising, or fast computer chips. Up until now, the world lived with disease and the limited potential of the cards you were dealt. There would be controversy about playing with fire, and regulations to control sensitive issues, and breakthroughs for those whose fate was sealed at birth.

CHAPTER
THIRTY-EIGHT
FANCY MEETING YOU HERE

ROBBIE'S CARE was almost 100% around his blood work. He was now on a regime that included blood panel screening at UCSF and the Berkeley Clinic every other week. He was on a gap year in medical school and trying to make the best of a bad situation in the Bay Area. It wasn't being sick that bothered him, but rather the inconvenience. In his mind, he had planned the gap year around a handful of exciting places to visit, exotic restaurants to enjoy, and more time with the adult Saints and their crazy fun lives. During a recent Discord chat with the guys, he wrote, "I really enjoyed your visit to the Bay Area and the chance to see the local sites and some crab at the Crustacean."

"I can't believe you ordered and ate a full crab," said Luke.

"I'm still amazed we rode in a robotaxi with no driver," said Joseph. "I'd like to try again down Lombard Street!"

"I'll be in the Bay for at least another 6 months, and you should come back soon," said Robbie. "Let's plan another set of events, this time to a professional sports event and some rooftop bar venues."

"We should try a few Michelin star places," said Paul. "Let's take Jack to a nice French restaurant."

"I know you all have terrible schedules to coordinate, so I will request this. Let's plan for either the second Saturday of next month or the one after, with no excuses for attendance," said Jack. I will reach out to Jack as soon as we all decide and I'm sure he will join."

The Discord chats bounced back and forth until they agreed on a date three weeks away. It was a Friday to Sunday afternoon arrival/departure with a multitude of fun packed into the 48 hours. Robbie invited Jack to join as much as he could spare.

"Maybe we should put a few more trips on the calendar," said Michael. "We can also look into Las Vegas or Los Angeles."

"I vote for Vegas and the Bellagio," said Paul. "I could stare at their water show forever."

"If we go to Vegas, let's plan an extra day and watch the sunrise at the Grand Canyon," said Robbie.

"How about we explore one of the ranches too," chimed Michael again. "Maybe Bunny, Chicken or Mustang would be nice."

"Then you need to bring some extra spending money," said Joseph.

The Saints wrote back and forth for another hour with lists of ideas to fill the next few field trip vacations. The convo would have continued longer, but Robbie was on the clock and needed to get to his doctor appointment.

So, what were the odds that Ava and Robbie would meet at UCSF? Today's visit was to UCSF and since parking was such a hassle, Robbie took BART across the water and then Uber to the clinic. The UCSF campus was very well organized and decorated as one of the finest cancer research institutes along with Cedars-Sinai and Stanford. Robbie's appointment was at 2pm and he arrived fifteen minutes early. His infusion therapy usually took about an hour. As he entered the procedure room, he carefully scanned the various patients with tubes, wires, and needles galore. Robbie's chair was the only open one remaining and as he walked towards the station, he heard, "Hello Robbie." He turned and saw Ava with her arms on the armrests hooked up with blood-flowing tubes. She smiled and nodded and whispered, "This is the last place I thought we would meet each other."

"I've never met anyone I know at these clinics," said Robbie. "I'm guessing you're not here to give a pint?"

"No," Ava said. "I've recently been diagnosed with an aggressive immune disorder. The doctors want to rule out diabetes, rheumatoid arthritis, or lupus. Sorry if this is too much detail."

"Not at all. I understand the needle pricking, blood-sucking, and diagnosis shopping procedures," said Robbie. "It is my pleasure to visit not one, but two clinics and battle the ugly commutes. However, today, I will remember the lovely chance to see you." he smiled.

"Well, it was lovely to see you too," said Ava. "Jack talks about you constantly and probably wishes he was here with us now."

"He was going to be here, but I told him it was routine and didn't want to pull him away," said Robbie. "Besides, hospitals are for sick people," he said in a statement. Robbie opened his iPad and brought up a new audiobook called "Palo Alto." He inserted his Air Pods, started listening, and kept another close eye on Ava. He wondered if Jack knew about her situation and then decided not to worry about things he could not control. The hour flew and his cycle was completed. His nurse removed all his equipment, applied his band aid, and started walking him out. Robbie leaned over to Ava and whispered, "Why don't vampires use autocorrect?" She smiled and nodded. Robbie continued, "because they love Type O's."

Ava's drip was slower, and she was still in her session so they both gave each other a soft hand wave and blink. It was 3:30p and just in time for the horrible commute back to Berkeley.

CHAPTER
THIRTY-NINE
RED, GREEN, & BLUE

INTERNALLY, there were 3 Herman variants including Herman-Red, Herman-Green, and Herman-Blue. Blue was for babies through age 18 and considered the least critical for launch. It would be developed and tested alongside the other variants and be available for unique trials to help curate the database. Green was the base platform. It was being developed with the most sophisticated data sets and what was considered "routine" medical challenges, including monitoring common pathogens, minor genetic diseases, and the "starter package" for markers. Finally, Herman-Red was designed for the most challenging medical diagnoses across the full gamut of known diseases, all flavors of cancers and other terminal diseases or sicknesses where today's treatments are at best, only slowing the disease. Red also meant any research with terminal diseases was managed with hazmat suits and extreme protection. Jack made the team watch "Hot Zone," and appreciate the threat of a body fluid transmitted disease and the added risk category of air-borne diseases such as Anthrax, RSV, or SARS.

Seres had multiple campuses in the Bay Area including separate buildings for Herman Green and Red. Corporate headquarters were in South San Francisco where several employees were from Genentech, one of the bay's largest biomedical employers. The green and red campuses were near UCSF and Stanford Hospitals, respectively, and had arranged early trials in their facilities.

Although the business plan was laid out with four initial phases, the most significant of all milestones was the results of the trials. In the case of Seres, there was also no precedent and the FDA had to be creative between drug trials, gene editing, general diagnostics (e.g., diabetes), screening (e.g., ancestry), and whether there was a regulatory body for applications such as a health exchange platform. It was all new groundbreaking territory and would be met with excitement and resistance.

There is a well-documented process when performing clinical trials which covered the terms and conditions, consent, and pages and pages of obligatory verbiage to spell out the potential risks. The least time is spent on the potential outcome which in most cases is some sort of potential new treatment, drug, or medical device that may eventually improve or save lives. Typically, these trials have an excellent safety record and are beneficial to medicine.

The Green trials followed the outline for drug trials with 4 phases and sizes ranging from 50 to over 1000 persons. For the early trials, the lengths of each phase were short (about a month) with limited or no side effects to worry about. The early trials allowed patients to monitor their health on their smartphones with information never provided by the doctor. The phone accessory took in body fluids (saliva, pee, or blood) and processed the information in the Herman cloud. The phone app began populating patient results with full panel screens in less than an hour. The Seres UI team had built several user-friendly interfaces to explore the best results for the patient. Like many complicated applications, the desktop version was more robust and was available for more thorough formats such as graphs and data display. However, the phone app was the target for success.

Feedback during the first phase was very positive, with patients being able to immediately monitor their personal care between doctor visits. This was obvious for those with chronic illnesses such as arthritis, diabetes, and more complicated blood disorders. Green was powerful and could detect anemia, sickle cell, cancers, and was developing new models to potentially monitor the internal organs functions such as the liver, heart, lungs and bone or bone marrow. During the trials, all diagnostics were turned off for the patient and only used in the lab for internal purposes. The app would provide basic blood sugars, hemoglobin, and even aspirin, alcohol or cannabis levels - that seemed to have special interest.

In the Seres labs, and by customer consent, the teams evaluated any severe disorders, organ health, genetic markers, and compared the new patient samples with extensive database information. They also monitored any change of status such as reduction in T-cell count, heart rate monitoring, and if there were any saliva or urine samples, advanced information on the liver, kidney function, PSA for prostate, etc.

Herman-Red was even more challenging. The front end including body fluid sampling and setting up the patient screening was exact to Green. The major difference was that all Red clinical trials involved patients with known diseases. The consent was carefully written to let those in the trial know that this was not a cure or to be a substitute for doctor's care. Jack knew the Red trials were the most exciting and dangerous. Initial Herman trials, of any color, were to test the initial thesis of obtaining the most valuable bioinformatics data from both patient and real world databases. The Herman exchange would eventually add care modules, including connections with your doctor, consultations or second opinions, and advanced, extremely confidential, health exchange options. This last option was ideal for those suffering from either life-threatening or highly disappointing genetic destinations. For example, a Herman Red patient might find their results suggesting a blend of gene editing and substitutions that would change the course of their lives by suppressing, curing, or removing a disease. And for Robbie, the question was whether Herman can act on AGS quickly. Jack would keep his brothers' anonymous samples at the top of the review list. His case was personal and had the least research or data to act upon. Jack asked if JT could carve out extra cycles to monitor his brother's results throughout the trials.

CHAPTER
FORTY

CELEBRATE ME HOME

AFTER SIX MONTHS OF TRIALS, there was overwhelming evidence that the Seres team was on to something big. Most of the 3,000 patients found the constant updates in their point of care Herman application useful. There were enough common success points that Jack decided to create additional backdoor access by the medical community as long as he maintained strict confidentiality between patients and their data. One of the positive feedback statements from a patient read, "I have never had a single application as wonderful as Herman that allows me to have all of my health data all in one place. I now have daily access to my whole health and reduce the hassles from a dozen doctors, who have never offered any form of digitized health data." This was both positive and a bullseye for what the team hoped to accomplish. There were many reasons no one has ever attempted to collect (from multiple sources) and present patient data in a single interface. It was like asking your urologist, cardiologist, general physician, and perhaps anesthesiologist into a quick Zoom call to discuss one of many things. It just wouldn't work, ever. But this was the new digital age, and Seres would revolutionize patient care by starting with patient bioinformatics and new algorithms that may be more powerful than humans. Jack's first discussions with Eagle said he wanted to leverage several critical technologies and markets into one super converged platform. To borrow the words from Joni Mitchel's Both Sides Now, "So many things I would have done, but clouds got in the way," which loosely translated to Jack knew his challenge ahead would be daunting. Still, if somehow, he could pull off a few miracles, then the outcome of his plan would justify all the effort.

Unbeknownst to anyone other than Jack, Dr K, and JT, the backend platform of Hermes had already presented solutions to over a dozen patients with terminal illnesses. A few were gene editing out certain genetic markers and others including first-ever gene replacement therapy using genome information from other patients. Not to put this lightly, however, the intellectual property for how to edit out or replace genomic data to remove markers for cancer, was likely worth billions of dollars in the future.

Tonight, was celebration time and a chance to roast and award the team. His favorite party planner, Naomi Yang, had been with Jack for years and knew how to pull together a team party. She picked a local ax-throwing place to give the team a host of fun games including ax throwing, darts, shuffleboard sawdust, and a private room for 25 guests. Jack asked if Ava might want to join and show off her throwing skills. "Of course, I'd love to come," she said. As a positive indication of support, everyone made it to the venue before 6:30p. A few had already started sharpening their skills and took a break to grab some protein munchies. Jessica was the MC and had special envelopes prepared at each person's table setting. She mentioned some work highlights and handed the mic to Jack for his brief speech. He reiterated their plan for changing the healthcare universe, world domination, and the belief that now was "their time." This company was built at just the right time for the crazy convergence of humanity, medicine, and digital intelligence to reshape people's futures. He finished his speech with reminders that in a very short time, the company had developed a platform from which miracles would be created. He mentioned with caution that they had unpublished clinical results that would forever change people's lives and that the Herman platform would one day become the most common application for use by over a billion people. He closed with a caution to be ready for a meteoric rise in downloads and demands that would easily put Seres in the running for awards such the Nobel prize for medicine, and a "most down-loaded path" for an American company (referencing TikTok as Chinese) that will surpass Instagram, Facebook, WhatsApp and Snap-Chat. For the first time in history, a non-social media app would be the most popular and most influential for the health and well-being of the lives around us. He returned the mic to Naomi, who granted them access to their envelopes, including a $10,000 cash bonus and additional stock grants.

Jack raised his glass for a toast, "I am forever grateful for the amazing people in this room without whom this achievement would not be possible. I thank my lovely girlfriend Ava for putting up with my crazy schedule, and finally to my wonderful family, Robbie and the Saints, for their constant support to this dream."

Everyone was in a great mood after encouraging words from their CEO, along with cash and stock. After a quick toast, it was time to head to the games for the real competition. No amount of coding expertise could help with the throwing of an ax or the sending of a shuffleboard disc. Some of the team took their gaming very seriously and it was safe to say that it was "game on," for the rest of the evening.

Ava reached over and said, "That was a very lovely speech to the team. You can tell by looking around that the group loves working for you. And you were very generous."

"Being generous with this team is easy," said Jack. "In addition to all their work, I have included a unique trial with Robbie to try and get to the bottom of his disease. Robbie thinks we are just shadowing his therapy, but I am pushing to see if we can slow down or kill the AGS enemy. Unfortunately, our strength is dominating information fusion, and there is not enough info on AGS to draw conclusions or suggest experiments. Sorry, this is too much info for tonight."

"No, that's alright," she said. "I want to know how your team is doing and I want to download the application for my use too," she said jokingly, but she secretly wanted into the mix."

"Look love, I have the keys to the castle and you're welcome anytime to join in the fun."

"Ok then, I'd like that," said Ava. Later in the evening, Ava told Naomi that Jack would allow her into the trials and if she could sign up as a new Patient X. Naomi knew this was an extreme exception and would make it happen. "I'll send you the link to sign up in a text. There are a few online DocuSign's I need you to fill in to ensure we cover all our bases for confidentiality and liability. Sorry about the lawyer talk, but we run a tight ship with the FDA and adding you will just be routine as long as we follow the protocols," said Naomi.

"I completely understand these are sensitive trials and thank you for your help," responded Ava.

CHAPTER
FORTY-ONE
I GOTTA FEELING

ALTHOUGH JACK and Robbie were twins, their lives grew more and more independent with age. They spent their first 10-15 years near and shared activities, travels, and mischievous adventures. Perhaps their most elaborate troublemaking was in high school when they were first learning about fire and dangerous mixing of elements. It was Chemistry Class and time for mixing sodium's (acetate and hydroxide) in a dish over a flaming candle. This was considered an experiment. However, for the boys, it was all about the thrill of early pyrotechnics and controlled chaos. The directions were simple: gently stir the sodium crystals overheat until they became liquid. Apply a small flame to the liquid and "voila" a torch is now lit. It resulted from forming methane gas and acted like a peaceful dish of flames.

Robbie spoke: "Wow, this is a blast. We just pushed a bunch of hydrogen atoms around and made methane. How cool is that…?"

Both boys knew their elements and reactions from middle school. Understanding basic principles early in life was mandatory in the Moore family. However, their school system was a bit slow in applying lab exercises, which was a treat.

"You know what this means…?" replied Jack.

"No, not really," from Robbie.

Jack spoke with a movie star accent. "There is a challenge here amongst the Lords of the Flame. Let history be our reminder, that when male twins are introduced to the power of the flame, there must be a contest to determine its ruler."

"Oh, I see," Robbie questioned. "Is this from Ancient times in Bull-shitville or perhaps the lesser-known territory of ImGonnaKick-YourAss...?"

"How poorly you jest, my flame-challenged competitor." Jack said. "We have less than a fortnight to prepare for battle and we must defend the pride of our ancestors and whoever conquers the flame shall wear his crown of dignity."

"As Master Hothead," Robbie laughed.

The boys gave it a little break and cleaned up their chemistry mess. After school, their banter continued, and it was determined that Saturday evening was the date of the challenge. As always and even in competition, they shared just enough about making their inventions to perfectly pull the other one along.

"I'd like to add one rule," mentioned Robbie.

"Sure," replied Jack.

"Whatever craziness and chaos we create, we cannot harm any creature or building such that there are no aftereffects of our battle." Robbie made it clear.

"There goes blowing up a school bus," Jack smiled. "I'm ok with that rule and fully agree."

"And if you'd like to keep this a fair fight," Robbie made a gesture and hand wave.

"Ok what now," said Jack.

"We can share our ideas before the event, pick the winner and then pull together the best ideas to make it superlative," again the gesture from Robbie, this time with his other hand.

"OMG let's make this complicated again," said Jack with a head bob. "So, I'm gonna vote for mine, and you're gonna vote for yours, so it's a grand tie.

Robbie began with a calm, decisive voice, "In all that we do, there is a purpose. Through purpose, we deliver on our promise to create, build, amaze, reveal, impress, articulate, discover, and energize the senses to a new height. If we went to a famous museum, we would certainly have some excitement to see well-known historical treasures or a new city with new landmarks. However, this event concerns the intersection between creative chemistry and shocking the senses. Our winner will combine these two for a lifetime memory. And it will be clear from the ideation phase if there is a path to stardom."

"Geez, you sound a bit stoic these days, Professor of Exotic Philosophy," Jack responded. "I'm not ready to concede my idea, but you've laid down a bit of a gauntlet here. Tell you what we should do to vote for the ultimate winner. Should a tie occur, we will open a sealed envelope with the following inside. Each of us will create a list of qualities in the other person. We will choose a handful of qualities, say 5 and write them down in order of perceived significance. The person guessing the most in order wins."

"But what does this have to do with the contest?" questioned Robbie.

"You said it yourself. This is about purpose and what better example of purpose than to evaluate each other's best qualities in life," Jack quickly replied.

"Ok, it's probably a corner case, so I will regretfully agree to your terms of engagement," Robbie sneered. "Let the challenge be recorded on a single sheet of paper, front side only. In ten days, we shall meet and reveal our smashing, world-colliding flaming inventions."

On the ninth and final planning day, Robbie waited patiently for Jack before their trek home. Amongst the normal stress of schoolwork, sports, family matters were the quiet backdrop of the fortnight challenge. Robbie's brain was wired for dates, times, places and faces. Having a deadline was just another line in his computer chip, but this time he had a bit more than usual excitement in his mind.

"So, how was your day?" Robbie asked Jack.

"Pretty good. Got a reminder to start college applications. Mrs. Rappaport (Biology) reminded me that I scored well on the SAT's and that she had two professors at UofW that would recognize her name on a letter of recommendation. It was sweet but added pressure to an otherwise busy day. How about you, how was class…?" Jack replied.

"Mine was good too," said Robbie. He couldn't help himself and blurted out, "You know what today is don't you?"

"Ya, it's Thursday. Why?"

"In the fortnight challenge, we agreed to meet on day 10 to reveal our creations."

"Ok, so that makes for some fun on Friday night." Jack grinned.

"Yes, but we might consider a Premier," said Robbie,

"You know you're impossible in these contests. I suppose you have an outline of the guidelines for a "premier," replied Jack.

"Well, yes." Robbie nodded. "I know this is mostly secret planning in solitude, but we might add a few items since I seldom get to beat my brother in competition."

"That's only true because we never go head-2-head on anything in real life. If we did, I'd get killed and I'm not giving you any gimme hints here." Jack made it clear, but with a smile.

"No, it's not about that. In Latin, premier is first in importance. Before we ink our plans, we should share a premier item or two," Robbie shared.

"Ok, with all this hype, you need to go first my friend," said Jack.

"My event occurs in a magical place where not all flying boats have wings," Robbie proudly delivered.

"What kind of premier is wrapped in a riddle…? Jack said. "Ok smart ass, let me try my best on you. A rainbow can come in how many shapes…?

There begins the battle between two brilliant kids about rainbows and flying boats. Somehow their genius is reduced to fantasies and hints that only leave the other guessing about what will be put on paper. Friday morning at breakfast, the boys glanced at one another like friendly adversaries and again at lunchtime, only this time, they were separated by tables and chairs. Each was a masterwork and finished before evening when the boys rejoined at the dinner table. Tom had prepared spaghetti with meat sauce, fresh parmesan cheese, and plenty of garlic French bread. The three of them said prayers and dove into the yummy food.

Tom asked, "You two seem distracted. Is everything ok at school?"

"Oh yes," replied Jack, "we are just tired after a busy week and ready for a break." Robbie nodded in agreement.

"Ok, let me do the dishes and you two are free to enjoy the evening," said Tom.

"Go get your paper," said Jack, "and meet me in the living room."

When they returned, each had just one piece of paper lying face down. This was more than a made up game amongst competitors, it was "a document between kings," with intellectual rights as risk.

Robbie gestured, "As I created this adventure, I shall also end it. For this reason, your creation will be revealed first and mine will follow. When you are ready, please proceed."

Jack turned over his page and recited, "There are few reactions in nature that are magical and expand in happiness from when we are children until old age. When we see our first rainbow in the sky, our eyes are captivated, and our minds explore each vibrant color across the arches. The combination of sun rays and raindrops bring us joyous reflections across a rainbow of colors. Double rainbows are the rarest and appear close to one another for an amazing effect. In China, a "rainbow cloud" was seen where the colorful rings appeared as a reflection above the cloud, similar to a colorful ring above the cloud. If a rainbow was just 8 variations of red, it would be a "red rainbow" and have a much less effect than all the colors in a true rainbow. Our eyes and minds are trained to love all of these colors.

It is no secret that scientists have created man-made clouds by seeding the atmosphere with silver iodide causing water to condense into rain drops. Let's assume we can create the perfect raindrop and have them fall where we want. For now, don't assume this is H_2O. Then, let's paint the town streets with gallons of acids (red, pink, orange, yellow), bases (green, blue, purple), and a thin film of excitement on top. Immediately after sunset, let the fun begin, seed the clouds, make it rain and have the drops hit the ground with a burst of colored excitement!!!"

"How does this reaction occur?" questioned Robbie.

"We use a thin film layer of methane trans glucamate to ignite a small flame of color as the drop hits the paint," replied Jack.

"And I suppose you have the chemical formula for this reaction?"

"Of course, it's in my notes at the bottom of the page," replied Jack.

"Hmmm, that does sound truly amazing. Each drop ignites a small colorful flame that lasts about a second and then is washed away. I like it," said Robbie.

"Ok, now, it's your turn my friend. Show off your magic," Jack requested.

Robbie started with a leading statement to seal his fate. "For my creation, I combined the joys of the 4th of July fireworks for Mom, imaginary floating boats for Dad, and a climactic big bang ending for overall showmanship. In my setup, we make lantern boats (with name tags) with a parachute on top, a can of fuel in the boat, and a special section on the bottom known as "kaboom." There is a ring of string about 20' in diameter that connects all the boats with spokes that lead to a center ring about a foot round. The center boat is a bit larger than the rest and has a second smaller boat on top to match the other boats. It's a rather complex circle of fun, and I've tried to arrange the timing for a grand show. Picture the following; as the sun sets, we meet at the dock and lay out the "Circle of Boats," lighting each of the small boats in the round. To keep the boats from collapsing upon one another, I've added a gentle stiffener ring in the mesh to keep them in the same horizontal plane. We then light the center boat and attach to a toy boat in the water. After pushing out in the lake about 50', the tether is freed, and the circle of lights rises upwards. Each lantern has a soft yellow glow from its parachute as the candle burns down. Then, after only about 30 seconds, the small boats burn through to a colored reaction of salts that are each of the colors of the rainbow. Each boat now glows from the bottom with its own magical color of red, purple, green, yellow, blue, magenta before the center boat transitions. A few seconds later, the candle on the large center boat burns through and a fireball explodes bigger than the entire ring. A finale of flames."

"Wow," said Jack. "Guess you thought this one through like a genius. But you did kinda forget one important effect."

"Oh, what's that? Said Robbie,

"You're missing a song to be played from the dock. Fix this, and we have a winner! Conceded Jack.

"I think you may win for the scientific breakthrough of methane trans-whatever you called it?" replied Robbie.

"Ya, I added a few yet-to-be-developed achievements which can be discovered in the next few days," added Jack.

Before the evening ended, they exchanged their tie cards as a courtesy. Jack read the 5 from his brother in order: Brotherly love, Patient love, Unquestionable love, Unending love & I will always love you.

On Saturday, the boys loaded Jack's car with the "flying boat contraption", a small tool kit, a blanket, and a small cooler and Robbie brought his drone. It was still light out, but the sun was going down in the coming hour, giving them enough time to reach their destination.

"Which way are we heading," asked Jack.

"To the water where the sky opens to the heavens." replied Robbie.

As was instructed, they laid out the circle of boats, loaded the candle cups, arranged everything in meticulous order and then launched from its tethered tugboat. There was very little wind and the circle floated gently upwards. Act one was the glowing yellow parachutes - Jack called over to Robbie to start the boom box. He pressed play and the music began. It was Crazy Love[1] by Van Morrisson.

I can hear her heartbeat from a thousand miles,

Hear the heavens open every time she smiles,

And when I come to her, that's where I belong,

Yet, I'm run into her like a rivers strong.
You gimme love, love, crazy love.

~

When high school ended, the boys knew a transition was coming in their lives as they were all college-bound. Interestingly, Jack stayed local at UoW and Robbie attended UC Berkeley, remotely. The Saints attended schools from the Pacific Northwest to Southern California with hybrid attendance. During the formidable years from ages 17 to 22, they stayed connected through the internet, birthdays and a group visit near Seattle whenever possible. Each team member attended graduate school and completed business, economics, law, and science degrees. Then came the dynamic mid-twenties, each with their own path to work and personal happiness. Robbie had been their steadfast leader, athletic coach of sorts, and key instigator plus event coordinator. The AGS setback pushed some of his ad hoc responsibilities to the group or Jack.

Managing the trip to the hospital on Thursday mornings was getting easier as Jack found the ideal route UCSF and played the parking dance after lunch. He wanted to arrive by 1:30p to meet Robbie in the cancer ward. Unfortunately, the term "Stage 4 Cancer" is common when you're in the waiting area. Male or female, old or young, married, unmarried and even the happiest can find themselves in this place. It is not by desire that anyone would wish to come to a place where disease has no cure and limitations are put on one's life expectancy. Jack took his seat and texted Robbie for his ETA. Robbie's reply was "In Uber, 5 min out." He arrived looking very professional for a doctor visit with dress jeans, a sport coat, and matching brown shoes and belt. As soon as his eyes met Jack, his face lit up as he walked over to sit together. "Good to see you," said Robbie.

"The pleasure is all mine," Jack grinned. He noticed Robbie's walk was slower than expected and Jack wondered if this was normal.

"The nurses are usually busy with the 1pm and 1:30pm "needles", and they will come for me at 5 or 10 minutes past the hour."

"How are you feeling?" asked Jack.

"I'm just ok," said Robbie. "The doctors seem to know what they are doing. The serum seems to help my joints, but I don't have any arthritis. I've asked them to address my headaches and backaches."

"How bad are the headaches, and how often do you get them?"

"Unfortunately, they are coming often and although they aren't too painful, something affects my eyes and sometimes my legs. I think the AGS weeds may be growing faster in the brain mush."

The nurse came to get Robbie and Jack asked if he could sit with him in the clinic area. They asked the "only family members allowed" questions and let him come in. Robbie quickly scanned the room looking for Ava to no avail. He proceeded to his chair and Jack to a seat beside him. They got Robbie's all "hooked up," and Jack pulled out his iPad for a read. Mom, Dad, and I agreed that we should spend more time on some bible verses, and I will read some of our favorites to you. Both boys had read the bible several times and could converse swiftly on both Old and New Testament. The following hour included passages from the Gospels, Wisdom and Solomon songs, and Psalms poetry. As Jack read aloud, Robbie often repeated or aligned his words in sync with him. At the end of the session, Jack walked Robbie out to the curb and hired his own Uber Black to take him back across the bay. "Your carriage awaits you fine sir," Jack joked. "These guys will take you back in the fast lane. Get some rest and I'll check in later."

"Many thanks to my eloquent Christian orator," Robbie bowed. "May the time spent away from the office provide you with many golden returns." It was a cheesy and perfect good afternoon adieu.

Before Jack returned to the office, he sent the Saint's group chat text to round up the cavalry. He provided 2 possible dates and within 30 minutes, they had all agreed. Jack called his office admin and made all the arrangements for 2 weeks out for arrival into SFO. They would arrive by late afternoon and into the Ritz Carlton on Stockton Street. Jack liked the hotel's elegance and the simple pleasure of getting adjoining rooms.

In this new era of hoteling and limited services after Covid, he wanted to make sure the field trip meant all together, all the time. As the date approached, he also made plans for Robbie and Ava to join what looked like an outing or two throughout the weekend. On "Thursday therapy," Robbie and Ava would join him for a special dinner in the city. And, on this particular day, Robbie had a needle-pricking chair next to Ava and they caught up on dirty little secrets about Jack. There were very few secrets. However, Robbie provided some scary boat time stories, insider views on lame high school girlfriends (who could not hold a candle to Ava), and that he was a mommy's boy. He shared that Julia was also his favorite and that growing up as a twin in the Mohr family was a dream come true. Between a lifetime spent with Jack, the attention and caring from his sisters, and the forever love glue from Tom & Julia, Robbie could not ask for more. Then he played the humble card. "However, there is one thing we both need: more time," said Robbie. There was a fine line between being sick and dying and Ava and Robbie were playing musical chairs not knowing how severe their conditions were heading.

Jack made arrangements for Robbie to be picked up and brought into Seres before dinner and he arrived at the campus around 3:30p p.m. There was a badge waiting for him, and a quick trip up the elevator to the top floor. Seres rented half the 10-story building and Jack's office was in the corner facing the bay. Robbie went to the window to gauge the view from the Golden Gate down to the South Bay.

"Nice view, eh?" said Jack.

"I see why you picked this office," said Robbie. "It's really nice."

"We are in the south part of the bay and the water is filled with container ships."

"Yes, but even they serve a purpose and bring their colored little boxes from all over the world. There are up to 24,000 twenty-foot containers on the large vessels with a profit of nearly $1,000 per container. That's a cool $24 million," said Robbie. "These barges are worth over $100 million when loaded."

"So, what is your favorite color container?" asked Jack.

"Did you know there is a container color chart like Pantone? It is called RAL and dates back nearly 100 years. I would go with a dark blue or green, but I would pay extra for a cool camouflage print!"

"I agree with having more fun with that metal real estate. Perhaps offering some advertising for the containers that face the shore. Did you know they offer a vacation cruise on some cargo ships. My boss, Steve (Anderson), took his wife from SF to Tahiti on a 5-star cargo excursion."

"Hmmm, wonder what the food tastes like?"

"There is a good reason for it to be a 5-star vaca. The rooms are massive, and the food and alcohol are served like a cruise line, 24/7. Top-of-the-line buffets for just 10 or 20 elite passengers. Hey, hoping you're ok to stay for dinner tonight? Let me shut down in a few and we can head out."

"Ok," said Robbie. "Let me watch a few more boats."

Jack texted Ava about dinner and booked her Uber to pick her up at her place. She asked what to wear and he filled her in on the Saints surprise and now the weekend invites made a lot of sense. She responded with heel and long dress emoji's and said she would be at the restaurant before 6pm. It had been a long time since she had been with the Saints and when she arrived, they were at the bar. Paul was first to spot her and while turning said, "Wow, you look amazing." Ava always looked beautiful and in high fashion, and tonight was extra special for Robbie.

"It's great to see you all. May I join you? I hear there is a party here tonight," smiled Ava.

"Yes, but it's invite-only," grinned Michael. "It's kind of a Seattle thing."

"Oic," said Ava. "Do I need a championship ring or tattoo?"

"Let me see if I can speak to the manager," Michael said, quickly sending a fake text. His phone alarm sounded as the text replied. "Ok, so we have made arrangements. However, there is one thing you must do."

"Ok, I think," she said.

"Apparently a mandatory kiss on both checks is required!" Ava made her way down the bar with obligatory and lovely kisses to the Saints. They were each thrilled to see her and know she was a part of the weekend festivities. "I see you guys picked an amazing spot for dinner," said Ava.

"This was all put together by Jack," a rare comment from Luke. "We were told what clothes to bring for the weekend, but not many details. I'm guessing there will be some time on the bay."

It was a fairly short drive to the restaurant and Jack knew the best valet for his fancy car. Robbie enjoyed his brother's extravagant taste and first-class attention to detail. When they arrived at the restaurant, they headed straight to the bar where they were met with smiles, hugs, and lovely kisses. Robbie winked at Ava saying, "Lovely to see you here. Much better than our other meeting place."

"Oh, I agree," said Ava. "Let me get you a drink to celebrate."

"My brother will want a Manhattan, so let's make it two." Ordering through Ava was easy as the bartender kept an eye on her for all the right reasons. Ava raised her glass when all the drinks were filled, smiling to the Saints, "This is your weekend, and we are so happy you are here."

Jack said, "I am especially excited to see everyone and hope we can do this more often. Mi casa, tu casa!"

"You mean, my Ritz Carlton is your Ritz Carlton," smirked Michael. The party moved to a table near the window to the bay and two hours of constant chatter about everyone's lives and plans. A few softballs were thrown to Jack about his startup empire, with an underlying curiosity about his groundbreaking platform. At one point, he volunteered a walk through the labs over the weekend and a chance to show off his work in progress. Jack had many plans for the Saints with the centerpiece of a boat ride on the bay including a chartered trip on an 80′ Magnum Series luxury speed boat. The after-lunch treat included everyone taking turns at the wheel and the unforgettable sights of Ava (who also brought a few girlfriends) sunbathing. With speeds up to 60 mph, the real challenge was not hitting any other boat as they zipped by. It was like a Ferrari in a Safeway parking lot with too many horses and insufficient open water. Robbie asked to make a quick U-turn around the Golden Gate Bridge and easily turned the eighty-foot monster in the mouth of San Francisco Bay. During the weekend, they ate at nearly a dozen restaurants, held a sleepover on Saturday night at the Ritz, visited the Seres plant of innovation, hot fudge sundaes at Ghirardelli on Pier 39, cable car rides, and a finale brunch at Barrio's in Fort Mason, walking distance from the Marina.

During the 3 days of events, no illnesses were mentioned. Ava was secretly sick, but Robbie was dying. However, this was not an intervention or a prayer group. Jack and the Saints knew very well about Robbie's progression with AGS, yet the topic was sidelined for the weekend. This time was about special moments with the most amazing friendships anyone could ask for. Lots of exciting photographs blasting across the bay, messy ice cream sundaes, windblown hair traveling in cable cars pretending to be in car chase movies up and down the hills of the city, and a group of mid-twenty-year-olds hoping to enjoy these memories forever.

PART SEVEN

CHAPTER
FORTY-TWO
LETTER TO THE IDIOTS

THE HERMAN RED team had saved or successfully altered the disease trajectory of hundreds of clinical trial patients. There was mounting evidence that the exchange platform could identify a patient's illness and provide several essential recommendations towards a cure. With Herman's immense amount of data, analytics, and the engine to produce new genome types, there was new hope for chronic illnesses. However, Ava and Robbie's situation was within the trial data database. Ava's autoimmune condition was treatable with HIV medication. However, her condition meant she would also pass along the virus to any offspring. In her case, she had more time to improve than Robbie. His Red results suggested aggressive bone marrow transplants or a mix of gene editing and replacement therapies. Jack knew AGS was hereditary and had the team monitor Robbie's results alongside a parallel study of his blood work. Unfortunately, his data showed no signs of any disease.

The Seres team conducted weekly assessments of the trials and presented recommendations to Jack and a host of medical advisors. This included everything from a simple course correction for existing therapies to complete reversals and ideas for new paths to cures. A key part of the data review was any condition that was changing rapidly.

In these cases, there were likely mutations or other uncontrolled variables significantly altering a patient's health. Robbie, who was on the "top ten watch list," had risen to the top of concern, or Code Red.

Jack called his folks to fill them in on Robbie's care. "We are in unfamiliar territory with his illness," said Jack. "Our team has been monitoring him for the past year in parallel with his doctors and there are new concerns about his condition."

"Just how bad is it son?" asked Tom.

"As you know, our company is working on a new platform that allows patients with chronic diseases to have hope for a cure," said Jack. "It is still early in development. However, we have made significant progress such that we can say that we have saved lives. However, most of this is using brilliant algorithms on past data that allows us to correct certain disease pathways. In the case of AGS, there is limited information, especially on adults, and even less on people as unique as Robbie. I have a team dedicated to his care and a network of doctors I communicate with weekly about his situation. I just want you two to know that we are in a race to save him."

"What do you recommend we do?" asked Julia.

"I'm not sure yet, but I wanted you to be aware in case we have to act," said Jack.

Jack spent the coming 2 months sharing as much time with Robbie as possible. He was open about his concerns and told him he wanted them to be together. Robbie was happy to oblige as it meant more doting over him, and he would always love more time with his brother. In addition to the usual food and fanfare, they read books or passages from their past aloud. Jack also hosted a recital for Ava with he and Robbie playing the piano and guitar. A little James Taylor, Tracy Chapman and UB40[1].

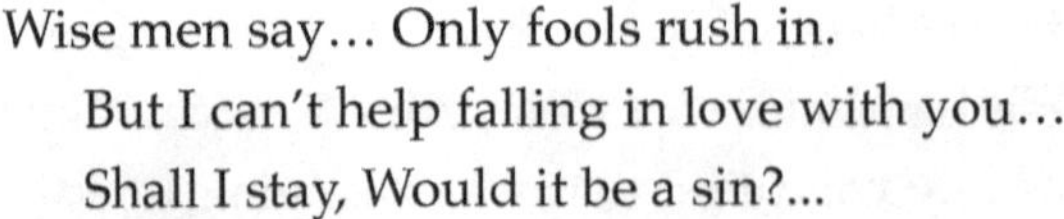

Wise men say... Only fools rush in.

But I can't help falling in love with you...

Shall I stay, Would it be a sin?...

If I can't help falling in love with you.
As the river flows, Gently to the sea,
Darling so it goes, Some things are meant to be,
Take my hand, Take my whole life too,
For I can't help falling in love with you.

Jack bought a carrom board to play at work, flew an RC plane over the water at Golden Gate Park, and bargained for several dozen PSA 10 Pokémon graded cards on eBay. Robbie asked if they could try archery, attend a Warriors game, and hope to get a Steph Curry autograph and a Chinese warrior tattoo on their inner biceps.

"Are we filling up our bucket lists?" asked Robbie.

"I think bucket lists are overrated," said Jack. "We should live with our dreams on our sleeves and see what journey they take us on. A Shaolin monk spoke on a TEDTalk and described a traveler's experience interviewing folks after a mountain climb. After hearing about all their journeys to the top, he decides he no longer needs to climb and will be satisfied knowing about the mountain from intimate conversations. However, as the monk points out, only climbing to the mountain will allow you to push through our hindrances."

"You played the monk card to convince me that you are excited to spend more time with me?" said Robbie. "Sounds like maybe you need the brain scan instead of me."

In less than thirty days, Robbie died peacefully in his sleep. This would be one of the saddest days in the Mohr family. They hosted the funeral at their home and people came from all parts of Robbie's life including childhood in Reston, the hospital crew, college friends, the Saints, and Ava. Jack, Gianna, and Amara wore traditional black outfits with a boat lapel pin. They toasted Robbie with the Lyle Lovett song, If I had a Boat[2].

And if I had a boat,
   I'd go out on the ocean,
   And if I had a pony
   I'd ride him on my boat
   And we could all together
   Go out on the ocean,
   I said me upon my pony on my boat.

The dynamics of losing Robbie were terrible. He was the Saints ad hoc leader and his brother's closest confidant. The Mohr family was a mom, a dad, two sisters, and twin boys. How does 6 become 5? How does every family activity, fond memory, digital photograph, or Robbie belongings fade away. Age 27 was too early to die, leaving a lifetime for those to remember him. On his flight back, Jack held Ava's hand most of the flight. Tom had given him an envelope with letters from Robbie to read. They were simply marked "One" and "Two." He opened the first letter and it read as follows.

"Dear Beloved Jack, I could not ask for a better brother to share my life with. Reading this note means we are separated, but I will always look down on you sending love and kindness. I wish I had more time with you and even more adventures. Most bucket's include exotic travel to the wonders of the world. However, my list is to "go out on the ocean on my boat." I will never forget you in my colorful dreams.

There is one favor I need to ask. Please use my body to save the lives of others. I have given instructions to a neurologist at UCSF who will perform my autopsy with specific instructions to provide unique information to you and only you. Like you, I know your Herman invention is real and will change lives. My situation was driven by a time clock and your algorithms could not work as fast as my disease. For my contribution to science, I will add posthumous data from an autistic, twin, male specimen with the most unique properties.

After the funeral and some autopsy chops, would you spread my ashes over water. Please bring Don McLean's Vincent[3] with you - I don't want to honor suicides, but more importantly how the canvas speaks to hope and suggesting.

Starry, Starry night
    Paint your palette blue and gray
    Look out on a summer's day
    With eyes that know the darkness in my soul
    Shadows on the hills,
    Sketch the trees and the daffodils,
    Catch the breeze and the winter chills
    In colors on the snowy linen land
    Now I understand,
    What you tried to say to me
    How you suffered for your sanity,
    How you tried to set them free,
    They would not listen, they did not know how.
    Perhaps they'll listen now.
    For they could not love you,
    But still your love was true,
    And when no hope was left in sight on that starry, starry night
    You took your life as lovers often do.
    But I could have told you, Vincent,
    This world was never meant for one as beautiful as you.

A division known as Herman Plus was formed to evaluate postmortem data. It wasn't an easy climb due to confidentiality, and many patients or families were reluctant to have their data swirling around. In less than 90 days, there was enough excitement to announce that the Herman Red Plus team had discovered a dozen new implementations. Robbie's new data brought new angles to brain, immune, and to a lesser extent, arthritis disorders. In fact, with insights from Robbie's cells, Jack used a highly targeted therapy on Ava and reversed her HIV condition to normal.

Jack opened letter number two - and it was sent to the Saints. It read, "I will miss each of you every day from now on. The only thing greater than my departing sadness is the hope that we will someday be connected again. I know that brilliant minds don't often do well with religious beliefs in places such as heaven, but I do believe that we were all brought together for a reason. The odds are slim that my brother and I would push to work at a hospital where you were patiently waiting for us to appear. And then, over the next 10 years, we thrived and remained the Five Saints. My sacrifice in life will bring strength and happiness for many lives to come. And I know there is no replacement for the love from Michael, Joseph, Luke and Paul. As my brother is likely reading this to you, please bring him into the Saints circle and remain the Fabulous Five."

In the mortal words of John Denver at age 23, he was Leaving on a Jet Plane[4].

All my bags are packed, I'm ready to go.
   I'm standing here outside your door,
   I hate to wake you up to say goodbye.
   But the dawn is breaking, it's early morn.
   The taxi's waiting, he's blowin' his horn,
   Already I'm so lonesome I could die,
   So, kiss me and smile for me,
   Tell me that you'll wait for me.
   Hold me like you never let me go.
   'Cause I'm leaving on a jet plane,
   Don't know when I'll be back again.
   Oh babe, I hate to go.

Jack folded the letters and put them back into the envelope. Ava spent the night at his place noticing objects around his condo with Robbie effects. He poured some white wine for them to relax and celebrate his amazing brother. His face teared again as he whispered to Ava, "I'm really going to miss my brother."

"Yes, I know, but it will be ok," she said. "I guess that you may miss him forever."

"Thank you for being in my life right now. I need your love."

"I'm here for you," she said. And after a long and emotional weekend, they rested.

43. MedEx Launch

In the coming months, Jack was head down in work. He spent nearly a year refining and expanding Herman's core strengths. The Herman color scheme worked well and eventually filled half the rainbow. There would be new groupings based on age, race, gender, and sub-markets based on disease population and growth rates. After the trials were completed, the full commercial launch of Herman was set. In his careful fashion, Jack had already market-tested the application variants including North America, UK, and the valuable techie markets where patents were in process including Germany, France, Spain, Israel and Italy. Translations and currency exchanges were included in the testing and all market feedback on the launch was good.

Jack hired a marketing specialist from Apple & Google and created a campaign with extensive branding. Focus group results suggested the company name was acceptable with new emphasis on tagline, logo, and product name. Herman was a great internal code name, but an overhaul was needed. In less than 100 days, the company had relaunched their website, logo, tagline and corporate colors. The

Herman SKUs were rebranded under the new platform name "MedEx." The messaging stressed a clear, minimalist-like style with every piece of content adding to the company's new image. After setting the stage for print and digital promotion, the campaign fueled social media, SEO optimization, targeted promotion based on personas, and traditional cable advertising. Every outbound play was monitored with call-to-action links, lead generation and scoring. The Google expert was an analytics guru with every campaign linked to an associated set of metrics.

Jack held a pre-launch meeting with all staff worldwide. He outlined the goals in detailed slides, demonstrated the application on his iPad, and projected on stage. The team had been through months of development and software releases and was now ready to "go live." He closed with a tv advertisement including some background prompts and short speech. "I cannot thank this team enough for being a part of this amazing journey to develop one of the world's most valuable apps for healthcare. From today forward, the world will have access to controlling, modifying, and improving their health destination. We've rebranded to MedEx, and I am pleased to announce our brand ambassador. Joining Jack on stage was Patrick Dempsey. Jack handed the mic to Patrick whose charm and smile took over. "As many of you may know, I was born with a genetic disease commonly known as dyslexia and managed the best I could. And, after my mother died of cancer, I created the Dempsey Center to help those suffering from and surviving cancer. When Jack called me to represent Seres, I said I seldom put my name on endorsements. However, I know from my 10 years of experience that saving lives can be exciting and humbling. I am also the least technical person in this room and hope to manage to get my parking validated." His speech was from the heart, and it was clear that he would represent the company well. Patrick pointed his mic towards Jack and said, "Roll tape," and the tv advertisement was played. After 30 seconds, the crowd applauded until Jack returned to center stage to shake Patrick's hand. Jack summoned a few more folks to the stage including Dr K., JT, Naomi, and the marketing team. Strategically planned for maximum exposure, the 10am Tuesday launch was ready. He announced, "Go Live," and the worldwide launch was on. A fresh new face was revealed for Seres.com, and the world began to enjoy the MedEx experience. Metrics were off the charts as millions of downloads grew to 10's and then over 100 million before the end of the first month. There were still several app's with over a billion downloads and Jack wanted world domination. The next milestone was 500 million, taking a few extra months and careful launches into Asia.

There were multiple paths to monetize MedEx including traditional point-of-care services, genome analysis, doctor networking, and several specialized modules for advanced healthcare. Seres was at the forefront of establishing the world's most accurate and dynamic genome database. In addition, the software provided a life-changing diagnosis to every patient.

Although there were skeptics, the medical journals corroborated the results and encouraged the app's use. The list included the New England Journal of Medicine, Lancet, JAMA, Nature, and 10 or more cancer research journals. The Seres algorithms were likely more complex than those from Google, Facebook, Apple, Samsung, and the Mayo Clinic. Analysts suggested that the IP alone put the company's valuation over $10 billion and climbing.

CHAPTER
FORTY-FOUR
ONE TRUE BUYER

FOR JACK'S 29TH BIRTHDAY, he took the day off and showed up at Ava's with his favorite coffees and flowers. She greeted him with a kiss and welcomed him in.

Ava guided him upstairs. She turned down the sheets and waved him over to her. She untied his shoes, loosened his belt, and removed his pants. He unbuttoned his shirt and handed it to her and laid down. She proceeded to give him a back and neck rub. She removed her clothes and added more body rubs mounting his back butt cheek to butt cheek. Jack could feel her sensual touches as she spun around and worked a little on his hamstrings. Her hands wandered playfully through his legs and aroused him. It was safe to say he was feeling much better and as he rolled to his backside, she managed to hold on to her cowgirl position and rode him to completion. She carefully dismounted and brought back a warm washcloth and cleaned him up.

"You're welcome to rest here for the day," said Ava.

"I just need an hour," replied Jack. "Maybe we can go out later for lunch?"

"I'll be downstairs if you need me," said Ava. "I'm in the middle of a new project." That was code for a new art piece.

Jack awoke to a text from Alex that read, "Just saw the news on MedEx. Congrats!!!"

He replied, "It's been a wild ride this past year and the team pulled out all the stops to deliver."

"You have time to meet soon?" said Alex.

"I'm heading out with Ava after lunch, maybe we can grab a coffee."

"How about the Carnelian Room around 3pm?" texted Alex.

"Yes, perfect," said Jack. He went downstairs to the art studio and carefully interrupted Ava's work. "Alex has invited us to a fancy lunch downtown. Would you join me?"

"Oh, that sounds lovely," said Ava. I need a bit longer for this piece and will shower shortly. Maybe you will join me?"

"Mmmmm, yes I'm ready when you are," said Jack. He would never pass up time in the shower with Ava, and today was becoming increasingly a special day off work. Their shower time was luxurious, including lots of hand washing of each other's intimate body parts. Ava was a little dirty from the welding, but Jack wanted extra time to caress and massage her. As she rinsed off and turned to face him, Jack knelt and began licking her. The shower rain ran down her flat stomach and across his face as he continued his oral extravaganza. She pulled him up and whispered, "Would you like some afternoon delight time?"

"I had my release earlier. This is your time," replied Jack. He turned off the shower heads and followed her sexy naked butt to the bed.

"Maybe you should save some strength for lunch," Ava grinned. Jack positioned her on the bed and said, "Oh, I'm feeling fine right now. Let's see about you." He pulled the sheet over him like a cape and returned to his favorite position tonguing and tasting her. She was wet from the shower and getting juicier by the moment. As Ava climaxed, she interlocked their hands and squeezed while her body shivered. She turned their bodies sideways and interlocked her legs with Jack's. She held him close and whispered, "You need to take more days off."

They drove downtown and reached the top of the Bank of America building where they met Alex at the Carnelian. Alex made it a point to host the Eagle clients to fine SF dining and today was no exception. Ava and Jack followed him to a window table and a bottle of iced champagne waiting for them.

"So, what's the occasion?" said Jack.

"We have a lot to talk about and I thought we might start with some bubbly," said Alex. He grabbed the bottle. Ava raised her glass and Alex poured champagne for each of them.

"A toast to the amazing Seres team," said Alex. "And the launch of MedEx, and perhaps one of the hottest new platforms in the world."

"I really appreciate your support," said Jack. "I remember grinding through business plans and endless fundraising activities."

"Those days are over for you," said Alex. "Over the past 24 hours since the launch, Eagle received over 30 unsolicited offers to buy the company. Steve mentioned a few were from large public companies that could fund a cash and stock deal without ever going to process. I'm surprised you didn't get approached directly."

"I was trying to take the day off today," smiled Jack. He pulled out his phone to see several pages of missed texts and phone calls."

"What does all this mean?" asked Ava. "Are you going to sell the company?"

"I don't know, but because we are here with my best friends, I suggest we eat some food first." said Jack. Alex and Ava smiled and agreed to review the menu and order late lunch. After a bit more small talk, Alex reminded Jack, "You should enjoy today. It may be the last day your feet touch the ground. When you get a break, Steve would like to visit you and discuss next steps to handle the frenzy.

In the coming week, Steve and the Eagle team paid several visits to the Seres headquarters and nearby campuses. They collected their diligence information and summarized their data into a pitchbook for the other partners. The Eagle deal team also managed the inbound excitement from hungry buyers who wanted to get closer to the team. Things were moving quickly, and Jack was managing the exchange platform's hypergrowth and processing the prospective buyers' excitement. He also knew the paperwork grind from the lawyers often follows the euphoria from the bankers.

He had missed a few calls from Simon and sent him a text, "Sorry for the delay, too much craziness in the pit."

"Np, I am in town this weekend and wanted to invite you to dinner," said Simon.

"Excellent, I'd like that," said Jack.

"I just bought a property in Sea Cliff and Teresa will be with me to help fill it up with furniture and art. You should bring Ava as I don't believe you two have met my wife."

"Let us know the time and place and we look forward to it," said Jack.

The upcoming Saturday evening, Simon hosted them at his new home. In his usual high-end fashion, he bought a 6 bedroom, 7,000 sq-ft mansion with an ocean view. As they arrived, Teresa met them at the door and invited them in for a tour. Other than the need for a bit more furniture, the place was gorgeous. "We wanted to spend more time in NorCal, and it came down to properties in the Napa area or San Francisco," said Simon. "The owners of this home had lived here for over 50 years, and we grabbed it before it hit the market. It always pays to have a large down payment," he smiled.

"Your new home is lovely," said Ava. "I have some artist friends who can help you decorate with their works."

"Yes, please," said Teresa. "You can see we have quite a bit of space. Let me get you some more wine," and she guided them back to the kitchen. "Are you ready for some appetizers?" They put on a spread to host Jack and Ava including a pork tenderloin, seasoned vegetables, sweet potato gnocchi, mixed green salad, and chocolate mousse. Jack joined Simon on the patio to watch over the barbecue. "So, I hear Seres is going very well for you?" said Simon.

"Yes, it's been crazy," said Jack. "Last week's launch created a buzz. We have had over 300 million downloads and are heading towards half a billion. We have broken every record for fastest growing application on both Apple and Android platforms. The market had been anxious for the right point of care information and MedEx fit nicely into the gap."

"What do the folks at Eagle say about their investment?" said Simon.

"They are the majority outside shareholder at 30% and are thinking of cashing out," replied Jack.

"Are you selling the company?"

"I'm not sure. In less than a week since launch, we have several attractive offers from folks with deep pockets," replied Jack.

"Are the offers sincere?" said Simon.

"Most are Letters of Intent (LOIs). However, one term sheet with an offer has a purchase price range that ties directly to our sales projections."

"What is the range?"

"From $8 to $15 billion, with additional earn-out."

"I have a counteroffer for you," said Simon. "I will purchase 51% of the Eagle shares assuming they own 30% of $8 billion. Let's say $1.2 billion goes back to Eagle, they net a 20x return with an additional 9% left to ride."

"What will you do with the company?" said Jack.

"As you know, we lost our child to a brain tumor years ago. The tragedy forever changed the way Teresa and I view the world. As we consider adoption, we continue to wonder about alternatives and I'm guessing MedEx might be a path for us. We have been a huge fan of your talent and believe there is much more success in your future. To that end, I've been in touch with the folks at Goldman Sachs and they want to take you public. This would give you the best of both worlds as you would have the freedom to run a public company, or you could run a process and sell later, which could be less than a year in this market."

"Sounds like you've done your homework," said Jack. "I think the Seres team will start getting poached soon and I need to secure them beyond stock options."

"There are a few ways to help retain them pre & post IPO," said Simon. "Why don't we get back to the ladies and our dinner and talk again tomorrow."

The men returned with a delicious beef tenderloin and the four enjoyed a wonderful dinner. Simon said a toast, "To old friends and new, and to sharing time in the Bay Area."

On the drive home, Jack filled Ava in on the business conversations and expressed excitement about working with Simon. He spoke without using numbers and told her this path made sense. Ava smiled and already knew that Simon was a person who can help make dreams come true.

On Sunday, Jack texted Simon, "Ava and I wanted to thank you and Teresa for a lovely evening at your new home. Next time is our treat. I also want to circle back on our conversation and have a few additional ideas to discuss."

Simon responded, "Let me rearrange my Monday and come to your office." Simon stayed the week with visits to Seres, Eagle, Goldman, and some furniture shopping. Ava and Teresa also spent time together; they were ready to celebrate by Thursday evening. After several long back-to-back 18-hour days, Simon had completed his transaction with Eagle and the Goldman deal team had been assigned to build the S1 filing. The IPO process had begun with a kickoff that morning and an evening out was in order.

Ava and Jack decided that an unforgettable evening out with Simon and Teresa was in order. They scoured the restaurant scene and reviewed the latest, hottest places in the city. Jack recalled taking the Saints to the Ritz and many rooftop bars with Ava. After careful review, they decided on Mastro's on Geary. The four met at the restaurant in classy cocktail fashion. Ava and Teresa wore their glam outfits with strapless, see-through, stilettos, and looked like runway models. Jack and Simon followed them to their table and enjoyed a fantastic meal. "We are so happy to have you in San Francisco and hope we can have many more occasions with you," said Ava.

"This has been one of the more exciting weeks of my life and we welcome you back to the city anytime you wish," said Jack.

"Our friendship started on the common ground of wanting a special evening, which happened to be at the B&W Bar. The timing may have been by chance. However, the reason we are here together is from the heart. I hope we can turn the amazing business you have built into some financial freedoms you so deserve," Simon said, raising his glass of red wine.

While IPOs typically take 6 to 9 months, Seres went public in less than 100 days. Their market capitalization rose to $10 billion in the first month. Simon had turned his initial $1.2 billion into $1.8 billion and climbing. In the S1 filing, Jack Mohr was the largest shareholder at 12.5% or $1.25 billion. At age 29, Jack had become a billionaire.

CHAPTER
FORTY-FIVE
ME UPON MY PONY

BEFORE JACK TURNED 30, the stock price doubled, and his net worth grew over $2 billion. The company continued to receive offers to buy the company and the investors including Eagle, Simon, and the founders including Jack, Dr K, and JT decided to keep their positions and the stock symbol. The app has reached over 500 million downloads, which only 80 other companies in the world have achieved and over 80% of these are from Apple, Google, Samsung and TikTok. Jack's plan of record was to reach over 1 billion downloads within the first year, and they were tracking towards this peak.

MedEx was designed to help people monitor their daily lives with digital healthcare at their fingertips. Millions of users were checking their vital signs with a new perspective of owning their own options for better health. Many users received hours of wasted time from waiting in doctors' offices for simple results. And for others, it was truly saving lives with the ability to reverse chronic conditions or change the biological future such that markers could be dealt with through gene therapy.

One of Jack's dreams while growing up was to save lives. He didn't know how to do the lifesaving, but it would forever be his passion. His greatest influence was his brother Robbie and their lifelong friendship.

If possible, Robbie would say he knew his brother in the womb and even describe how he looked in the uterus. Jack could remember everything about his brother at every stage of their life. The highlights include sneaking off for a double date and their first girl kiss, winning a music recital in middle school with Jack on guitar and Robbie on piano, and helping out at the hospital in high school. Robbie was the reason for the formation of the Saints and the default leader by appointment. These gifted five were highly connected through friendship, love, and kindness. On several occasions, they offered each other help including organ donations to survive. The team stayed even closer to Robbie after his AGS diagnosis. However, not even the miracles of MedEx could help save his life. Robbie's unselfish ask through his autopsy was yet another act of kindness towards his brother and the entire world by extension of this exchange platform.

Jack wondered in hindsight if he would have lived his first 30 years any different. Perhaps more time with Robbie, the Saints, or with Ava. He chose a very demanding career and knew there would be challenges with extra free time, but there was always reflection about a do-over. Maybe he should have stayed in Seattle or taken more trips with his closest loved ones. His sacrifice was to pour his life into his technology and be ready to change the world. It took a little over 5 years. However, he accomplished his dream and now it was time to give back.

Jack's first give-back was to donate money to Tacoma General Hospital for a new library. The hospital was where the Saints were formed and in an unusual book-reading fashion. Jack clarified that the library could extend to a new wing and that Robbie, Paul, Julien, Joseph and Michael would be part of the structure in name or design.

His next giveback was to get the Saints together for a special meet -n-greet. He flew to Seattle and had the boys meet him near the Bell Harbor Marina, slip 22. When they arrived, they walked down to the docks and followed the path to slip 22. There was an ice chest with balloons and a note on top. Joseph opened the envelope which read, "I'll be joining you soon, meanwhile have a drink." The guys enjoyed some imported beers and wondered when Jack would arrive. From a distance, they could see a large yacht approaching along the mouth and slowing its engines down inside the marina. It was over 60' long and heading towards the end slip. As it reached the docks, Jack appeared from the dark glass cockpit and waved. "Need a little help," yelled Michael.

"That would be great," said Jack. As the ship came closer, it got bigger and bigger in the eyes of the Saints. Jack put his reverse thrusters on the engines and the yacht gently maneuvered to the edge of the dock. They tied down the yacht and helped lower the retractable stairway. "Welcome aboard," said Jack waving them on.

"Now, I know why you needed an end slip," said Paul, carefully looking from front to back at the beautiful yacht.

"I'm guessing you couldn't park this beauty in San Francisco," joked Luke.

"Please come join me on the upper deck," said Jack. "So, how do you like this view?" Each took turns looking around and enjoying every minute of the Seattle harbor.

"I hope you guys like amenities on this baby. Each of you have a stateroom and bath," said Jack. "The food is excellent too! Lunch is served in 15 minutes in the main galley." This gave them each time to investigate the ship from tip to tail. They rejoined again at the buffet, filled their plates and then Jack appeared with a large envelope. "I have a small favor to ask from each of you," said Jack. The guys looked up with eager attention as to what he could possibly need. "Since Robbie died, I've focused the past year on our startup and launch. I know I haven't been much of a friend lately and want to change that now. With your permission, I'd like to become one of the Saints."

"You've always been part of the Saints," said Michael.

"Maybe it was through Robbie, but this is from my heart," said Jack.

"I think we all knew that you were a bit different from us. The Upside Down Idiots club kept us safe from a complicated world and allowed us to form our bonds of togetherness. As we grew up, the friendships lasted through different schools and other family directions, and we managed to always be there for one another. For the past 10 years, I have had a text from one or more of you every single day," said Joseph.

Jack turned to Paul and Luke and said, "How about you two?"

"I've always thought of you as our Super-Saint. As much as we care for you, you return your love and friendship to us unconditionally," said Paul.

"Like the others, I will miss Robbie every day. But I also know that whatever emptiness we have from him leaving is easily consumed with you. My life changed the moment you two came into my life and I would be overjoyed if you were part of our group. I vote yes!" said Luke.

"Then it is settled," said Joseph. "You are a Saint and the smartest from the Upside Down," he smiled.

"Ok, this is wonderful. Now, I can fill you in on a few new things," said Jack. "I'm sure you all know that MedEx was a success and has given me more freedom. Buying this boat was more than a purchase, it was my commitment to all of us enjoying time together and for Robbie, to be on the water. I still need your help with a name, but assume from now on, you are all part owners in an 80' superyacht." The team all smiled and started whispering about a name for the boat.

"I also want you to know that your names are part of the new library wing at the Tacoma General Hospital. I'm hoping there will be many other "saints" formed through this facility. And lastly, our key investor Simon informed me that he will match any funds I gift to each of you." Jack opened the large envelope with 4 notes with the Saints names. He handed them out and finished his speech. "Financial analysts will tell you it takes between $3-$5 million to retire depending on lifestyle and longevity. I have no idea what the future will hold for each of you, but this should help you on your journey."

They opened their letters which read, "On behalf of Jack & Robbie Mohr and Simon Bilteau, you will each receive $50 million. The rest of the letter covered the details and a lawyer+banker paragraph.

"As you might imagine, there are some business, banking and tax discussions, but please know this is your money." After moments of stunning excitement, it was time to head out on the yacht. Jack summoned his new crew to release the ropes and start the engines. They cruised around the bay for a couple of hours and each Saint had their time at the wheel directing their mega yacht through the obstacles and then back to slip 22. Jack mentioned that he would spend the night on the boat, and they were all welcome to stay or return with their pj's. They all agreed to be back by 6pm in time for dinner and a movie in their onboard cinema room with 12 lounge seats. Afterwards, they each made their way to their staterooms and began making themselves at home. They ate a light breakfast before departing, each $50 million richer. Jack fired up the engines and set his course for San Francisco. He sent Ava a text that read, "Heading back to SF and hope to see you in a few days. The new boat is amazing. The Saints and I had a blast and spent the night on Saturday. Missu lots."

Ava responded, "I look forward to seeing you soon. Just let me know when and where and I will come to you."

The trip was longer than expected and Jack wished he had brought Ava. He made it to the mouth of the San Francisco Bay and through the Golden Gate Bridge. He was on a waiting list for the closest slip to his condo. However, things were about to change for his home address. With $2 billion, the world is your oyster, and every realtor is your best friend. The Marina Yacht Harbor had over 700 berths with 15 end ties for those berthing up to 90' length overall. Jack arranged for a month's rent of an end berth until he could swing a permanent spot.

He sent Ava a quick text and a pin drop for his new location. She arrived in less than 30 minutes and received the royal treatment to come aboard.

In the morning, they enjoyed coffee and looking out over the bay. Jack said, "We should plan a trip soon. Maybe head down south for a while."

"That sounds wonderful," said Ava. "Let me check my schedule," she smiled.

"I think you should spend more time with art and less with work," said Jack. "I've been meaning to ask if you would like to help me with a few art projects?"

This was a first and Ava paused before saying, "Ok, I'd be happy to help. What do you have in mind?"

"Well, there is certainly a need here on the boat, and I may have to find a new home since my condo looks pretty ragged. I also need help with this." He extended his hand with a gift bag and as she reached to grab it, he knelt on one knee. Ava looked inside to see the teal blue Tiffany's box and pulled the beautiful box out. Jack spoke softly, "I am incredibly in love with you. There is no one in the world I would rather spend my life with, and I hope you will have me?"

He paused as Ava's eyes teared up. "May I go on?" he asked. She nodded. "My life is complicated through work (he smiled), but that was a means to an end and for all my dreams to come true, I need you in it. I will promise to love and cherish you forever and ever again."

Watery eyed Ava replied, "I love you too,"

"Will you marry me?" Jack requested. He was wobbling on one knee and hoping for a quick answer.

"Yes, I will," she replied.

When Jack and Robbie were born, they shared DNA as fraternal twins. They were handsome, magnetic, and gifted. For over 25 years, their lives would be filled with a pure essence of love and devotion that was uncommon and unforgettable. Robbie's early departure meant that Jack would need to find solace through the Saints, Ava, and the rich memories of his brother. The glass was half full, the glasses were rose-colored, and he would celebrate that their time together was fulfilling enough to last a lifetime. He named the yacht, "Me Upon My Pony," bought a large enough house to fit a grand piano in the living room, and finally got his bicep tattoo.

Sitting on his boat, he breathed in the misty salt air and the smell of marine diesel. He texted Ava, "Let's get out of town. Can you meet me at the pier?"

"Of course," she replied. "I'd love to spend more time with my lovely new husband."

NOTES

CHAPTER 7

1. "Carolina in My Mind," James Taylor, 1969

CHAPTER 36

1. "Wedding Song (There is Love)" Paul Stookey, 1971

CHAPTER 41

1. "Crazy Love," Van Morrisson, 1970

CHAPTER 42

1. "Red Red Wine." UB40, 1983
2. "If I Had a Boat," Lyle Lovett, 1988
3. "Vincent," Don McLean, 1971
4. "Leaving on a Jet Plane," John Denver, 1966

ABOUT THE AUTHOR

LEO MAXWELL lives in California with his wife and two amazing children.

His artwork includes fiction writing, abstract mixed-media painting, poetry, and engineered puzzles.

When not thriving in creative activities, he enjoys walks on the lovely beaches of the Pacific Ocean from Big Sur to Fort Ross.

Favorite sports teams include the 49ers, SF Giants and the Golden State Warriors.

Always searching for the finest Cabernet, a savory filet steak, and a loaded baked potato.

26.2 < 3, Brie, Camaro, Caymus, Discus, Forty-Love, Picasso, Rochambeau, Route 432